Cruel HONEY

ALSO BY PIPER CJ

Cruel HONEY

PIPER CJ

Orders by U.S. trade bookstores, wholesalers, and all other business inquiries, please connect at pipercj.com
Film & Media, please contact: Alex D'Amico

Paperback ISBN: 979-8-9998383-2-2

Cover: Chris Welch
Graphic Design: Helena Elias
Editor: Kathryn Wolhpart
Formatting: Zachary James Novels

For everyone wondering if *Eat the Rich* could be a vacation activity — yes, but those hidden fees will kill you.

CONTENTS

1

A WET RAMEN NOODLE PLOPPED FROM MY FORK ONTO MY CHEST, which pretty much summed up my day. Maybe I shouldn't have been eating microwavable junk food while lying on my back, but life was shit and I needed to cry on the floor. The mindless cooking video that kept me company while I wolfed down my depression meal clicked over to an ad for an all-inclusive couples' resort in Turks and Caicos, which added insult to injury. You needed to be in a couple to attend a couples' resort, and since Amanda had tumbled fingers-first into her coworker, I was bitterly single. You also needed money. And the will to live.

Then again, I'd probably prefer to cry into my cup-o-noodles on the beach.

I shivered, wishing to all Hell that I'd grabbed a blanket before resigning myself to the floor. Depression and laziness battled against any sense of self-preservation, and I surrendered my flesh to goosebumps, shaking as whatever was left of my body heat escaped into the threadbare floor.

The Denver winter slithered in through the cracks in my window, cold enough that I could see my breath, but not enough to justify turning on the heater and running up the bill.

I breathed in a mildewy cloud of rotting wood and the mold growing near the shower. In the hallway, a cockroach made an ambitious sprint from the baseboard to the corner, its shadow long and jittery under the weak overhead light. I stared at it, too tired to chase it off, too dead inside to care.

Four months prior, things had been different. Happy, even.

Goddamn, I hated thinking of Amanda. I hated the stupid, warm smile that spent years plastered on my lips. I hated thinking of the scent of sautéed garlic and onions when I came home to her in the kitchen, knowing she spent all day cooking what I liked. I hated the collection of sensory-friendly stuffies she'd gifted me to provide hugs and warmth whenever she was away. I hated that she'd filled my belly with butterflies, making a fool out of me as I floated through my days in love.

Now, thinking of her was like sipping cyanide. Bitter almond, faux sweet, and guaranteed to end in my demise.

I was living with my ex, waking up on a comfortable queen-sized bed to coffee from the corner bakery before classes, a fully stocked fridge, and three-to-five partnered orgasms a week. She was an insatiable top who had insane skills with the strap; I was a pillow princess in love.

I was a goddamn idiot.

Apparently, Amanda's appetite was too insatiable for one woman.

She didn't even apologize. She just explained that she'd realized she was polyamorous, and that it was abusive of me to force her into compulsory monogamy.

I had told her to drop dead, packed my meager possessions, and now outsourced all my orgasms to PornHub and the Hitachi Magic Wand.

I had never been lucky, but I was on a particularly shitty losing streak. It was hard not to feel like my parents were right. I should have stayed in Colorado Springs. I could be living with them for free. Maybe, in another life, I would have gone to community college and gotten my M-R-S. Maybe, in that version of events, I would have been straight instead of the rebellious queer atheist they accidentally raised. But no, I had to be a broke-ass med student drowning in debt who only called her parents on Christmas and Easter.

My phone rang.

I groaned.

"Yeah?" I answered, already dreading. I moved from the floor to the squishy cushions of my secondhand couch, the kind that had been passed through at least four Craigslist ads before it landed in my apartment.

"Cassidy Finch."

My landlord.

The nasal scrape of his voice sent a fresh pulse of dread through my skull.

"Listen, before you say anything—" I started, but he was already rolling over my excuses. I plopped the now-bloated Styrofoam cup of ramen on the armrest, appetite long gone.

"Your rent is late, Finch. Again. You think I'm running a charity here?"

I bit my lip, staring at the peeling wallpaper as I pressed my fingers against my temple. "I just need another week."

"You said that last month," he grumbled.

"I mean it this time."

"I don't give a shit what you mean. You got three days. Three. After that, you're out. You understand?"

I hung up the phone and blocked his number. Him calling every ten seconds wasn't going to make the rent come any faster. I dropped my phone onto my lap and exhaled through my nose. I had nothing in the city. No family with spare couches. No emergency fund. No backup plan. I was too broke to function, and, apparently, too stupid to fix it.

Still, I did what any desperate girl in a downward spiral would do: I doom scrolled.

Videos blurred past my fingertips—vacation vlogs, aesthetic apartment makeovers, women in cozy, oversized sweaters making fresh bread in kitchens I could never afford. Then, a girl popped up on my screen, smirking into the camera, glossy-lipped and diamond-studded, mouthing over a trending sound.

The caption read: *I'm a sugar baby, and I never have to sleep with them.*

I snorted. "Liar."

She claimed I could be one too, but only if I followed her affiliate link. Which is code for: *I'm selling a product and getting paid for your gullibility. Sign up to sell your body and give me 10% of your registration fee.*

A notification pulled me back to reality. A text from my manager:

Hey, I hate to do this, but the health inspection did not go well. We're shutdown for at least a month. No shifts. Sorry, Cass.

My stomach plummeted. That was it. That was the last life raft yanked away, and now I was left in the freezing, open water of reality. No job, no rent, no options. The universe was really about to make me drop out of school, move home, and become a doctor's wife.

I scrolled past wedding photos from my college friends, all smiling in white lace, all honeymooning in Mexico with margaritas and infinity pools. I locked my screen and let it drop onto the couch beside me.

The silence that followed was suffocating.

The MLM Sugar Baby scammer offered false terms, but hope dangled like bait at the end of a hook. Sugaring was real, right? It was real work, real money, real high-risk behavior that ended with my face on 60 Minutes and an anchor telling people I used to light up a room. All I had to do was cross a line, be alone with a stranger, and wonder if I could live with myself.

Fuck it. I had nothing to lose.

My fingertips trembled as I punched in the keys.

I warred against every survival instinct I had, reopened my phone, and typed into Google: *sugar baby websites.*

It was horrifyingly easy.

My mouth was dry. My heart rate ticked up uncomfortably.

I skimmed past the ones that felt like obvious scams until I found something that looked…legit enough. *Discreet Arrangements*. Sounded professional. Whatever that meant.

I chewed my lip, fingers hovering over the keyboard before I started typing.

Hi, I'm Cassidy.

I hit delete and chewed on the slot for first names. I wasn't sure if this was legal or not. Was sugaring technically prostitution? Would this ad get me on a list for solicitation? Then again, I wouldn't have to pay rent in jail.

I rolled the dice and picked a new name.

Hi, I'm Juniper. I'm friendly, open-minded, and love witty banter.

"That sucks," I muttered to myself. "Are you also going to tell the potential sugar daddies that you like long walks on the beach? Hang on. Actually…"

I'm more of a "sangria on the beach" person than a "snowboarding the Rockies" kinda girl and would love to get cocktails with you. I'm a third-year med student and just need a little help covering tuition and rent. Open to arrangements. Text me.

And, like an absolute idiot, I typed my real number.

I uploaded a handful of pictures that showed my starving-student body and partially obscured my face, then hit submit.

And immediately closed the site.

What was I doing?

I spent the next three hours cleaning like a madwoman, if only to distract myself from the anxiety of the world crumbling at my feet. I was terrified of things staying the same. I was equally terrified of change, should the site mean I become someone else. Someone doing things I'd never thought I'd do. Someone I may not recognize.

I was in the middle of scrubbing rust from the oven when I heard a knock at the door.

I was in rubber gloves, sweats, and had a frizzy bun that had migrated from the top of my head to somewhere near my ear. I wasn't wearing makeup, I hadn't showered, and I wasn't expecting company. I debated chugging the lemon cleaner to get out of interacting with a stranger.

Another knock, harder this time.

Shit.

I crept toward the door and peeked through the peephole. My stomach turned. My landlord stood outside, his pudgy face twisted in irritation, knocking with more insistence.

"Cassidy, I know you're in there. Tenants don't get to block my number and expect to keep living in my building. Open up."

Fuck.

My phone buzzed. I hastily plucked off a rubber glove and snatched it from the counter.

A text.

> Unknown Number: Juniper? Hello. I saw your ad and have a proposition for you. I'd love to meet.

Already? How was that possible?

I was going to be sick.

I slipped on my shoes, grabbed a coat, and pressed the phone to my ear.

Cracking my door open, I lifted a finger to tell the landlord to wait as I faked a call. "Oh, hi, yeah! What? You have shifts for me after all? That's amazing, thank you!" I slipped out into the cold before my landlord could wedge his boot in the doorway.

"Sorry! Gotta go! Work emergency!" I called over my shoulder.

"Cassidy Finch!" he bellowed after me.

"This is good news!" I shouted again. "I'll have enough to cover rent by the end of the shift!"

I didn't stop walking until I was three blocks away, breathing hard against the bite of winter air.

Then I looked at the message waiting for me again.

My fingers hovered over the keyboard before I finally typed back.

Juniper: Where and when?

I wandered the streets for a while to clear my head. Denver's winter was brutal; the wind sliced through my thrift-store coat like it was made of tissue paper. My fingers were already numb when I found myself outside the 24-hour diner on Main.

I ducked inside, relishing the warm blast of greasy air and coffee. The waitress barely looked up when I slid into a booth at the back. I wrapped my hands around the chipped ceramic mug she set in front of me, watching as steam curled up into the dim lights.

My phone buzzed again.

Unknown Number: Let's meet at The Rosewood, 8:00 p.m. My treat, of course.

I swallowed. The Rosewood? That was no cheap bar—it was high-end, expensive. The kind of place that didn't let you in unless you had a black card or a last name that meant something.

I tapped out a response.

Juniper: How will I know you?

A pause. Then:

Unknown Number: Wear something red. I'll find you.

I shivered, but it had nothing to do with the cold.

This was really happening. There was no turning back.

2

Jenna's apartment smelled like vanilla and expendable income. I stepped into the bright light and high ceilings of someone who had their shit together. It didn't serve me to be jealous, but dammit, I would trade places with her in an instant. She was the chic sort of lesbian that they made queer media about—a polished, upscale gay who we used as marketing to convince the straights that gays were members of the Illuminati and secretly controlling the banks. Her place was always clean, always pristine, with sheer curtains that softened the harsh winter light spilling through the oversized windows. I had never felt more like a stray dog dragged in from the cold.

She squished me in a hug the moment I walked through the door. "Babe, you look like you're falling apart."

"Thanks, Jenna, you look great too," I coughed into her cloud of perfectly straightened platinum blonde hair. She'd had her life together from the moment I met her. She was the most organized sophomore in our undergraduate dorm; a girl with a life plan from which she did not deviate. Now, she was out of school with a great job in marketing while I continued to whither in class.

"I just mean, you need a break. Get out of that shitty place of yours. You can crash here." Jenna pulled out of the hug. "If my roommate's okay with it."

I didn't bother getting my hopes up. "She's not. Your roommate sucks."

"Yeah, she's the worst." Jenna sighed, already rummaging through her closet. "But your message said you're here for a dress, not my couch, right? Got a hot date?"

I nodded, perching on the edge of Jenna's plush, white bed. I was never comfortable in places like this, places where people could afford matching furniture and seasonal decor. "Something red, please."

Jenna plucked a short, ruby dress from her rack, holding it against my frame with a scrutinizing eye. "Jesus, Cass, do you even eat?"

I shrugged. "When I can afford it."

I bit down on my inner lip to keep from showing any emotion at the comment. Mentioning someone's weight was usually a shitty move. When Jenna did it, I knew it was because she was threatening to move into my sorry excuse for an apartment and cook me three square meals until I was on my feet again.

"You're all sharp angles." Jenna turned me toward the full-length mirror. "Look at you. That balayage is just grown-out roots, isn't it?"

I attempted a half-smirk. "Balayage sounds trendier."

Jenna sighed, stepping behind me, fingers already in my hair. "You are so lucky you're naturally pretty, because you have no idea what you're doing."

I clamped down on my inner lip, harder this time.

It wasn't that I didn't know how to be pretty. It was that I couldn't afford the Beauty Industrial Complex and whatever it was selling us from month to month. I barely budgeted for under-eye concealer and lip balm. I'd be the first to get a boob job, eyelash extensions, and a blow out if I won the lottery.

I wasn't ugly, but I wasn't the type to turn heads on my own.

My hair, long and brown with subtle caramel streaks, had been a happy accident of neglect rather than salon expertise. My frame was rail-thin, my chest small, hips slightly boxy. I was pretty sure that I'd figure out makeup when I had room on my credit card, and that my persistent disastrous state was a function of my wallet. Jenna, ever the fixer, was happy to take over.

"So, what's this dinner?" Jenna asked, dabbing foundation onto my face. "Girl or guy?"

I released a shaky breath before admitting, "I put up a sugar baby ad."

Jenna froze mid-brushstroke, then let out a short laugh. "Oh, hun." I braced myself for judgment, but Jenna just smirked, setting the brush down. "I did that once, you know. Junior year."

My brows lifted. "No shit?"

"No shit. It just wasn't a good experience, so I never talk about it." Jenna rifled through her drawer for mascara. "The guy smelled like Hamburger Helper and cried halfway through because he felt bad for cheating on his wife. But hey, it paid off my car."

I made a face. "Yikes."

Jenna finished the last swipe of lip gloss and pulled back to admire her work. "Yeah, never again. But you do what you gotta do." She turned, grabbing her phone. "Speaking of bad decisions…"

She pulled out her phone, then grimaced.

"What?" I extended my hand for the device.

"Never mind. I shouldn't have said anything." She shook her head.

"For fuck's sake," I grumbled, snatching the phone from her, holding its staticky glow an inch from my nose.

The room around melted as the bright, neon rectangle took over my vision. My stomach twisted.

A picture of my ex-girlfriend, snowboard in hand, all

wrapped up in a cozy lodge selfie with the girl she cheated with. They were kissing, all lips and grins and helmets and snow.

I couldn't breathe. "Wow."

Jenna squeezed my shoulder. "You okay?"

I forced an unconvincing smile. "Yeah. Just nice to see that I got replaced so fast. Glad our years together were so meaningful."

Jenna's eyes softened. "Babe, skip dinner. Stay here with me. Let's get takeout and watch romcoms and drink too much wine and cry over your asshole of an ex. We need to process."

"I don't want to process. I want to become a badass doctor and make her regret it, so she crawls back to me in a decade, and I get to shoot her down."

"Hun…"

"Thanks for the dress, Jen. I gotta go."

I CHAFED MY SKIN FOR WARMTH, DANCING FROM HEEL TO HEEL AS I rallied the courage to enter the restaurant. "Pull it together. Maybe Cassidy is a broke coward, but this Juniper chick?"

A valet looked up from his stand with a furrowed brow. I ignored him, ignored the frost on the sidewalk, ignored the fancy couples in their fur shawls and designer jackets as I dug deep.

"Whether it goes well or not doesn't matter. You literally have nothing to lose."

The truth of the last statement plummeted into my gut, as if the frost had permeated my stomach. I straightened my shoulders, marched toward the door, and the valet sprinted to open it for me just as I reached for the handle.

"Thank you," I muttered.

"Good luck," he said.

Warmth leached into me the moment I crossed the threshold.

The Rosewood was everything I had expected: dimly lit, sleek, and filled with men in tailored suits who didn't check their bank accounts before ordering. I handed my coat to the hostess, suddenly hyper-aware of how much skin I was showing.

I took an uncertain step toward the tables, scanning for a man who, if my experience was to be anything like Jenna's, smelled like Hamburger Helper.

"Juniper?" asked a low, husky voice behind me.

I turned and struggled to suppress my shock.

I don't know what I'd been expecting, but I would have been less surprised to see an eighty-year-old white man with a gut and a wedding ring than this young, tanned, well-dressed gentleman.

I sucked in a breath.

The man was beautiful in that effortless, untouchable way. Dark hair, sharp features, the kind of looks that felt deliberately sculpted. He had the sort of permanent tan that stood out against the sunless winter. His watch alone could have bought me two cars and a night on the town. He was too refined to be here for someone like me. His cologne reminded me of sea breezes and something fresh, green, and foreign. Not a hamburger to be had.

I hesitated.

I forced myself forward, heels clicking against the marble floors.

"Lovely to meet you," he greeted smoothly, offering his hand. When I took it, he swept mine to his mouth and brushed a kiss against my knuckles. Electricity ran from my fingers, through my arm, up my neck, sending goosebumps sprawling across my back at his kiss. "I'm Denning. We're seated this way."

"Your name is…Denning?" I asked, still trying to gather my

composure. The man led me to a table in the corner where he pulled out a chair for me. I slid in while he took the seat across.

He arched a brow. "Why? Not a believable name? You're the one going by Juniper."

I bit the inside of my cheek, still tingling from the innocuous kiss. "Fair enough."

Denning leaned back, signaling to the waiter without a word. I'd come here for an arrangement, prepared to meet a monster, but this man oozed sex. I struggled to breathe around him.

The server appeared a moment later, pouring wine into our glasses before slipping away. I scanned the menu, trying not to look at the prices. My stomach grumbled a little too loudly for my comfort. This place was all oysters and steak tartare and other raw foods with the sort of names incomprehensible for a girl with a weekly $20 budget.

When the waitress returned to the table, Denning ordered for both of us. He got the wagyu steak and grilled lobster for himself, and the truffle ravioli for me. "You look like you could stand to gain a few pounds."

I shifted self-consciously, then reached for an artisanal bread, if only to pick off the seeds.

It'd be great if everyone stopped making underhanded digs at my body. I wanted unfettered access to food just as much as the next person.

He buttered a roll of his own, and the motion exposed the black ink of a tattoo around his wrist. It appeared to be script, though it was a language I didn't recognize.

"Cool tattoo," I said.

He let out a low laugh, as if at a private joke. He tugged the sleeve over the ink and asked, "Do you have any?"

"One," I admitted. I thought of the purple, pink and blue moon I'd gotten on flash sale during the last pride. "On my ankle. I'm planning on getting more, but I'm waiting until I pass the boards. Then I'll get one to celebrate."

"Can it be easily covered? Yours, that is?"

I was surprised by the request but wasn't about to look a gift horse in the mouth and question him over something so minor. "Sure, I can do that."

"Before I explain my proposal, I need to know if you can take a week off of school. Your ad mentioned that you're studying medicine?"

I cleared my throat. A week? They flayed me alive if I missed a single day. "Not without a doctor's note."

"That's not a problem," he said. "I'll have my private physician write something up. We'll need a full day of travel in either direction, and then five days on our trip."

Sure. A normal solution to normal problems.

"Let's get the awkward part out of the way." Denning slid an envelope across the table.

I swapped the roll for the envelope, picking it up hesitantly, feeling the weight of cash inside.

"A deposit," he explained. "To be perfectly frank with you, I have no interest in paying you for sex."

I thought of the sugar-scamming liar, knowing a trap when I heard one.

The restaurant's din hummed in a blurred, foggy sort of way, as red smears and candles and the idle chatter of the wealthy hummed around us.

His lip twitched into a half smile. "Don't get me wrong. You're quite lovely. I'd be thrilled to grab that dress by the collar, bend you over the table, shove your head into the bread, and fuck you right now in front of the buttoned-up dinner crowd."

Holy shit.

My cheeks heated, and I could only imagine they were a shade lighter than my red dress. Suddenly, my chest wasn't the only place with a heartbeat. I squirmed in my seat. I was certain my face was as red as the dress. I managed to sputter, "And scandalize the waitress?"

"I'm sure she's seen worse," he said. "But that is not why I need a companion on this trip. I need a real person. Someone with a history, a backstory, who can convincingly play the part of my girlfriend."

I blinked. "Then why me? Why not hire an actress?"

"Because my ex-wife's private detective breathes into her ear like a dragon," he rolled his eyes. "If you had any experience in acting—even a whiff—she'd be onto our ruse before you tasted the hors d'oeuvres."

I thought of Amanda—of seeing her smug, cheating face as she gloated atop a snow-capped mountain with the girl she threw away our life for—and balked at the idea of a former lover knowing that much about my life. "Do you always travel with your ex?"

"Come on," he winked. "Isn't revenge sweetest when your ex can choke on your happiness? You have to let them know you won the breakup. And if I bring you…"

If my face wasn't red before, it certainly was now.

I struggled to imagine that I could make a wealthy former spouse jealous, and yet… I had to admit, I'd love for Amanda to be the one gripping a friend's phone as she stared at pictures of me grinning alongside a chiseled millionaire. She'd always hated that I was bisexual. Maybe she deserved a salted insult to injury.

"Unfortunately, she's part owner of the island," he explained. "This is an annual trip. She's hoping I'll sell her my share, but it's not going to happen."

I wondered what it would take me to give up my stake in a private island…then I wondered what it would be like to dive, headfirst, into a vault of gold like Scrooge McDuck, and whatever sort of unhinged questions the wealthy asked of themselves.

"If you were a professional escort, they'd discover you in seconds," he continued. "No, it has to be this. Which, while I'm on the topic of discretion, I would appreciate if you took down your post until our arrangement is finished."

I swallowed. "So, what do you need?"

"I hate traveling alone." He exhaled, rolling his glass between his fingers. "My ex-wife has already moved on. I'd prefer not to arrive by myself."

He slid his phone toward me. I glanced at the screen. Pictures of a tropical island—clear turquoise waters, white sand beaches, the kind of place that only existed in travel brochures. I half-wondered if his scent was cologne at all, or if being this wealthy meant he'd just absorbed the essence of the tropics.

"It's a privately owned island—one of the Gilis," he said. "Off the coast of Lombok, Indonesia. If you don't mind a jaunt across the globe."

I stared at the photos, heart pounding. What was that old adage about something seeming too good to be true?

Denning took a sip of his wine, watching my reaction. "All I need is the full, pampered girlfriend experience. You play the part, memorize a few details about me, get ready to answer some questions about yourself, and make it believable."

"So, for all intents and purposes, we'll be dating?" I asked, still staring at the screen. I wanted to ask if that meant sex was *off* the table, as I was pretty sure that nothing made me hornier than being drunk on mojitos, relaxing in a beachside mansion with a staggeringly handsome millionaire.

"Indeed." The slow smile played at the corner of his mouth. "You'll be mine, and I'll be yours."

His words made me dizzy.

"And…if I get uncomfortable? If I feel like I'm in over my head?"

His lower lip lifted, contemplative. "Safe words are for more than sex. We could choose one that signals we need to stop. You can get out at any time."

I looked over his shoulder at the window, recoiling at the

yellow streetlight that reflected off of the dirty snow. "How about 'winter'?"

His mouth curved in a polite attempt not to laugh. "We'll want a word that doesn't get said in regular conversation. The goal is for it to be jarring enough that it stops whatever's happening, no matter the context. Winter may be a little too common."

I understood his amusement. I'd given myself away: I'd never chosen a safe word before. "How about 'tundra'?"

"Already choosing safe words." His hand moved toward mine. His palm twitched, hovering above mine, before withdrawing. "Does that mean you're in?"

I'd be crazy to go, right? And equally crazy to say no.

He went on. "Feel free to post about the trip—just wait until after you're back. Not that you'll have much of a choice. The Wi-Fi is rather spotty on the island."

I looked back at him, the weight of the moment settling in.

This was insane. Reckless. Dangerous.

But God, that island was beautiful.

And I had nothing left to lose.

I exhaled, reaching for my glass, then lifting it for a toast. "Alright, Denning," I clinked my glass against his. "Tell me everything I need to know."

3

FUCK, FUCK, FUCK.

I rushed home, heart pounding, and tore through my drawers, looking for the small, blue book. Getting a passport was one of the last nice things my parents did before abandoning me to med school. My fingers skimmed over the cover before I flipped it open, exhaling when I saw the expiration date was ages away.

One crisis avoided.

Packing was another story. I had never traveled internationally, much less to an island, much less to an island with a man who had handed me an envelope of cash and expected me to play a part. I shoved a few necessities into my suitcase before realizing my threadbare jeans and faded t-shirts weren't exactly 'rich man's girlfriend' material. Especially a man as fine as Denning…I couldn't help but wonder what might happen if the trip went well. If I was the perfect girlfriend, maybe we could continue dating. Maybe this would be the first of many…

I'd only been with two men, though, and my blowjob game left something to be desired. Good thing he knew he was hiring a broke med student instead of a professional.

Jenna's text came through as I sent her my itinerary:

Jenna: What the fuck am I supposed to do with "one of the Gilis"? That's not specific enough if I'm on the phone with the Indonesian embassy trying to retrieve your body.

Cassidy: Could you be a little more positive?

Jenna: Sure. I'm positive he's about to kill you and wear your skin.

I snorted and tossed my phone onto the bed. I didn't have the time to panic. Denning was on tonight's redeye. Meanwhile, I'd been given homework. I was to get highlights, a manicure, and enough designer pieces to look the part, all on his dime. I didn't know how special you had to be to have Amex add a line of credit in your name and overnight the card, but I was told to put some miles on the borrowed piece of plastic.

I counted the stacks of bills and exhaled with the sort of relief I hadn't felt since I was six years old—a kid with no responsibilities, no obligations beyond to be playful and learn my alphabet. He'd given me four times more than I needed to turn things around, and this was only the deposit. My mind reeled over what it would mean for me if I could afford to move out of this place, if I could stay on top of tuition payments, if I didn't have to choose between paying my phone bill and eating dinner. I counted out a quarter of the stack and marched to the landlord's office, pounded on his door until he answered, and shoved the overdue rent towards him.

His fingers closed around the wad of cash.

"I want a receipt," I said, refusing to release my grip on the money. "I'm not gonna let you pretend I didn't pay you as some excuse to kick me out."

"You've got a lot of nerve, talking to me like that after the stunts you've pulled."

I yanked the cash back, counted it in front of him, then

crossed my arms and waited. After a disgruntled beat, he fetched a pen and paper from the table by the door, scribbled down the confirmation of payment, and signed it. Victorious, I stormed back to my apartment with an assignment.

First, get some beauty rest.

Then, turn my life around.

DENNING HAD BOOKED ME AT A SALON AT 9:00 A.M. FOR MY RICH bitch glow up. Five hours later, I had an official bronde balayage instead of the low-rent knock-off I'd been rocking for the better part of two years, a nude, almond-shaped manicure, and a rosy-pink pedicure.

I didn't know where to find designer stores in Denver, but I'd been in Nordstrom enough times, skulking past the Louis Vuitton and Hermes kiosks—if that's what you called a brand's presence in a department store when their prices started at a thousand—to find a few pieces. The plan was to pretend the airline had lost my checked bag and pillage the island's luxury guest closet from there.

I didn't realize that designer stores sold beachwear, but a nerve-wracking hour later, I had a white and beige Fendi swim-suit, a sporty bag with the logo printed on the strap, a cover-up, and pale wedges. I picked up a carry-on luggage from Gucci, a matching black sweat set from Balenciaga, along with their iconic shoes-that-look-like-socks for the plane. I got my jewelry and perfume from Chanel, and with it, a stress migraine to last the ages.

The shopping spree cost nine months of rent and gave me such debilitating imposter syndrome that I spent the entire time worried about being thrown from the premises, but I did it.

A few hours later, I walked into Denver International Airport, stomach twisting with anticipation. I had half of the designer pieces on my back, and the other carefully folded in the luxury rolling bag. The sleek silk, the delicate lace, the impossibly expensive price tags—Denning had told me to look the part, and I was now Rich Bitch from head to toe.

First-class check-in was smoother than I had ever experienced, mostly because I had only flown twice before, and both times had been in the cramped, sneeze-filled nightmare of economy.

He'd texted to remind me that my ticket came with access to the sky lounge, which meant another hour of cosplaying as a nepo baby before takeoff.

It was a world away from the overcrowded terminal chaos I was used to. Plush leather chairs, complimentary champagne, soft music playing over speakers that weren't blasting distorted flight announcements. I sank into one of the oversized seats, stretching my legs as I sipped on something fizzy.

Another ping. I checked to see if it was from my new Sugar Daddy but was surprised to see Jenna's message along with an attached photo of my date.

Jenna: Is this your Denning?

Cassidy: That's him, yes. He's gorgeous.

Jenna: Too gorgeous. Nathaniel Denning Rothschild, III. His parents are in the hotel industry. Father is from New York. Mother is from Mumbai. I can't figure out what he's doing in Denver.

Cassidy: Damn, Sherlock.

Jenna: I don't like it. Look at these articles. It makes it sound like they're under water with debt. They've closed eight locations in the last year alone. How does he have the money to hire you for this vacation?

Cassidy: You know what they say about looking a gift horse in the mouth?

Jenna: To do it with a magnifying glass! This is your life, girl. Don't throw it away.

I knew she meant well, but she couldn't understand how broke and desperate I was. Her advice was coming from a place of someone with options. I had none. I closed my phone and ordered another flute.

Maybe it was the nerves, or just being told it was complementary, but I downed three glasses of champagne before stumbling to my gate.

By the time I boarded, my body still wasn't used to the level of privilege I was now experiencing. My seat—if it could even be called that—was a fully enclosed suite with a lay-flat bed, a flatscreen larger than the one I had at home, a personal minibar, and what felt like more space than my first apartment. As the plane took off, I lay back, staring at the ceiling and trying to process how the hell my life had shifted so fast. Now that I was on the cusp of having everything, I began wondering what terrible things I would do to keep from waking up from this dream.

The flights from Denver to Narita, then Japan to Indonesia gave me a chance to concentrate on my assignment. I would memorize everything: the names of his nannies, his siblings, his jobs, his boarding schools, his drink order, how he liked his steak cooked, everything. For one week, I would be the best girlfriend the world had ever seen. I would study the information Denning had given me as if my life depended on it, because the way I saw it, it may as well have.

JAKARTA'S HUMID AIR HIT ME THE SECOND I STEPPED OFF THE plane, thick and salty, carrying the dust and sweat of thirty-four million residents in its smog. I'd marveled at the gray-green mist enshrouding the concrete jungle on our descent, and in another life—one where I could backpack through Asia and savor the sights and foods and smells—I'd like to stay and appreciate the madness. As it were, I was glad I was only here for the time it took to locate the private jet.

It belonged to Denning's friends—Roman and Clementine, he'd said—though we were welcome to use it.

I'd slept most of the flight and followed an influencer's skin care tips for waking up glowy, but I still felt like a sweaty, unwashed mess as I hurried through the terminal. I was too single and too thirsty to show up to meet a millionaire while looking like a gremlin. I sent Jenna a selfie of me beneath an airport sign printed in three languages as proof of life, then told her I'd touch base when I could.

Denning was waiting for me just beyond customs, looking completely unbothered by the heat in his linen shirt and expensive sunglasses. I caught the tattoo once more—partially obscured by his watch, but now without the benefit of a long sleeve to hide it—and guessed that it was written in Sanskrit. His smile was easy, practiced, and as soon as I stepped into his reach, he leaned down and pressed a kiss to my cheek. I tried to remind myself that this was just business, but the heat spreading from my face down my chest suddenly had nothing to do with the tropics.

"We're almost to paradise." He slipped an arm around my waist and guiding me toward the next leg of our journey: the private jet waiting to take us to the island. I savored his touch on my lower back as he asked, "Are you ready to play the role of a lifetime?"

4

ISLAND: DAY ONE

I'D ONLY SEEN PRIVATE JETS IN MOVIES. THIS ONE HAD THE SAME beige carpeting, wood panel strip with muted light, and stuffed leather recliners I'd come to expect from films. It also came with a polite, beautiful woman in a matching uniform and little sailor hat who served us snacks and drinks throughout the flight. Maybe if things didn't work out with my sugar daddy, I'd double back to the airport and catch her number.

She handed me a steamed, ginger-scented towel. "Can I get you anything before takeoff?"

As I returned it to her, I noticed that she, too, had a thin strip of ink around her wrist—daintier than Denning's, but unmistakably similar. I pointed to her tattoo. "What does that mean?"

She gave me a glassy-eyed smile. "It means I'm part of the island. I'm sure you'll see many of these in the days to come. Perhaps you'll end up with one, yourself. Now, may I get you anything?"

I shook my head and closed my eyes, braced against a small patch of turbulence.

"Nervous flyer?" Denning asked.

"I don't know what kind of flyer I am," I said. "This trip is the most time I've ever spent in the air by a longshot."

He remained polite, if a bit cool, during the final two-hour flight.

Then again, I was nervous, which made me chatty.

"You're going to do fine," he assured me. He flagged the stewardess—the only one aboard the jet—for two glasses of champagne. "Liquid courage."

"I think shots of tequila would be better suited for the kind of courage I need."

He lifted his finger once more. "Ma'am? Two shots of tequila for me and my girlfriend."

My heart skipped at the word. He was already in character. It was time for me to be, too. I took the plunge and reached over, squeezing his hand. "Thanks, dear. You always know just what I need."

She brought over a small wooden plate with two carefully balanced shot glasses, four slices of lime, and a small pile of sea salt. I forewent the hand-licking and simply dipped one of the green wedges directly in the salt.

I didn't miss the pleased look on his face. "Bersulang," he said.

"Na zdorovie," I replied. An explosion of acid, sour and bitter salt, burning liquid, and I waited for the cough that never came as down the hatch they went.

"Damn, that's smooth," I marveled. Then asked, "What should I expect?"

He considered the question. "My friends are quite nice, most of the time. I'm sure they'll love you."

"And if they don't?"

The engine whirred beneath us, vibrating pleasantly as fluffy, white clouds bobbed beyond the window. Clean, white light illuminated him, making him look like an angel as he replied.

"They will. If they don't, then the next thing I'm going to

say is irrelevant. But if they do like you, and I'm certain they will, we do an initiation ceremony of sorts—one that christens you into the island."

I gnawed on my lip. "What does that mean? That I can come back?"

"It's just a tradition in the friend group," he shrugged. "We've all gone through something similar."

"And this…ceremony…is it scary? Fun? What are we talking about?"

"It's a once-in-a-lifetime experience. I'd be shocked if you didn't love it."

Denning redirected the conversation from there. He quizzed me on a few basic things a girlfriend should know about her boyfriend, and before I knew it, we were arriving. He sipped champagne as a chaser before pointing out the window. "There it is. Which means we're low on time." He lifted a finger for the flight attendant's attention. "One more shot before we descend."

I raised a brow. "Starting the party early?"

"It's for you," he said as she handed me a second clear shot of tequila.

"Oh, I'm okay." I gave the flight attendant a polite grimace for having wasted her effort.

But she didn't pull the tray away, and Denning didn't budge.

His gaze held mine. "Drink it."

Was he serious? I tried to shake my head again, to reject the shot, but the flight attendant continued staring at me with that eerie, glassy smile. Denning watched, waiting for my compliance. And the shot stared back at me, filled to the brim.

"Are you going to make me say 'tundra' already?"

He didn't look away. "If that's how you feel, I'll drop it. Or we can come up with a second word. If 'tundra' means our unequivocal stop, then perhaps we need its opposite: a word that means 'trust me and go with this.'"

I looked at the tequila. "And you want me to blindly trust you to take a shot? Why?"

A smile. "Things are so much sweeter, June, when you relinquish control."

I swallowed. "I like control."

"All the better," he said. "Consider this my Hippocratic Oath: in stripping your control, I will do no harm. I'm willing to bet you'll see it my way."

My pulse hiccupped as I looked at the shot—at what it represented. *Was this his game?*

"Hippocrates?" I asked, lightly touching the shot glass, as I offered a word.

"Hippocrates," he echoed, confirming our second safe word.

Alright. If I was going to be trapped on the island with rich fucking assholes, I might as well be drunk for it.

I narrowed my eyes, grabbed the shot, abandoned the salt and lime, and tossed it back.

"There's a good girl."

I wasn't sure if it was the liquor, the weird mind game, or his words making me hot, but I was glad for the visual distraction as I glued myself to the window for the last ten minutes of the flight. Then, at last, we were on the ground.

I had no sense of perspective from the sky, and the lack of buildings didn't help. Unlike Jakarta's skyscrapers and booming industry, I couldn't find a single building on the island. As we landed, I spotted the first two structures: a small shelter with a golf cart and a single attendant parked underneath, and a hanger—little more than a glorified garage—for the jet to refuel.

As we headed toward the modest means of transportation, I spotted the first of Denning's friends. A glamorous woman in a gold gown waited just in the treeline. I reached for his elbow, grazing it to get his attention as I gestured to the dark-haired woman.

"Which one of your friends is that?" I asked.

I looked over to the trees but, by the time he followed my gaze, she was nowhere to be found.

"It must have been one of the groundskeepers," he said dismissively.

"A groundskeeper in so much jewelry I could spot it from the plane?"

If the rest of his compatriots wore anything that gawdy, I was in for a treat.

I eyed the forest for a moment longer, but there was nothing to be seen amidst the dangling vines and larger-than-life monstera leaves, so I traded green for blue. The sapphire horizon of sea and sky bled together, an endless, indigo line between us and civilization.

This was what it meant to be in the middle of nowhere.

"Selemat malam, sir," the attendant greeted Denning. "Someone is on the way for your bags. Please allow me to escort you to your villa."

"Selemat," Denning echoed. He gestured for me to take a seat in the back of the shaded cart, then rounded the corner and slid in. Sweat was already beading between my breasts, but Denning didn't look dewy in the slightest. I wondered how he managed it.

"Do you live here full time?" I asked the attendant.

He turned around and smiled cheerfully, then faced forward without responding.

"Most of the staff speaks limited English," Denning explained. "Ni Luh is the head of staff, so if you need anything, you'll be able to tell her, and she'll relay the message."

"But he was just speaking perfect English a minute ago," I argued.

"No. He's memorized useful phrases. It's okay if it feels a little unusual at first. I'm sure you'll get the hang of it in no time."

"Is it the same with the flight attendant?" I asked.

"Hmm?"

"The flight attendant…when she used the word 'belong' like that, I assumed it was lost in translation. Humans can't own humans anymore, right?" When he didn't immediately jump in, I began to spiral. "Oh god. Please tell me I'm not complicit in some sort of human trafficking—"

Cord-like vines dangled from the branches overhead, running their tendrils along the top of the golf cart. The sound was jarring enough to get me to shut up, as if the tree itself had lifted a silencing finger to its lips.

He chuckled. "No, no, it's nothing like that. I think you'll understand once you've spent a few days with us. Once you've worked here, lived here, or visited here, it's hard to envision yourself anywhere else. I'm pretty sure she doesn't even deplane when we land in Jakarta. She has no desire to be in the city."

"You know her pretty well, then?" I asked, unsure as to why I was feeling a pang of insecurity when he spoke of the pretty stewardess. He was just playing the role of my boyfriend. In reality, he was nothing to me. I needed to remember that.

Maybe that's why he didn't answer.

I let my gaze fall away from him and wander to the jungle.

Thirty-foot palm trees swayed in the breeze. Glassy, blue water splashed over volcanic rocks. We had landed close enough to the ocean for both me and a seabird to spot a few fish. Waxy pink, white, and yellow flowers—jepun, Denning told me—adorned the thin, twisty trees. An electric fuchsia flower dotted the bushes. Shiny, rubber-looking lilies lined the brushed concrete path. A jewel-toned bird chirped an exotic melody, and a second answered.

I pinched myself to ensure I wasn't dreaming.

"This is unreal," I breathed, marveling at the hibiscus, the birds of paradise, even the moss and ferns coating the retaining walls.

"Is it what you expected?" he asked.

I didn't know how to tell him that no, it wasn't. I wasn't

capable of expecting this. I wasn't even capable of fantasizing about a place this perfect.

"How long is the ride to the villas?" I asked.

"The whole island is a thirty-minute golf cart ride across. The villas are on the western peninsula, so the sunsets are out of this world. We'll be in eyeshot of the main house when we round the next bend, so this is your last chance to make a run for it and dive into the jungle."

I chuckled nervously, looking at the dense foliage. "Are there any animals in the woods?"

"A couple of monkeys." He looked up and to the right while he dug through his memory. "Geckos, bats, bugs…and Lemon owns a jaguar."

"Lemon?"

"My ex."

I'd fixated on the wrong part of the statement. Did he say a jaguar?

I wasn't prepared for the view as we turned the corner. What lay ahead could hardly be described as villas, rather a compound of luxury buildings—all brushed concrete, glass, and gauzy curtains, divided by fresh cut grass and walkways made of polished stone—blossomed into view. I caught my first glimpse of a tawny woman in a flowing orange dress and felt a shock run through me.

"Denning," I whispered his name urgently, reaching over to squeeze his knee. "How did we meet?"

He leaned toward me but did not match my intensity. With smiling ease, he said, "As a third-year med student, you've already begun your clinical rotation, right? You were shadowing a doctor when I went in for stitches, and when he left the room, I asked for your number."

I swallowed. "But what do you—"

He tapped his forearm. "A boating accident sent me to urgent care four months ago. I was too far from home to go to the family physician. The story works."

The woman in orange spotted us and began to wave. "Denning! Darling, get over here!"

The attendant stopped the golf cart just in time for her to run up and give him a peck on each cheek, which he politely returned. "Indie, how are you?"

"I'm in paradise! How do you think I am?" She popped off her sunglasses to eye me, face filled with the sort of over-the-top excitement that either meant she was a treasure or a nightmare. She flung out her arms for a hug. "And you must be the girlfriend! He's been keeping you all to himself. I'm Indie. Indie Demirci. And you are?"

I was instantly glad for the Balenciaga getup, as I felt frumpy in Indie's presence even dressed top to bottom in designer pieces. "Juniper," I cleared my throat, buying just enough time to supply my middle name in lieu of my last. "Juniper Mae."

"Now *there* is a charming name." She pulled away but did not release me. Her hands remained on my elbows as she shot Denning a wink. "You always did know how to pick them. Hopefully, you'll be a peach and share her." With that, she blew a kiss and headed back for the villa.

"You okay?" he chuckled at what was surely my shell-shocked expression.

I shouldered my purse as we walked toward the eco-chic building. "She was way too pretty to be that nice," I said.

The cocked half-smile stayed on his lips. "Well, you're gorgeous, and I guarantee she wants to fuck you."

I nearly choked on my own spit. "But as far as she knows, I'm your girlfriend."

"Indie is in the lifestyle. Everyone here is now that I think about it."

I repeated the word. "Lifestyle? Like…socialite?"

Another laugh. "Yes, she's a socialite," he put a hand on the sliding glass door and guided me into modern luxury. "But lifestyle is shorthand for the…*adventurous*. Usually, the term is used to describe swingers, swappers, and the sexually open. You'll neither offend me, nor blow our cover should you wish to indulge."

I stared at him, eyes bulging, for any indication that he was joking.

He was not.

I took a few cautious steps around the villa, taking stock of everything. Bamboo fixtures, the straight lines of tropical minimalism, and the elevated reds and golds of what I could only assume was a priceless tapestry were all a far cry from Jakarta's bustle. We'd left the sweat, the pollution, the grime of millions of bodies behind for air conditioning, the soothing rhythm of crashing waves, and hibiscus-scented linens. Clean sun filtered through spotless glass to illuminate our home for the next week. One king bed. One canopy. One white sofa tucked in a nook with a coffee table. One bar cart with coffee supplies on top and alcohol and a wine fridge on the bottom. An enormous television. A writing desk built into the wall that ran the length of one side of the room. A three-quarters dividing wall, separating the sleeping area from the bath area. A closed-off water closet, and on the other side, closed-off indoor-outdoor shower. A terrace with a small, submerged soaking pool. A daybed. And by the door: a golden statue of two women. The first had four arms, with two hands pointing up clutching something that might have been flowers, one hand flattened up as if to stop us from advancing, the other palm flattened out to receive. The second, a woman with six arms tilted in action, stuck out a serpentine tongue, held an archer's bow, and appeared ready to strike

A woven-leaf basket filled with offerings sat beside them.

A small plate of artfully displayed food, a smoking stick of incense, an elaborate boutonniere of flowers, and something shiny that caught my eye. I moved closer to inspect and my jaw dropped at the sight. Atop a small gold plate was an unmistakable pile of precious gems—emeralds, rubies, sapphire and diamonds.

"Holy shit," I said, extending a finger toward the jewels.

"I wouldn't touch their things," Denning said from over my shoulder.

I dropped my finger. "Whose things?"

"The goddesses'." There was a frustrating nonchalance to his tone that let me know he hadn't intended to explain.

"I'm going to need you to give me a little more than that," I pushed. When my frown was unyielding, he offered a short, defeated sigh, then gestured toward the altar.

"The majority of Indonesia is monotheistic—Islam is the dominant religion. Bali is the exception, which is pretty much exclusively Hindu. You'll find a decent mixture of Buddhist saints, Hindu gods, and even a decent splash of animism in the polytheistic islands. These are two of their goddesses. They bless the island."

"We're not in Bali."

"We're not in the rest of Indonesia, either," he replied.

I hadn't grown up religious, nor had I spent any meaningful time learning about the faiths of the world, save for the elementary school unit on Greek Mythology when I was eleven. I had a thousand more questions, but before I could ask one, Denning changed the topic.

"It looks like our bags are here," he said, nudging the gauzy curtains to the side and looking out the French glass door. "I'm going to track down Clementine and let her know that your checked bag was lost and see if we can't rustle up some beach attire. Help yourself to the minibar—it's not a hotel, there's no charge—and I'll be back in a bit."

I wanted to protest, but to what end, I wasn't sure. He was my only lifeline on a remote rock in the sea filled with sex-crazed strangers. I didn't know how to act normal or relaxed while navigating this impossible scenario. I was still wrapping my head around flying overseas, let alone jetting to a private island. The woodwork, stone accents, earthy tones, and rain-forest felt too big and too small all at once.

The attendant entered with my Gucci carry-on and Denning's proper luggage just as my date slipped out. I uselessly tried to engage the man in conversation when a pair of moving figures rounded the corner and stopped short.

Two men—both over six feet and with their botanical shirts unbuttoned to show the world their rippling abdominals—grinned at the sight of me.

"You must be Denning's girl." The first man grinned. He was just pink enough from the sun to pass for blushing. I relaxed as he spoke, catching the vocal inflection I usually heard in gay clubs. I suddenly wished my tri-colored moon was on my wrist instead of my ankle, so I'd have an organic way to tell him we flew similar flags.

The other man was the first to extend a rich, brown hand. "I'm Odie," he said. "My partner is Flick."

"Charmed," Flick said. "So, tell us, how are you finding the island?"

I answered honestly. "I have no idea. I've only been here for ten minutes and am already so overwhelmed."

"Oh," Odie tsk'ed his regrets. "Jet lag will do that."

"Don't nap, though," Flick cautioned. "Or you'll never get adjusted to the time zone."

"Would you like a wake-me-up?" Odie asked.

I cocked my head to the side. "I'm sorry?"

"A bump," Flick explained.

At my uncomprehending stare, Odie said, "Of coke, babe. To help you stay awake."

My eyes widened. "Oh! No, I'm okay."

"Are you off nose candy?" Odie nodded knowingly. "They'll fuck up your septum. I've got some Adderall in my bag, if you'd prefer."

It was as if they were speaking English, yet weren't. Colorado had led the charge on the legalization of recreational weed, and mushrooms were sure to be right around the corner. When it came to hard drugs, I'd been raised to believe that capsules, powders, and pills were peddled by wormy, back-alley figures in trench coats. D.A.R.E. hadn't prepared me for the peer pressure of sexy rich people on vacation. A white seabird flapped behind them, offering a high-pitched whistle in place of the proverbial cricket chirp.

"I'm…all good…on drugs. Erm…thanks."

My response delighted them. Flick flashed his partner a set of bright white teeth. "Ah, he brought a *good* girl. Ever's gonna *love* her."

"Lemon's going to *hate* her," Odie replied. Then, "We'll let you settle in. Tah, dear. See you at dinner."

"And remember," Flick added, *"don't* nap. It's the worst thing you can do."

"Well, one of the worst," Odie added. "You're already here with Denning, after all."

The men shared a chuckle as they departed, vanishing as quickly as they'd arrived. Left me with knots in my stomach over the idea that Denning's ex-wife was predestined to despise me. I wasn't sure why I thought it would be any different. Hell, it was batshit of me to agree to go to an island with a sugar daddy in the first place, let alone one where a former spouse would be present.

I returned to the bed, sinking slowly onto the corner and flopping backward to stare at the canopy. What was I doing?

I closed my eyes, only for a second. Just for one second.

Just…for…one…

5

Had I forgotten to pay the electricity bill? It was so fucking dark.

I reached for my bedside lamp only for my hand to flap uselessly in empty space. I rolled over to hit the cheap, naked bulb on the thrifted nightstand only for reality to come crashing back.

I wasn't in Denver. It was no longer the dead of winter. I was no longer the girl who'd left her shitty apartment behind.

I sat up in a panic, struggling to ground myself. Where was Denning? Where was I, for that matter? I struggled to connect with the earth, as if fighting to get back in my body, until something orange caught my eye. A curling, snapping light pulled me out of the darkness.

Something was on fire.

Like the fabled moth, I got up from the bed and cracked open the door. Dewy humidity beaded on my skin the moment I abandoned the air conditioning. I took shallow sips of the muggy night air, following the light as I looked for answers.

The night air was thick with patchouli smoke and the scent of burning citronella. I stepped barefoot onto the villa's flat stone path, each rock still emanating sunbaked warmth from the day, and followed the flickering line of tiki torches that curved through the gardens. The distant hum of laughter and music guided me, growing louder with each step, until I emerged on a sprawling lawn where a massive banquet stretched beneath a twisting banyan tree, its branches and vines dotted with dangling lights.

The table was obscene in its decadence. Platters of ripe tropical fruits—mangoes sliced in perfect crescents, pineapples carved into delicate fans, glossy cherries still clinging to their stems—sat among an ocean of sushi. Thousands of dollars of prime sashimi cuts gleamed under the lights, hand rolls adorned with edible flowers and slivers of mango, delicate bowls of miso soup beside plates of sushi-grade wagyu, and an endless spread of Japanese appetizers I couldn't name but desperately wanted to devour. I briefly wondered where they ordered Japanese food on a private island, before remembering that they employed a small staff—surely one that included one, if not several, chefs.

A ripple of applause and laughter spread through the group as I arrived.

"There she is!" someone called.

I was instantly self-conscious.

I'd arrived with mussed hair, in smudged and travel-damp clothes, among a sea of veritable supermodels wearing, what appeared to be, resort attire. My feet moved forward despite my hesitation. I had a part to play, after all, and that fact alone plastered a smile on my face. I wriggled my fingers in a reciprocal greeting.

Denning stood, beaming at me like I was the only person in the world. "Come, meet the crew."

My eyes scanned the table, snagging, not on a living member of the island, but on the large statue of two golden women nestled in the banyan tree, overlooking the table. It appeared to be the same women—goddesses, rather—as the ones with the offerings in our villa. I hoped he'd introduce me to her, too, when we finished the rounds of pleasantries.

His extended arm was an invitation I couldn't refuse, and for a moment, I forgot it was all an act. I crossed the grass, stepping into his space as he slid his hand against the small of my back, his warmth bleeding through the fabric of my wrinkled airport garb.

"You've met Indie." He jutted a thumb to the woman from earlier in the orange dress, who blew a kiss in greeting. She went back to taking pictures of the elaborately plated food, seemingly taking her role as influencer very seriously.

"Odie and I had the pleasure of bumping into her earlier today," Flick added with a wink.

Denning gestured to a man and woman seated at the center of the table. "These are our hosts—Roman and Clementine Locke."

Roman was tanned, his button-down crisp, despite the humidity, an easy smirk playing at the edge of his lips. Clementine, by contrast, was porcelain-pale, her red hair swept up in an effortless twist, eyes sharp as she took me in.

"Thank you for letting us use the jet," I said, my voice smaller than I wanted it to be.

Roman waved a dismissive hand. "Any friend of Denning's."

"And the other half of the citrus sisters—" Denning turned toward the woman watching me with a smirk that was just this side of cruel. "The infamous Lemon."

I hoped my face didn't reflect how anxious I felt as I turned to take in the ex-wife. She was older than I thought she'd be— Denning's age, if not a smidge older than him—with perfectly highlighted hair, red painted lips, and a golden dress that suited the fruit after which she was named.

"Charmed, I'm sure." Lemon lifted her glass lazily. Her blonde hair gleamed in the candlelight, her expression unreadable.

The man beside her lifted a single finger. "Wei," he said simply, offering a nod before returning his attention to his drink. He was younger than Lemon by at least a decade, his frame broad and muscular, his shirt unbuttoned just enough to make it a statement.

The statement was: I'm young and hot, and I belong here.

"What's your insta?" he asked, pulling out his phone. "I'll add you."

"Wei has 1.3 million followers," Indie supplied. "It's a big deal if he follows you."

"Oh, I'm not on Instagram," I said. "Besides, I haven't gotten my phone to work yet."

Wei stared at his phone, baffled. "Not on socials? Are you a caveman?"

"Probably," I muttered. Before I could explain myself further, a pair of arms wrapped around me from behind. My pulse jumped at the surprise attack, but the mix of smirks and bemused expressions around me let me know that whoever had crashed into me was doing nothing new.

"Last but not least, meet Ever," Denning said as I stiffened.

"Evergreen," came the name in a bright, British accent. I fought the urge to squirm out of the surprise hug as the woman rested her chin on my shoulder. "But everyone calls me Ever."

I counted the attendees. "Is this everyone? I thought, maybe, I'd see the woman from earlier."

"This is everyone," he nodded. "Save for the attendants."

"We employee a full staff," Clementine said.

"At least eight are here at any given time. More, if we have guests," Roman added.

Indie chimed in, "One or two extra now that Lemon keeps her cat here. Who knows, June. Maybe if things go well between you and Denning, he'll buy you a giraffe to add to the little menagerie."

The others chuckled, but I was still reeling from how out of my depth I felt. I was both confused and grateful when Evergreen tugged on my arm for my attention.

"I hear we have a lost luggage situation on our hands?" she said. "Come, come, let's put you in something suitable for dinner while these old hens squawk."

Before I could protest, Ever was dragging me toward a nearby villa. I said something or other about how she didn't have to, about how nice this was, then about how it was quite warm, and it might be nice to get out of the Balenciagas as she led the charge. The burbling dinner party winked out behind us as we rounded three corners and disappeared into a space perfumed with jasmine and luxury. She unclasped herself from me to flit through a closet with purpose, pulling out one dress after another—pink, then black, then finally, a soft blue number she held up with satisfaction.

"This one," she declared. "It's perfect for someone named Juniper."

I gave a breathy laugh, still overwhelmed. "First the citrus sisters, now if you and I sit next to each other, we've got half a forest. Juniper and Evergreen."

"Isn't that neat?" Ever grinned, handing me the dress. "It's not so bad, right?"

I peeled off the sweaty outfit and stepped into the dress. I wiggled it over my hips, then struggled with the ties in the back as I said, "Everyone's been...really friendly. Denning mentioned something about a welcome ceremony. Is that tonight?"

Her smile widened as she helped me tie the dress at the back, her fingers lingering longer than necessary. She smoothed the fabric along my waist, her hands trailing up my arm, her fingertips barely brushing the side of my neck. A shiver ran down my spine.

Oh.

So that was what this was.

"No, no. I'm sure it'll be on your last night if it happens...

though, looking at you, I'm quite sure it will. Now," she dropped her hand, "let's do something about that makeup."

My stomach grumbled. "Do we have time?"

"Time is what you make it, sweetheart! But no, I'm not going to keep us from the food. Let me just..." she fished what might have been micellar water from a drawer and dabbed it on a cotton round before handing it to me. "For the mascara."

I was embarrassed, and I told her so.

"Nonsense. You haven't seen the crew piled on top of one another after a three-day bender. Lip gloss?"

"Please and thank you." I dabbed the rosy shade on my mouth, then ran a borrowed brush through my hair, still grateful for everyone's kindness. That said, I wondered if Ever was the sort of person I would be friends with if I had met her under any other context. Was she truly nice or was she just nice...*considering*.

It was a question for later.

On our way out, I asked her about the statue, as she had one in her room as well.

"Oh! Indonesian Hinduism is polytheistic. They're the goddesses of this island," Ever explained. Everything sounded better in her accent, so I prodded for more information.

"Like...they keep storms away? Provide...fresh coconuts?" I struggled to participate in the conversation without sounding insensitive.

Ever's laugh was like tinkling bells. "Something like that. It's a little unusual for someone from the west, but you'll get used to seeing them around."

By the time we returned to the table, the wine was flowing, the food vanishing at an impressive rate, and the mood had shifted into something looser, more indulgent. My eyes flicked across the table, noting the matching black tattoos on everyone's wrists. A simple band, delicate and inked in a curious, looping language. I wasn't quite drunk enough to risk asking what sort of friend group got matching tattoos, but maybe a buzz would give me the courage.

I reached for the sake drink and took a long sip.

And another.

I was certain I'd never eaten that much sushi before in my life.

No, I was certain no one had ever eaten that much sushi in their life.

My DNA had morphed to be 50% salmon belly by the time I was served a lychee martini. Then another. Then another.

Indie grabbed a bottle of champagne and handed Evergreen her phone. "Record me!" Then to Wei, she said, "Your followers will love this. Take off your shirt and get over here!"

She began to shake up the champagne then scrunched her face against the inevitable pop, prepared to spray it all over Wei's muscled body. When she couldn't quite get the cork, she brought it close to her body, sticking out her tongue, grunting slightly as she struggled. She succeeded at last and the champagne sprung free, arm flailing, bottle hitting Wei squarely in the middle of the face.

"Fuck, Indie!" A sparkling, beige shower of champagne sprayed over him while he grabbed his nose, blood already streaming down his face, dribbling onto his chest. "You broke my fucking nose."

"Holy shit, Wei, I'm so sorry! Shit, shit, shit," Indie set the bottle on the table as the last pressurized bits frothed over its glassy green neck.

"It's just a little blood." Lemon rushed to his side. "Tilt your head back."

"Here," Roman held out a cloth napkin.

Years of med school took over. "No, don't tilt your head back." I moved to the open space beside him. "It's a common misconception, but it doesn't stop the bleeding, it just makes the blood go down your throat. We don't want that. Lean forward."

I took the napkin from Roman and moved between Lemon and Wei, applying pressure, examining him like he was my patient. "It doesn't appear broken. Lemon's right. It's just blood."

She drummed her fingers against her hip. "Like I said."

I was pretty buzzed, but I knew from her tone that I'd overstepped. I'd let the alcohol get the best of me and moved in on her man.

"Here," I motioned for her to take over with the pressure. "The bleeding should stop any second."

Clementine walked over with a second bottle of champagne. She tucked a ginger lock behind her ear and asked, "Shall we try again? Maybe no shaking, this time?"

Two, four, six glasses of something strong, something sweet, something sparkly, something, something, something later, I could barely remember my own name. My faux pas between Lemon and Wei was long forgotten. I drank anything that was handed to me.

"If you don't slow down, I'm going to have to carry you off this lawn." Denning swirled his drink.

"Then carry me," I replied.

Flick, already loose from the alcohol, pulled a small tin from his pocket, flicking it open with an easy motion before passing it to the person beside him. It made its way around the table, the atmosphere humming with anticipation. When it reached me, I hesitated, the little white pill resting in my palm.

"None for us," Denning said, his voice smooth but firm as he plucked it from my fingers and passed it along.

Flick pouted. "Come on. Don't be a buzzkill."

"I can do it," I said, emboldened by the sake, by the attention, by the rush of feeling like I belonged.

Denning's voice lowered. "I think we should go to bed."

"Come on." My smile flickered as I did my best to wave him away.

"It wasn't a question," he said.

The shift in his tone sobered me. I kept my expression under control as I searched his gaze for any hint of jest. When I found none, I nodded.

Denning stood, clapping his hands together. "Please excuse us, but we're still a little tired from the trip."

Indie shot me a look, then back at the tin in Flick's hand. "Tomorrow, then?"

"We'll see," Denning said, sliding his arm around my waist. "Goodnight, everybody."

A chorus of goodnights followed us as we left the party behind, the sounds of laughter and revelry swelling in the distance. I focused on the path ahead, my pulse a little too quick, my mind a little too hazy.

Denning's grip was firm as he led me back to the villa, the night quiet save for the rhythmic crash of the waves against the shore. When we reached our door, he turned to me, his eyes scanning my face like he was searching for something.

"You okay?" he asked.

I exhaled, pressing a hand to my forehead. "Yeah. Just a lot to take in."

He nodded, stepping inside and holding the door open for me. As I walked past him, I felt the weight of his gaze, heavy and unreadable.

"You're doing marvelously," he murmured. "Better than I could have dreamed."

I had the feeling that despite all the excess, all the wealth, all the beauty of this place—Denning was the most dangerous thing on the island.

6

The flickering of lanterns cast soft shadows against the stone walls of the villa as we approached. I could still hear the sounds of partygoers, but their voices were drowned by the rustle of palm fronds in the breeze. The moment the doors slid shut and we were safely in the air-conditioned sanctuary; it was just us. Just me and Denning, standing on opposite sides of the room, both hyper-aware of the way the air between us crackled like an unstruck match.

He loosened the cuffs of his sleeves, rolling them up with practiced ease before unbuttoning the front of his shirt. My gaze lingered, dragged helplessly down the defined planes of his chest, the faint shadow of curved muscles creating an Adonis-V that disappeared beneath his waistband. His movements were self-assured, like he was used to being watched, used to people hanging on to his every motion.

"As a reminder," he mused, eyes cutting to me as he slid the shirt from his shoulders. "You're under no obligation to sleep with me."

My mouth was suddenly dry. "I know."

He shot a glance to the cream sofa. "I can take the couch."

"No," I blurted, then winced at how quickly I'd said it. I

45

cleared my throat, feigning nonchalance. "That's not necessary. It's your bed."

He tilted his head slightly, like he was seeing something amusing in my reaction. Like he knew exactly how long I'd been staring. He didn't call me on it, but he didn't have to.

I turned away under the guise of gathering my things, needing a moment to breathe before my pulse made my ribs shatter. "Go ahead and get ready for bed. I need to shower, then I'll meet you there."

"And we'll…"

"Sleep," I said.

"Right," he agreed seriously. "Sleep."

The bathroom continued the clean, modern lines, wood, and brushed concrete. I wasn't surprised in the least that the villas had a rainfall showerhead and savored the gentle cascade as it washed over me. I scrubbed away the remnants of travel, of the lingering scent of smoke, of the buzz of alcohol. My fingers worked shampoo into my scalp, then conditioner, then body wash—anything to keep myself occupied, to force myself to focus on something other than the image of Denning unbuttoning his shirt.

I couldn't stop myself from procuring the razor, even if I had no intentions of getting laid tonight. I still wanted to be dolphin-smooth and ready for the tropics. I shaved, taking my time, dragging the blade over my legs, my underarms, my more intimate places, making my skin perfectly soft in a way that made me feel a little more in control. When I finally reached to turn off the water, I realized my mistake.

No towel. No pajamas. Nothing but the steam curling around me and the chill creeping in from the open bathroom door.

I exhaled sharply, pressing a hand to my forehead. "God, you idiot."

I hesitated, weighing my options. Could I drip-dry? No, that was ridiculous. Could I wrap myself in the tiny bathmat?

Equally ridiculous. The only option left was asking Denning, and the thought of stepping out there, wet and vulnerable, made my skin prickle.

I'd begun to shiver before the chilly goosebumps made my choice for me.

"Denning?" I called; voice almost swallowed by the quiet of the villa.

A beat of silence. Then: "Yes?"

I scrunched my face, hating how uncool the next words out of my mouth were. "Can you bring me a towel?"

Another beat. Then, with maddening ease, he replied, "No."

My stomach flipped. "No?"

"Come get it."

I gripped the counter, heart hammering. Heat curled through me, slow and insidious, sinking into my limbs, pooling low in my belly. I wanted to stamp my feet. I wanted to pluck the shower hose from the wall and spray him. I wanted to curse him out.

Instead, I said, "I thought you said… I thought we weren't—"

"What did you think?" he asked, voice amused, like he already knew the answer. "Come get your towel."

I sucked in a breath, willing myself to stay collected; to not let him see just how much he was affecting me. But my body was already betraying me—my skin flushed, my pulse fluttering in my throat, my nipples hardening—whether from the cold or from his surprising command, I didn't want to admit the answer.

For fuck's sake. I had no idea what I felt.

I was going to kill him.

Or kiss him.

Or let the ground open up and swallow me whole.

I shivered for another five seconds, then ten.

"Fuck it."

I squared my shoulders, steeling myself, then stepped out of the bathroom, bare feet silent against the cool stone floor. The room was dim, golden light pooling at the edges, casting shadows against Denning's frame where he stood, leaning against the dresser, towel in hand. He held it lazily, smirking as I approached, his gaze dragging over me in a way that made my stomach tighten.

I stopped just in front of him, gaze locked onto his. I could have reached for the towel. I could have cursed him out for toying with me. Instead, I reached up, gathering my damp hair in my hands and, twisting it, let the droplets fall onto his bare feet.

He sucked his teeth, eyes gleaming. "Thatta girl."

I extended my hand for the towel and waited for him to concede before wrapping it tightly around myself, suddenly desperate for a barrier between us. But I didn't step away. Neither did he. "And now we're ready for bed."

"Not quite," I replied. I had a power move up my sleeve, as well.

"What are you doing?" he asked as I turned toward his suitcase. I was his girlfriend, after all, and what's his is mine. I plunged my hand into his personal possessions, rummaging through his clothes, his neatly organized packing cubes, his assortment of possessions.

"Getting a t-shirt to sleep in."

He didn't stop me. I could feel his eyes on me right where I'd left him. "Feel free."

I dug through his neatly folded wardrobe until I found a plain white shirt, soft and oversized. The scent of him—clean, sharp, something dark and masculine—clung to the fabric as I pulled it over my head. The hem fell to mid-thigh, teasingly short, but I refused to let myself think too much about it.

When I turned back, Denning was unbuckling his pants, sliding them off with the same casual confidence, leaving him in nothing but black boxer briefs that did nothing to hide his response, either to my naked body, or to his power game, or my obedience. Maybe all three.

His eyes met mine, unreadable. "Last chance to ask me to sleep on the couch."

My heart stuttered. One beat. Then another. Then another.

I shook my head.

The corner of his mouth lifted slightly, like he'd expected that answer. He hooked his thumbs into the waistband of his briefs and slid them off, standing before me completely bare. My breath hitched. My gaze dipped, my mouth went dry, and I swallowed, hard.

"Come to bed," he said.

I hesitated for a moment, then crossed the room, slipping beneath the sheets, my body humming with awareness of just how close we were.

Denning turned off the last of the lights, leaving only the moon to cast silver streaks across the bed. He lay back, his breathing steady, his presence impossibly large beside me.

"Goodnight, Juniper."

"Goodnight, Denning," I mumbled. But as I lay there, pulse racing, body wound tight with anticipation, I was confident I wouldn't be getting any sleep that night.

7

ISLAND: DAY TWO

A WOMAN'S VOICE STIRRED ME FROM THE SHALLOW WATERS OF fitful slumber.

"Cassidy…"

I groaned, swatting her away for another few minutes of sleep.

"Wake up, Cassidy…"

I reached for Amanda, only to find her place in the bed warm, but empty. I opened my eyes to the fluffy white duvet, thin canopy, and gentle sounds of rain. But Amanda wasn't my girlfriend anymore, and this was not the bed we'd shared.

I swiveled my head, gaze searching for who had called my name, but the villa was empty. I'd been caught between the wind and a dream, the jumble between the past and the present.

My sleep partner was still missing, however. I sat up, readying myself for my second day on the job. A job where my name was Juniper, I reminded myself, regardless of what my subconscious wanted to call me.

"Denning?" I spoke his name into the morning quiet, anxious not to be too loud. But there was no response. I slipped onto my bare feet and tip-toed to the bar cart to power up the portable espresso machine, but something didn't feel quite right. I listened to the mechanical whir and watched the frothing liquid fill the cup as I tasted something else on the air — something I couldn't name. It wasn't quite dread, not yet, but something more subtle—like the moment before a thunderstorm when the air thickens and the wind stills, the kind of silence that warns you before the first crack of lightning splits the sky.

A gust of wind sent a smattering of raindrops into the glass, and I relaxed.

It wasn't *like* a storm. It *was* a storm.

I carried my coffee back to the bed and settled between the sheets once more. I reached for my phone, only to remember that the Wi-Fi wasn't working. Damn. I'd hoped to google the rainy season in Indonesia to see if this was a gentle spritz that would pass, or the start of a meaningful downpour. I peered past the trees, beyond the lawn, past the beach, to the slate-colored waves breaking and foaming on the sand. The sea was a far cry from the previous day's calm turquoise waters.

Disastrous weather aside, the sounds were quite nice.

The morning light had a stifling, gray quality. The sounds I'd grown used to—the rhythmic waves, the chatter of birds—felt muted, as though the island was holding its breath. I sipped my caffeine, rubbing my eyes, my head still foggy from the night before. The party, the drinks, the strange electricity that hummed under my skin when Denning had looked at me, dripping wet from the shower, demanding that I stand naked before him like I was something rare, something to be possessed.

I looked at his side of the bed. The sheets were still rumpled, still warm.

I ignored the way my pulse quickened as I slid out of bed, padding barefoot to the sink to brush my teeth and start my day. The rainy noises separated from the sound of running water as I turned the corner and I understood what I'd been hearing. The rainfall showerhead had duped me as it blended in with the morning storm.

I'd barely reached for my toothbrush when Denning cracked open the door to the shower, shirtless, hair slicked back, with a towel around his waist.

He caught my reflection in the mirror and smirked. "If it isn't my golden girl."

I bit my lip, quick to tilt my head so the curtain of my hair concealed my face, but the flush in my cheeks betrayed me. "That's quite a nickname. You must be in a good mood."

"I had a good night." His smirk deepened as he leaned against the counter, arms folding across his chest. "You?"

I shoved the wetted toothbrush into my mouth, glad for an excuse as to why I was struggling to answer. I remembered the way my body had thrummed with awareness of him, the way I'd barely slept, too tangled up in the scent of him, the heat of him. "Fine," I mumbled through the brushing, voice a little too tight.

Denning didn't call me on it, but his gaze held mine a second longer than necessary before he tossed the towel aside. "Indie and Ever sent over a week's worth of outfits for you to choose from. Get dressed. Meet me for breakfast in the main house in twenty."

The unease from earlier hadn't left me. If anything, it had thickened, creeping up my spine as I dressed in a breezy white sundress left for me in the closet, as though someone had known I'd need it before I even did. The thought sent a shiver through me, but I pushed it aside. I ran my fingers through the material, marveling at how buttery-soft something could be when it wasn't fast fashion; incapable of comprehending what went into making clothes so that the ultra-wealthy could feel like their skin was kissed by clouds.

The rain stopped by the time I left the villa. I checked my phone but still had four flat lines where reception bars should be. I slipped into my pale wedges, dawned my jewelry, and had enough time to do my makeup properly before following the same path from the night before. The main house maintained architectural continuity of the villas, all with the same free-flowing indoor-outdoor living spaces. There were no women present at breakfast, but Flick and Wei were both settled into their respective seats as they drank their coffee and noshed on their meals. Denning was filling a plate from the spread of fresh fruit, pastries, and coffee laid out across the wooden table.

"Hey, sleepyhead," Wei said.

"Hey," I greeted. "I've been meaning to ask you: how have you gotten your phone to work? I can't seem to connect."

"Reception goes in and out," Flick said. "I'm sure you'll have a bar or two by later today."

I didn't love the answer, but there wasn't much I could do about it. I followed Denning to the table. He took a seat and began to pour me a flute of champagne before I'd finished selecting my pastries.

I slid into the chair beside Denning just in time to watch Flick reach across the table for the honey. As he did, his sleeve pushed up, exposing the matching tattoo. He caught me staring.

"Like it?" he asked.

"What does it mean?" I asked, forcing my voice to stay light, casual.

Flick opened his mouth, but before he could answer, Denning spoke instead. "It's a prayer," he said, stirring the honey into his coffee.

"To who?"

"To what," Denning corrected at my side. He slipped his hand down my leg, landing just above my knee. His thumb began to move in idle circles on the tender skin of my inner thigh, which was enough to distract me from the conversation at hand.

"Fortune," Flick said. "Prosperity."

Wei, who had been silent until now, let out a quiet chuckle. "Power."

I wasn't sure if it was something about the way they said the meaning, or Denning's rhythmic circles, but my skin prickled. I reached for my coffee, needing something to do with my hands. "So, like, a good luck charm?"

Denning's gaze was unreadable as he sipped his drink. "Something like that."

"Do I get one if I stay here long enough?" I asked.

"You? No," Flick said a little too quickly.

It was weird that his haste hurt me, if only a little. Why did I have an emotional response to the rejection? So what if they didn't want me in their club. I wouldn't have accepted the ink anyway…but it would have been nice to feel like I wasn't so ordinary, so far below the poverty line that I couldn't deign to be included in their wealthy, elitist club.

"It's for the best." Denning tapped my leg before he pulled his hand away. "You're subservient to no one." He paused, forcing me to look into his eyes as he added, "Except me."

I choked on my coffee, which seemed to please him. I let it drop, but the tab in my mind remained open.

The clouds parted just as Lemon, Roman, and Clementine strolled into breakfast.

Lemon draped an arm around her boy toy's neck, planting a kiss on his head. "How was your night, lover? Did you spend it with the girls?"

I was simultaneously glued to the answer and so uncomfortable that I wanted to scramble under the table. I wasn't quick enough, so I settled on studying the dragon fruit seeds as if I was deciphering the Rosetta Stone as he answered.

From my peripherals, I saw Wei crane his neck up to return the kiss. "Ever fell asleep right after dinner, but Indie and I played in the pool for a few hours. How was yours?" Then, politely, he extended the question to Clementine and Roman. "Isn't she something?"

Please, God, transport me anywhere but here for the next sixty seconds, or strike me dead, I begged. I shoved a croissant in my mouth and gripped my mimosa like my life depended on it. Denning must have noticed, because he slipped his hand over my knee and gave it a squeeze.

"Would you like to go for a walk?" he asked.

I tried to say "Please," but coughed up crumbs instead. He patted my back gently as he excused us from the table. I did my best impersonation of someone with pneumonia as we exited the main house. I was so relieved to be out of there that, in my distracted haze of gratitude, I ran headlong into Ever.

Her mug tumbled out of her hand, shattering against the stones into a thousand ceramic shards.

Her involuntary shriek turned the heads of the other breakfast goers.

"Holy shit." I dropped to my knees, grabbing for the largest pieces. "I'm so sorry."

Denning bent down and grabbed my wrist, forcing my hand open. The sharpened piece of ceramic nicked me on its way down. I looked up at him, bewildered. "That's someone else's job," he said. "You'll hurt yourself."

I tried to shake him loose while Ever giggled.

"Oh, hun, please don't fret. But you can make it up to me with a walk on the beach now that it's sunny. Denning? Can you spare your girl for a few minutes?"

I hoped he was telepathic and could hear my stream of "*No, no, please, let me stay with you,*" but he appeared not to be a mind reader, for he said it was no problem, as long as I was returned in one piece.

Great.

I watched him from over my shoulder, pouting helplessly as Ever looped her arm through mine and guided me toward the edge of the beach. The gray sky had definite streaks of blue by now. The waves had calmed substantially. The sand was warm beneath my feet, the water lapping lazily at the shore, but the storm within me had not passed.

"You're thinking too much," Ever chided, giving me a playful nudge.

I forced a smile. "When you get to know me better, you'll learn that's just my resting state."

"Well, stop," she said. "You're here to have fun."

Fun. That's what they kept saying. As if this was just a vacation, not a job I'd taken out of desperation. Fun, as if it wasn't terribly odd that everyone had matching tattoos and that they conveniently deflected whenever I asked for a translation. Fun, as if I hadn't been plopped in the tropics like a plump, suckling pig among lions when it came to fresh meat in the lifestyle. Fun, as if it didn't feel like there was something curling beneath the surface, something waiting.

Ever stopped abruptly, turning to face me, her gaze softer now, more searching. "You feel it, don't you?"

My throat went dry. Was *she* the telepathic one? "Feel what?"

"The connection," she said happily. "To this place. To us."

No, no telepathy here. Though, if I was being honest, a part of me did. There was something intoxicating about all of it—even in the fear. The anxiety was its own drug, for better or for worse. The beauty, the indulgence, the way they all seemed to *know* me in a way that felt impossible left me feeling inexplicably high, like I'd taken too many hits from the escapism blunt. But there was something else, too. If it had a name, I had yet to learn it.

Ever lifted my wrist, tracing her thumb absently over my skin. "It suits you."

"What does?"

She smiled. "You'll see."

8

Ever escorted me to meet Denning at the main house so she could get a fresh cup of coffee to replace the mug I'd broken, but the well-intentioned venture quickly roped me into a conversation that ended with threats to chuck me in the ocean.

"You've never been snorkeling?" Clementine gasped, her oversized sunglasses sliding down the bridge of her nose. "Oh, babe. We have to go."

My fingers twisted in the hem of my sundress. I deflected, "I'm a Colorado girl. Trails, snowcapped peaks, tents, s'mores…I haven't spent a ton of time near the ocean."

Clementine slapped my shoulder a little harder than I liked —the tinted print of coconut-scented tanner leaving a tiny mark on my shoulder. "You can't swim? What the hell are you doing on an island?"

"I can swim," I said, unconsciously rubbing the superficial injury. "And I'd kick all your asses if we were whitewater rafting. It's just…open water. Deep. Full of sharks. It's not exactly a mountain river, you know?"

Lemon snorted. "Oh, so you *can* swim, you're just a pussy?"

Ever stirred a scoop of sugar into her coffee. "Lemon, sweetie, don't be a cunt."

"Ever, *babe*," she lifted her mimosa, "don't be a simp."

I had a slew of unladylike opinions that I was all too ready to share, but I was on the clock. Instead, I gave her my cattiest, close-mouthed, eye-slit of a smile. "You know what? Maybe I will go. Snorkeling is just fancy floating, right?"

"Floating," Clementine agreed. "With flair."

Lemon tilted her head back against the lounge chair. "It's just floating until you inhale a mouthful of saltwater and embarrass yourself." She took a lazy sip of her mimosa. "But sure, yeah, go for it."

"Are you going?" I shot Ever a hopeful look.

"And ruin my hair? Nah, it's not for me. I'm sure you'll have fun, though," she said.

Denning stretched like he had all the time in the world. "I'll go with you," he said, flashing a grin. "It's a once-in-a-lifetime experience, June. We can't miss this."

My heart gave a traitorous little lurch. The words weren't meant to be intimate, but with the way he said 'we,' it did something to me.

"Exactly." Wei leaned back in his chair. "After all, who knows? This might be your last chance to do something like this."

My lip twitched in a scarcely controlled sneer. I didn't like his dig that I was unworthy of a life that might include snorkeling on the regular. He didn't know who I was, or what I'd earned. I couldn't let him win.

Clementine, Lemon, Wei, Denning, and I headed for the dock. I was ready for my Oscar-worthy performance as I prepared to play the most challenging role of my lifetime.

HOT, WHITE LIGHT PUNCTURED THE CLOUDLESS SKY, COOKING US under the frying rays. The sun was high overhead, bouncing off the rolling waves, casting bright, shimmering streaks across the open ocean. Seaspray kept the salty, humid air from being stifling. I would have loved to have felt an engine's low rumble beneath my feet, but the thirty-meter princess yacht cut through the gentle waves with smooth, noiseless power.

The boat was larger and more luxurious than my apartment in Denver. She possessed a deck, a combined living and dining room, and a queen bed in a private bedroom, each which reminded me just how little I had to my name. Lemon and Wei emerged from the bottom floor—presumably from fucking, given the snarls in her hair—and joined the rest of us on the captain's deck.

The engine rumbled, puttered, then cut as we came to a stop in the aquamarine waters. I'd expected rolling waves or some-thing choppy, but it was surprisingly calm. I peered over the edge and wondered at the depth. It was so clear that I could practically count the fish darting in and out of the coral.

"Are there barracudas in this coral?" I asked. "Poisonous jellyfish? Great whites?"

"Oh, she's scared," Lemon said. "It's not too late to take her back to shore."

The words were right. The tone was wrong.

Clementine reached across the seats and gave my hand a squeeze. She checked my fingers, my wrists, and my ears. "You're not wearing any jewelry, so you don't have the sort of flash a barracuda will care about. As for the rest, well…getting stung by a jellyfish is a rite of passage."

"You can't be serious." My shoulders wiggled as I worked through a chill.

Denning stood at the helm, one hand loose on the wheel, sunglasses perched on his nose. He looked like he belonged there—competent, self-assured, in control. Not like the other men on the island, who let attendants and captains cater to their every whim.

"I'll get you out of the water the moment we spot our first jelly," he said.

My hero.

I had no idea he had a boating license. He'd told me that he'd been in a boating accident—the scars of which were supposedly part of our meet cute—but I'd assumed he'd been a passenger, not a captain. I also didn't know that driving a boat was an aphrodisiac but watching him drop anchor in the open sea made me proud to be with the captain. Then again, in a boat this big, I sort of assumed there was an autopilot feature.

If I were better at my job, I would have sauntered over to him and draped an arm around his shoulder. It would have been the perfect opportunity to play the role of Relaxed Boat Babe. But I had more pressing concerns.

We made our way down the narrow flight of stairs to congregate on the deck. I shifted my weight from one foot to the other as I cast glances to the eerie, open water at the back of the boat.

They saw an invitation.

I saw a warning.

"You nervous?" Denning asked.

I glanced down at the mask and snorkel. "I just—" I giggled to keep it light. "More of a mountain girl, you know?"

Wei gave Lemon's hip a squeeze. "Aww, is Junie scared?"

Be so fucking for real, I choked down the urge to snap back. There was something about Wei's chiseled, dopey face that made the juvenile mockery all the more grating. He was the first male model I'd ever met, and with any luck, he'd be the last.

Lemon gave an exaggerated pout as the veritable high school bullies stared at me.

I kept the unbothered smile on my face, but was pretty sure I felt my eye twitch.

Denning cut her a look before tossing Wei the keys. "Get upstairs and take the wheel."

Wei blinked. "What? No, I wanted to get in—"

"See ya, suckers!" Clementine jumped off the side of the

boat and was swallowed by the turquoise waves in an instant. She burst free a moment later, waving her encouragement for the rest of us to follow.

"Be a man," Denning said to Wei.

I waited for a hint as to his misogyny, but something told me he was playing on Wei's toxicity. *Ask not what you can do for the patriarchy, but what the patriarchy can do for you,* I thought, reveling in the victory as Wei grumbled up the steps.

The instant karma was delicious.

Denning was already unzipping his…well, I wanted to call it a wetsuit, but it was more like a t-shirt, and I didn't have the oceanic vocabulary to know much about the accoutrements.

He turned back to me, tossing the shirt onto the bench before climbing onto the diving platform. His skin was bronzed from the sun, the muscles in his back shifting as he rolled his shoulders. He looked like a god carved from warm sand.

He glanced at me; hand extended. "Come on, June. I've got you."

I hesitated for half a second too long.

Lemon made her amusement known.

Her passive aggression made my blood boil hotter than any molten, island sunbeams. I hadn't been around such an openly unpleasant person since high school. I wondered if attitudes like hers were common among the wealthy. They had no incentive to grow as people, so they were permitted to stew in their childish misery.

If I was going to survive the trip, I needed to perfect the easy-going mask and learn to rise above the bullshit. I hoped my smile was convincing as I secured the flippers and strapped the snorkel behind my hair. I cast an uncertain look at the rippling blue ocean with no concept of its depth. The crystal-clear water might have been ten feet or one hundred for how perfectly I saw the bottom. If I thought about it for longer than a second, I'd chicken out. So, I took Denning's hand and took the plunge—literally.

The water hit me with a gentle warmth, nothing like the freezing cold lakes I'd been in before. It was like slipping into silk. I kicked my feet too hard at first, struggling not to panic as I fought to stay above the surface. Denning kept his grip on my wrist as I adjusted to the buoyancy, breathing through the snorkel experimentally. It felt wrong—like I was too aware of the air moving in and out of my lungs.

He popped up from beneath the surface, shook the droplets from his eyes. I wanted to describe what he was doing as treading water while I thrashed, but truth be told, it was more like he was floating. One hand on his goggles, he said, "Breathe slow. You're okay."

I gave a stiff nod.

"Trust me?"

A beat.

A warm wave broke against my cheek. Acrid saltwater burned my mouth. I couldn't relax with the wet, chaotic world below and the petty bitches above. Lemon slipped into the water behind us, joining Clementine a dozen or so feet away as they kicked effortlessly toward the reef.

Everyone's having fun except you, scolded the voice inside my head. *Maybe Cassidy can't do this, but Juniper can. Get it together.*

I nodded again. He shot me a wink as he pulled down his goggles. He dipped the snorkel in the water, tilted it in my direction, and sprayed it at my face. I splashed him back, grinning against the rubber bits of my mouthpiece.

We were normal. Playful. A real couple. It was nice enough to almost make me forget that I was in the middle of the ocean with a slew of complete strangers, inches from aquatic monsters.

Almost.

EVERYTHING CHANGED ONCE MY FACE SLIPPED BENEATH THE surface.

My heart skipped, my chest tightened, my skin tingled as everything shifted.

The world above disappeared, swallowed by an endless stretch of clear, electric blue. The sunlight dappled the coral below, flickering gold across ridges and valleys of delicate formations. Bright slices of yellow, orange, and purple broke through the aquamarine. Glittering schools of fish darted in iridescent waves—flashy pink coral, striking green stones, rich magenta scales. Tiny clownfish peeked out from a swaying bed of anemones, while a neon parrotfish scraped its teeth against the coral.

I had never seen anything like it.

The water was *alive*.

Denning and I drifted together; his hand still wrapped around mine. With each slow kick of our fins, we glided further into the reef. I forgot about the boat, about Lemon's voice in my ear, about all the ways this could go wrong.

For the first time in days, I let go.

Breathing through the snorkel was second nature, as if I'd always done it. Pulls of air came to me easily. I reached a testing hand toward the anemone, brushing my fingertips against the feather-soft tendrils. The fish didn't scatter as I'd expected. They moved around me, opening up to make space as they carried on their way.

I caught Denning flashing me two thumbs up from a cluster of coral and didn't miss the sparkle in his eyes as he smiled against his mask.

I mirrored the gesture, offering him two happy thumbs, when his expression faltered.

The glimmer in his eyes dimmed. He froze, no longer kicking, as his gaze snagged on something behind me.

My spine prickled. I struggled to turn around in the water,

unfamiliar with the odd kicking and whooshing, and I jerked my head to the side.

A shadow moved just beyond my field of vision. I cut my head abruptly, thrashing instinctively to spook the object, hoping to chase it away.

A large shape moved through the water, its body slicing past the reef with perfect, lethal grace. My heart stopped.

Sharp angles. Terrifying peaks and fins. A body nearly the size of my torso.

Oh fuck, oh fuck, oh fuck, fuck, fuck.

Panic took over as a shark curved in an arc toward us. Its pointed snout tapered into a sleek dorsal fin; its back marked with a distinctive black tip.

My mind was a nonsensical stream of garbled, sobbing curses. I flailed again, trying to scare it. As I did so, something in the deepest reaches of my lizard brain told me it was the wrong move.

Denning swam toward me, grabbing my arm to still the motion, which only heightened my panic. I needed my arms to tread water. I was going to drown. I was going to be torn limb from limb, bloodied and mangled, as I sank to the bottom of the sea. My bones would join the coral as little, colorful fish picked them clean.

He was gesturing a message to me. It was the flat, calming motion of a rancher trying to soothe a raging bull. The worry on his face was not for the shark, I realized. It was for me.

I looked at the shark again, and then at Denning. It wasn't the gargantuan monster I'd originally thought, I realized. Denning was calm. He was urging me to be, too. His soothing gestures awakened the tiny, logical voice that told me that blacktip reef sharks weren't dangerous. I had read it some-where before. I knew that.

But knowing and seeing were two different things.

I'd scarcely begun to calm down when the shark twisted toward us.

The instant my brain registered its path, my body panicked.

Once again, I kicked too hard, twisting in the water, sending up a swirl of sand as I tried to propel myself back to the boat. The snorkel ripped from my mouth as I gasped, sending a mouthful of seawater down my throat.

Denning caught me before I could bolt.

For half a second, I was certain this was it. That he was holding me in place. That he'd let me drown here. That I was never getting off this island.

I fought against my watery grave, my heart pounding, my lungs burning.

He shook his head sharply.

And then, right as the shark turned toward us, Denning moved.

Slowly, so painfully slow, he shifted his weight and extended the heel of his hand, nudging the shark's nose as it veered too close. The moment his skin met the sandpaper-like texture of its snout, it jerked away, twisting sharply, disappearing into the depths.

I watched, stunned, barely processing what had just happened.

He yanked me up and we both broke the surface, hair plastered to our faces, water dripping down our cheeks.

"Holy shit," I sputtered.

"If you swim away, you look like prey." He tapped my chin. "You're not prey. You need to learn to stand your ground."

I still couldn't breathe properly, but I was pretty sure he wasn't just talking about sharks.

"Let's get you onboard." He kicked back toward the boat, giving my hand one last squeeze before letting go.

I followed, my heart still hammering, my mind still catching up.

When I reached the ladder, Wei leaned over the edge, grinning down at me. "Did you see that thing? It was massive!"

"Of course we saw it." I battled the urge to plunge my face

beneath the surface to make sure it wasn't still loitering around the boat, waiting to eat my legs.

Lemon raised a lazy brow. "I don't know what you're talking about. Juniper and Denning looked like they were having a moment."

Denning shot her a glare before hoisting himself onto the deck, dripping water as he reached for a towel.

"You weren't exactly brave the first time you encountered a shark," he said to Lemon.

"Thank god we all have a white knight to rescue us," she replied, rolling her eyes.

I lingered, one hand on the ladder, still catching my breath. Still watching him.

I had no idea what had just happened.

All I knew was this:

Denning saved my life.

And I didn't know what to do with that.

9

It wasn't like I had somewhere to be.

No classes. No clinics. No sneezing children, leaking dicks, bleeding cuts, or everything else I'd been forced to attend in my third year of med school. No stalking Amanda's profile to see if she was happier with the new girl than she'd been with me (and especially no cursing out the girl she'd cheated with—it wasn't her fault, she was single. All the blame was on my ex's shitty, lying, cheating shoulders). No ramen noodles. No seeing my breath even while indoors. No texts or calls from the restaurant or the landlord or the school. Unfortunately, that also meant no texts or calls from Jenna.

What was a woman of leisure to do while trapped alone in paradise?

Clementine and Lemon stayed behind to leave footprints on the beach. Denning was still toweling off when I waved him away, assuring him I'd be fine. I just needed a little bit of time to clear my head.

"Still thinking about the shark? I wouldn't have let anything happen to you," he said.

"I'll remember that next time my life's in jeopardy," I joked, though I wasn't sure how convincing I sounded.

I left the dock and instead of heading back to the villa, began to follow the paths to see where they led. My arms and legs were noodles after the swim. My stomach growled. What I really wanted was a meat lover's pizza and to be left alone in bed, but I was pretty sure that retreating to my room would be a sign of defeat. I had to stay on two feet to keep moving forward, so that's what I'd do.

I waved at Flick and Odie as I passed their villa. I admired the koi fish in the lotus pond, then wondered how they'd imported so many non-indigenous plants and animals when there was only one jet that went to and from the island. I listened to the exotic songbirds, marveling at their plumage. Then, I followed the smells of grilled food and whatever must be for lunch as I rounded the corner to find a structure that looked too perfunctory to be for the guests. I approached what had to be an employee building.

I was barely thirty yards away before a young woman in neatly-pressed neutrals jogged out to greet me. Black hair slicked into a pony, smile wide and polite, and breath huffing through the impromptu exercise and waved me down.

"Can I help you, Miss?" She asked.

My nature was to apologize for whatever obvious inconvenience I'd caused her. I had to remind myself that Cassidy would fret over forcing an employee to jog, but me? Juniper was rich, and she kept her cool…though she'd remain dedicated to politeness when it came to those in the service industry, whether or not it was consistent with her role.

"No, I'm just exploring," I smiled. "What's your name?"

Her brow furrowed. "You need my name? Is something wrong?"

"No! No, god no. Nothing is wrong. My name is Ca— Juniper," I cleared my throat, hoping she wouldn't notice. "I'm just looking around."

"Miss Ca Juniper, I'm Ni Luh. May I help you with something? You want food? A drink? Need something cleaned?"

I shook my head, then had an idea. "Your tattoo. What is it?"

She lifted her wrist proudly. "We belong to the goddesses, Miss. Where is yours?"

"I don't have one yet," I said. I wasn't sure why I'd added the modifier for time, as I wouldn't be getting matching tattoos with the rich folk, but I liked that she asked.

She chewed on my answer, then said, "Would you like to see the jaguar?"

My eyes lit. I nodded excitedly. Ni Luh shouted something to the workers inside and a man came out with a bucket of fresh meat. She took it from him and asked me to follow her into the jungle.

I expected to find a cage—something sad and inhumane, like in the circus—but she led me, instead, to a single-wire fence overlooking a sheer cliff. I stumbled to a stop, a pebble coming loose and tumbling down the drop. It was no conventional pit like one might see in a zoo. It was an ecological marvel, as if she'd plucked the raptor pen directly from Jurassic Park.

Ni Luh called out in a high-pitched summons, voice moving rapidly up and down as she tossed a piece of meat into the pen.

"One moment, Miss. Ares will be along shortly."

"Aries? Like the astrology sign?"

"He is a god of war, Miss. One from far away. Do you know of the Greeks?"

I realized I couldn't name the Hindu god of war. I assumed Lemon, couldn't, either. With her blonde hair and blue eyes, she didn't exactly look Grecian to me, but I supposed appropriating yet another deity was precisely in line with everything I believed to be true about these wealthy island invaders.

I would have continued pondering war gods if the underbrush hadn't stirred.

I squinted through the green, tensed to see a flash of yellow spots. Instead, I was surprised by the powerful, onyx frame that approached. I was about to ask her if Ares was a panther, when he passed just close enough for me to see the grayish, hexagonal strips that ran between his black spots. I hadn't known black jaguars existed before this moment.

Ni Luh passed me the bucket, and I complied. Ares looked up as the meat arced through the air, rearing up and snatching it just before it hit the ground.

"It's just a pit? There's no way out?" I asked.

She pointed to an outcropping of rocks I hadn't noticed before. I followed the path with my eyes as it zig-zagged from my place on the cliff down to where he was on the cliff. "There's a gate," she said, "but we rarely use it."

"Does he always eat from the bucket?" I asked, suddenly sad for the captive beast.

"No, Miss. Sometimes, he hunts." I didn't get a chance to ask *what* he hunted before she dumped the rest of the bucket over the cliff. She smiled at me. "Come, now. We'll find your friends."

I assured Ni Luh that I could find my way back to the villa from the attendants' building on my own, and we parted ways, her with a bloody bucket, and me with certainty that I did not understand the choices of the wealthy.

A gray cloud blotted out the sun, which was a relief. Palms did their best to shade the path, but the sun here was unforgiving.

A glassy, blue butterfly with tiger-striped wings flitted past me. I followed it to its landing place on a fuchsia blossom, reaching with my fingertip, but knowing better than to touch. I couldn't resist the urge to stretch out my hand at every verdant wonder of the lush ecosystem. I felt like I'd tumbled into a National Geographic documentary and each and every jewel-toned plant, bird, or insect sent me into a renewed state of wonder.

Did the rich people know about the simple joys of catching butterflies? The ultra-wealthy wouldn't have to ship jaguars to remote islands for entertainment, if they realized there were already so many flowers to gawk at. I marveled at the jewel-toned insect, watching as it flapped away, leaving me alone once more on the path to the compound.

Though I didn't mind the walk, it was taking me a little longer than I expected to get back to my room. I carried on for a minute more, but the jungle seemed to be getting closer to the pathway rather than opening up to the main lawn.

I turned around and stared at the way I'd come.

Had I taken a wrong turn, somehow?

I felt a single droplet hit my forehead. Then another on my cheek.

A branch snapped.

My mind screamed a single word: *Ares.*

I jumped in my skin as I twisted toward the forest, searching the brush for a pair of yellow eyes and the black hide that would mean certain death.

"Cassidy."

My blood turned to ice.

I took off down the path, not caring if I looked foolish. No one on that island—not even Denning—should know my name. I didn't know where the voice had come from, but it was loud and quiet, near and far all at once. I picked up my knees and sped down the trail, gaining speed as my anxiety grew. The sky began to spit, intermittent sprinkles hitting me in the face as I ran. A dark shape appeared in front of me and I headed toward it, certain it must be the opening to the airplane hangar. Just as I rounded the corner, getting close enough to under-stand what I was seeing, my sandal caught on a rain-slick stone and I went skidding down the path, skinning my hands, my knees, the tops of my feet.

"Are you alright?" a woman asked.

I took in my surroundings, confused at where the path had taken me. I squinted at the dark hole in the rock that stared back at me.

This wasn't the tiny airport. The road was at a dead end. Its smoothed stones gave way to grass, to leaning trees, and to the gaping maw of a pitch-black cave.

I felt her hands against my skin before I saw who was speaking. It took me a second to see past the cloud of black hair, but I lost my breath when I looked into my helper's face. She was a supermodel. She was an A-list celebrity. She was the inspiration image that women across the globe printed off and carried into their plastic surgeon's office as the visual by which they hoped to sculpt their own face.

"You…I know you," I said.

She tucked a lock of inky hair behind her ear. Full lips pulled to the side in an amused smirk. "I doubt that."

"I do," I insisted. "I saw you when we landed. Are you…" I looked around for any indication that she was employed by the island—a hedge trimmer, a golf cart, a uniform—but she was in yet another shimmery outfit just like the one I'd noticed the day prior. I wanted to continue looking at her, but the rain was getting in my eyes. I held up a hand to shield them and asked, "How much farther are we from the villas?"

"You're lost." She urged me toward a blossoming tree with tangling yellow flowers. "Here, get beneath the cassia tree."

"The what?" I asked, letting her lead me. She pointed at the plant, and I repeated, "Cassia…tree...Cassidy. Oh."

"What is it?" asked the woman, also shielding herself from the rain.

"Nothing. Sorry. Who are you? What are you doing out in the rain?"

"I could ask you the same thing," she laughed. She pointed to the mouth of the cave, and for the first time, I noticed a pair of stone statues. "You're new, right? Have you noticed the little altars scattered around the island? This is the big one."

*Oh...*I waited for the pieces to click together. Denning, Roman, and Clementine had all insisted that anyone else on the island had been a member of the staff. I hadn't believed them, but then again, I didn't know anything about the religious iconography I'd seen strewn about the island. The jaguar had an attendant, after all, and now it appeared, so did the shrine.

"I want to ask you more about it, but—"

"But the rain!" she laughed. "Yes, yes. You'll come back here, okay? Come see me again. I'll tell you all about it. Do you know how to get back?"

The shrine at the mouth of the cave was the end of the path. The only way back to the villa was to follow it the way I'd come. This time, I wouldn't get distracted by butterflies and head the wrong direction after the worker's building.

"Good! I'll see you soon, okay?" She shouted over the rain. "Now, go! Stay dry! Enjoy yourself!"

"Okay," I said, then clipped off, out from the cassia tree, away from the cave.

I understood logically that nothing had been calling my name.

I also knew that Ares was safe in his pit.

But my nervous system refused to believe me, and no matter how hard I tried to convince the rest of my body, my gut insisted that we put as much space between me and the cave as possible.

10

I was under strict instructions to enjoy myself, and that was exactly what I was going to do. Once again, the rain had passed as soon as it arrived. The thick coating of dreary clouds lifted just in time for a pinkish sunset to take its place. I checked my phone on the off chance the Wi-Fi had been restored, but it had not. Instead, given the five o'clock hour, I gauged the sun must go down around six in this neck of the world.

I changed into one of the many string bikinis Indie and Evergreen had sent over and joined the others at the pool. The turquoise waters sparkled under the evening light. The surface rippled in the eighty-degree breeze. The humidity turned the already-hot hour into a sauna. The water, on the other hand, brushed against my skin like silk. I exhaled a sigh of relief as I kicked the bright blue surface, ready to drown myself in its respite.

Following my strange encounter with an apex predator, I was happy to down a few sangrias with my legs in the water.

Attendants flitted between lounge chairs, placing drinks into eager hands—coconut shells brimming with rum and pineapple, slender glasses of something green and citrusy,

Aperol spritzes, buckets of ice with bottled beer peeking out, and nary a bottle of water to be found.

I perched at the edge of the pool, cooling my feet. Lemon and Clementine reclined on loungers, stretching long legs, soaking up an afternoon tan. Indie and Ever splashed in the water, submerged to their chests, fingers curled loosely around the stems of their cocktail glasses. Others dotted the space—some on the steps leading into the water, others at the patio table overlooking the scene. The gathering hummed with the ease of people who knew one another intimately, who had shared in pleasures both obvious and hushed. Denning stayed near me, his thighs underwater as he sat on the top step of the pool.

"Thank you," I murmured to the attendant as he put a sweating Aperol spritz in my hand.

I stayed in Denning's orbit, but kept my attention on my drink while the group occupied itself in its separate conversations, some napping, others playing, until Indie clapped her hands together to get everyone's attention.

"I want to play a game." Her pouty lips curved up in a smirk.

Lemon made a face, already sinking deeper into her lounger. "I don't know if we can handle one of your games."

"Let's hear it," Roman countered, swirling the drink in his glass.

Indie smirked. *"Never Have I Ever."*

"You *have* ever'ed Ever," Evergreen winked.

A chorus of groans and playful boos filled the air. Flick leaned back onto the edge of the pool, shaking his head. "We'd all get shitfaced while Juniper stays completely sober."

"Well, hold on," Odie cut in, turning to me with an appraising glance. "Maybe that's presumptuous. How would you do in a game of *Never Have I Ever?*"

I hesitated, already feeling warmth creep into my cheeks. "Honestly?" I cleared my throat. "Not great. I was with the same woman for the last four years, and since the breakup, I've been too focused on my studies to do much dating."

Wei propped himself up on the chair to look at me. "You were dating a woman?"

I nodded.

I wasn't trying to make eye contact with Evergreen, but the way she bit her lip at this piece of information was so deviously un-subtle that I couldn't help the flutter it sent through me.

"Hot." He lifted his glass. "Good catch, Denning."

Denning half-smiled. The weight of his gaze settled on me as if he'd physically reached out to touch me. I wasn't sure if his expression was good or bad.

Ever leaned forward, dragging a wet hand through the surface of the water. "Let's stick with a classic. *Truth or Dare.*"

The pool's submerged electric lights clicked on as the sky darkened, setting our stage ablaze. It was apt timing. Her proposal was met with more enthusiasm—sly grins, the rustling of bodies shifting toward the game. A bottle of something dark and expensive was passed around, refilling empty glasses, lowering inhibitions. I took a slow sip of mine, nerves bubbling alongside the carbonation.

Ever flicked her gaze around the group before settling on me. "Since you're the new girl, you go first."

I swallowed. "What, I just pick someone?"

"Or," the word dripped from Denning's tongue, "we pick you."

A playful sound rippled through the group. I exhaled, rolling my eyes with a grin. "Fine. Truth."

Ever splashed me. "Tame."

Indie floated toward me, grinning. "Let me go, let me go! What's the hottest thing someone's ever done to you in bed?"

My pulse tripped, but I refused to back down. I could feel the eyes on me, the curiosity in their expressions, the silent invitation in some of them. I wet my lips. "I had an ex who liked to tie me up. Hands above my head. She'd leave me there and make me wait."

Clementine hummed, sipping her drink. "Patience is a virtue."

Denning's gaze was molten, though he said nothing.

Indie exhaled dramatically. "Alright, alright, our newbie tried light bondage. But I'm bored already. *Dares* make things interesting."

Flick smirked, slinging an arm over the ledge. "Fine, Juniper. Dare."

"Wait, that's not how it works," I argued. "Don't I get to ask someone else now?"

"They're hazing you." Denning leveled his gaze. "You're up for a dare before we can move on."

I hesitated, then shrugged. "Alright. Hit me."

Flick looked positively smug. "Give the straights a show, girl. Take off your top and toss it into the pool."

"The straights?" Ever scoffed. She teased, "Be a girl's girl. You know how badly we want to see those titties."

"*You* probably want to see them just as badly as her man," Indie giggled, winking at Evergreen. Then to me, she said, "Honestly, babe, do it for everyone other than Flick and Odie."

Flick's fingertips flew to his chest in feigned offense. "*Other* than Flick? As if I don't appreciate art when I see it?"

Laughter trickled around the pool. My stomach flipped, but I wouldn't give them the satisfaction of my nerves.

"You don't have to do it," Denning said. "If you pass on the dare, you just drink."

"Bullshit," Indie scoffed. "Give her a chance to be brave."

Indie was right. I wanted to be brave. I reached behind me, slowly pulling the straps of my bikini top loose before slipping it off. I held it in my fingers for a moment, then tossed it over the ledge, onto the brushed cement just beyond the water.

Ever clapped her hands. "That's more like it."

Heat curled in my stomach. The air was thick with something palpable now, something heady and charged. I slipped deeper into the pool, if only for a semblance of liquid modesty.

The sun winked out, leaving us with the lavender-gray remnants of daylight before we were plunged into total darkness.

The game continued. More truths, more dares. Flick was dared to kiss Odie—"like you mean it." Lemon had to whisper something filthy into Wei's ear. Clementine was challenged to pull Roman onto her lap and keep him there for the next round. The space between bodies narrowed, the energy shifting, thickening, twining into something electric.

Then, it was my turn again.

Denning spoke before anyone else could. "Dare."

I narrowed my eyes. "That's not how it works. I get to pick between the two."

He wore the same lazy, amused expression he had when making me walk for the towel. "I think it is."

A dare. From Denning. My skin heated beneath his gaze. "Alright." I straightened my shoulders. "Dare."

He leaned back against the edge of the pool, considering. Then, voice smoldering, he said, "Straddle me."

The group let out a collective sound of approval. My heart nearly stopped. Infuriating. Maddening. Unspeakably hot and equally humiliating. I'd been soaked for this man from the moment I met him, and the first time we were able to cross a line, he wanted me to do it in front of everyone else in some goddamn performance? Un-fucking-believable. My thoughts short-circuited as I fought the urge to cry out in protest, to splash him, to wrap my fingers around his thick neck and strangle him.

But I was paid to be here, and his dollar went a long way in handcuffing me from speaking my mind. I managed to spit out: "In front of…"

"Come here, babe," came the low, gravel of his command.

I wished he'd make it easy on me and grab me around the

wrist, yanking me to him, forcing me into his lap. I wanted him to take the choice out of the act so I could play the role of unwilling damsel, seduced despite herself. This, however…this was a new brand of torture.

I stared at Denning, pulse thundering painfully. He merely waited, unmoving, unreadable. A challenge. We were dating, as far as anyone knew, but that wasn't the dare. It wasn't about him. It was about exhibitionism, and to see how far I would go with an audience.

Fine. Fucking fine. He wanted to play? I was game.

The pool grew warmer as I waded into shallower waters. His eyes never left mine. My breath was shallow as I reached him, hands bracing against his shoulders. I felt the heat of his skin beneath my fingertips, the way his muscles tensed, coiled.

I summoned my swagger and gave the world a show. I swung a leg over his lap and settled against him.

My lips parted as I stared into his eyes, and my bravado evaporated.

His hands came to rest at my hips, calloused fingers slipping just beneath the string tie on either side of the bikini bottoms. His touch was firm, but I wanted more. My hips rolled against him as I tilted forward, the slow, crashing wave motion bringing him to life beneath me. He hardened under the movement, his mouth opening slightly to match mine as I leaned in. I sipped the breath of his exhale, savoring the taste as his grip on my hips tightened.

I leaned my forehead to his, skin to skin as we shared the same charged spark of air in the agonizing, never-ending moment right before the kiss. The hardness of his length electrified my core, building a hunger within me that tore me in half. This man was messing with my head, yet I couldn't drag myself away. None of this was real. I'm not his. He's not mine.

One hand slipped from my hip to the base of my neck, tightening as he pulled me for the kiss that I've been anxious to give. He stopped a hair's breadth from my lips, and I squirmed harder. The pain sent a jolt of electricity down my spine, straight to my clit.

This time, when he spoke, there was no cloying power in his voice. There were simply the words, "Kiss me."

That's it. I closed the gap between us, mouth slamming into his as I gave myself over to the need. One kiss wasn't enough. I moved on him, hips rolling harder this time as I savored his tongue against mine. This was supposed to be fake, a performance for his friends, but I felt myself melting beneath his touch, lost to his mouth, aching against his body. I drank his sweetness in like honey, and that made it all the more cruel.

I was lost in the moment. Lost in the show.

We were lovers, partners, dating.

We were strange, new, electric, terrifying, exciting.

I forgot the party, the island, the others, signing myself wholly over to the passion I'd felt for him since the moment he'd threatened to bend me over in the restaurant on our first encounter.

I would have kissed him forever if the whooping and excited calling behind us hadn't started.

"Oh, shit," Wei laughed. "You really *do* know how to pick 'em."

"I told you she was fun," Ever grinned.

I slipped out of his lap and onto the space beside him, breasts covered in droplets and glistening in the moonlight.

His fingers skimmed the bare skin of my back. "Comfortable?"

My stomach flipped. "I'm great." I looked at him until I said the magic word. "Hippocrates."

"Excellent."

We stayed like that for a moment too long. The game moved forward, but my body hummed with awareness of his.

The dares grew riskier, the air thicker, bodies closer. Someone suggested moving things to the hot tub. Another round of drinks appeared. I wasn't sure if I was warm from the water or the way Denning's touch still lingered against my skin.

I was breathless when the game finally broke apart, when people peeled away into smaller groups, some disappearing into the dark corners of the villa.

Denning stood, offering a hand. "Should we wash up before dinner?"

I hesitated, glancing around at the others—the looks exchanged, the knowledge of what came next as we headed back to the single room, single bed, of our villa. I took his hand, and let him lead me, hoping and praying I knew what would come next.

11

THE PATH BACK TO THE VILLA WAS QUIET, SAVE FOR THE RHYTHMIC hum of cicadas and the distant, crashing waves. The torches lining the walkway flickered in the warm breeze, casting golden light over Denning's sharp features, the slight smirk still tugging at the corner of his lips. He walked beside me, close but not touching, the heat from his skin nearly palpable in the thick, humid air.

"You were a good sport tonight," he smiled.

I huffed a small laugh, absently squeezing my thighs together. My pulse hadn't quite settled since the pool. "That's one way to put it."

His gaze flickered to me, sharp and assessing. "You enjoyed yourself."

I didn't answer right away, but I didn't have to. He knew. I could tell by the way his smirk deepened, the satisfaction there. He liked watching me unravel.

I exhaled, rolling my shoulders as if that would shake the tension from my body. "And you? Did you enjoy yourself?"

"Immensely."

The weight of that word sent a ripple of warmth to my pussy. I glanced ahead, pretending the shadows in the jungle weren't pressing in on us like silent watchers. There was always something watching.

We reached the villa, stepping inside, the contrast between the open, humid night and the cool air inside sending a shiver down my spine. I kicked off my sandals near the door, moving toward the bathroom on autopilot, already craving the feeling of warm water washing away the salt and chlorine clinging to my skin.

Denning followed, his presence pressing at my back without ever quite touching. He leaned against the door, arms folded, while I tested the shower waters.

"You're quiet," he said.

I turned the faucet, letting the steam curl into the air before answering. "Just thinking."

He moved closer. Not quite touching, but close enough that I could feel the heat radiating from him. "About what?"

I didn't look at him. "About you. About all of this."

He was silent for a beat, and when he finally spoke, his voice was softer, almost coaxing. "And what do you think?"

I let out a breathy laugh, shaking my head. "That's the problem. I don't know what to think."

His fingers skimmed the ends of my damp hair, deliberate, lingering. "Then don't."

The water was hot against my palm as I moved beneath its concentrated rainfall, but it wasn't as hot as his presence against my skin.

I glanced up at him, at the way the dim light from the sconces played over the angles of his face. The heat in his gaze was unmistakable, smoldering and patient, like he was giving me all the time in the world to step away—and daring me to stay.

I should have stepped away. But I didn't.

"That kiss…" I dared. "In the pool…"

One corner of his mouth turned up.

"I like when you listen."

His praise ran through me, lighting up every nerve in my body. I fought against the pleasure, trying to keep my thoughts straight so he wouldn't see how badly he was affecting me.

"You like when you push my boundaries," I countered. "Is that a…kink of yours? A power dynamic thing?"

"Maybe I just like watching you squirm," he said, trailing his fingers down my spine. "Maybe my kink is the moment when you overcome it and give in."

I reached for the strap of my swimsuit, my breath shallow, my pulse loud in my ears. "Are you going to stand there and watch, or are you getting in?"

His smirk was slow, indulgent. Predatory.

He toyed with the buttons of his shirt, slipping one free. Then another. I'd just been around his bare chest in the pool moments prior, but it meant something different now as he opened his shirt, revealing his rippled abdominals, his carved pecs, the pronounced line of demarcation running down the center of him. His dark gaze never left mine.

My heart was going to pound right out of my chest. My stomach twisted. My pussy pulsed. I was thirsty and quenched all at once. I hated what this man did to me, and I loved it more than I could explain.

I exhaled, trying to steady the nervous energy thrumming through me, but then he stepped beneath the water—and my mind went blank. He towered over me, water dripping off his hair and face onto mine as I looked up at him.

God, he was attractive.

Denning hovered inches from my face. His hands slid over me under the hot water, pulling my hips flush against his. Despite the steam, my body shivered. His fingertips flexed against my back as he pinned me against him, lips still a tantalizing gap from mine.

I could feel his hard length twitch between us, and all I wanted was more.

I tried to kiss him, but he pulled away just enough to reject the advance—teasing me, forcing me to cook in my own heat. I got to my tiptoes, desperate to close the tiny space between our mouths, but once again he moved his face just at the last second, refusing to allow me the satisfaction.

He planted one enormous hand on the shower wall behind my head and leaned over me while I waited, helpless, beneath him. I was consumed entirely by him, there was no space left for me to think any thought except how badly I wanted this, wanted him. His other hand moved from my back to my face, grazing my throat as he ran a thumb over my lips. It moved down my neck, down my front, trailing fingertips between my breasts, over my stomach, inching daringly close to my sex. My hips rolled off the wall toward him, hoping he would touch me in the place I craved, but instead he grabbed my hips, pinning me away from him.

If this man didn't kiss me, I was going to lose my mind.

I was on the verge of breaking when a heard a woman's voice—a familiar British accent—from somewhere near the door.

Fuck.

"Are you two having fun?" Ever called.

"We're in here, E," Denning replied.

My heart thumped painfully as I tried to understand what was happening. *Why would he let her interrupt our first time? Was he never going to kiss me? Did he want to kiss her, instead?* I was dizzy. I couldn't breathe.

I craved him.

I loathed him.

Ever's face appeared at the crack in the door, her eyes taking in our precarious position. I watched as a light spark danced across her eyes, and small thrill shot through my core.

She tilted her head. "Mind if I join?"

Denning paid her no mind, instead he weighed me with his eyes, a faint twitch of his lip. "I got you a plaything."

"I…" My voice choked up, confusion and arousal twining into a ball at the back of my throat.

"As long as you remember: you're *my* plaything. Do you understand?"

I gulped on the water.

Was he offering her to me?

"You can say no," he said. "You can stop at anytime. Or… you can see how good it feels when you listen."

I stared at him through the water and offered my hesitant word. "Hippocrates?"

"Hippocrates," he echoed.

The cracked open door sent a wave of chilly air slithering over me. I looked between Ever and Denning, no semblance of a clue as to what was going on or how I felt or what I wanted. I was confused, but it was more than that. The curiosity, the panic, the fear, the excitement wove themselves into a complex braid that started on my tongue, made its way to my breasts, then pooled between my legs in a powerful throb.

"Nod, Juniper," he commanded.

I obeyed.

"Tell me you're going to listen."

One second of the rhythmic sounds of water while he stared at me. Two. Three. At last, I nodded.

"There's a good girl." His praise rolled over me, melting my body. Then, he turned to Ever and cocked his head in my direction. "Come on in."

Confusion was a choking cloud. I didn't want to watch him choose someone else. I didn't want to see him kiss her, fuck her, touch her when he wouldn't do the same to me. I didn't want—

Ever stepped beneath the shower water, fully clothed. She stuck her hand in my hair and pulled me to her, her lips on mine, her tongue tasting my mouth, her free hand cupping my cheek as she pulled me in. Everything switched in an instant. My panic changed cadence. My body redirected. I melted, if only slightly, against her soft, perfect lips.

"Go ahead," Denning said. "Kiss her back."

Excitement and questions sparkled in Ever's eyes as she looked at me. "Is this okay?" she asked.

And the truth was, it was *very* okay.

My lips found hers again, eyes closed against the water as I began to kiss her in earnest. I channeled everything I felt for Denning into the kiss, pleading, commanding, exploring.

"E, make her feel good," Denning said. "I want to look her in the eye while she cums."

I barely had a moment to comprehend the order as Ever dropped to her knees. I fell backward into the polished cement, desperate for the support, as her mouth moved over me. She kissed from my bellybutton to my vulva, mouth moving from my outer lips to my inner lips, tasting, tantalizing, until she reached my clit.

My fingers buried in her hair, wrapped in the wet mess as I held on for dear life.

I let out a gasp as she worked two fingers inside of me, gently at first, then moving rhythmically. Her tongue swirled around my clit, then she began to suck.

Denning worked his hand underneath my head, supporting it so it wasn't forced into the cement, as he stood over Ever. "Breathe through it," he commanded.

I tried to inhale, but my breath was coming in shallow gasps. I was lost to the sensation, lost to the need that was curling deep in my ocean.

"She's not going to stop until you cum. Relax into it."

I continued taking shallow sips of air while her hand pumped inside me. The sucking. The fucking. The water. Denning's unbelievable body. Her soft lips. His strong hands. Her talented tongue. His flexed jaw. Her wet clothes. His dark eyes. Her on her knees. And at last, his mouth as he lowered his face to mine and gave me the kiss I'd been so desperate to have.

He breathed out, and I breathed in, inhaling him like a slow drag of smoke. His lips were hard and claiming. Up on my toes, down on the flats of my feet, trying to get closer, to relax, to draw him close, to let her touch me, pleasure me, use me. My tongue prodded his for that sweetness, that honey, desperate for relief to the fire he'd started within me. I gulped him down, lost on the tantalizing, dominant perfection of his mouth.

My mind unlocked, every pleasure center electrifying as I became liquid beneath him.

An involuntary cry broke the kiss as she brought me to the edge. The muscles within me clenched. I cried out again, desperate, needing, succumbing.

He pulled away, just enough to smile at me as he looked into my eyes, watching me tumble into oblivion as I came harder than I'd ever cum.

I shattered completely, a million pieces of my mind, body, and soul washing down the drain—Denning's to command.

12

I struggled to look Evergreen in the eye when we reconvened for dinner. She was breezy as ever, as if this was just another Tuesday.

The night unraveled in a blur of indulgence. Another elaborate dinner stretched into the late hours, the table overflowing with glistening fruits, exotic meats, and endless flutes of champagne. Laughter rang through the candlelit space, warmth curling around me like an embrace. I caught myself smiling more, leaning into the conversations, allowing the rhythm of the island to sink into my bones. Maybe I was imaging it. Maybe I was seeing what I hoped to see. But the others seemed to be treating me differently now—not as an outsider, but as someone slipping into the fold, adapting to the cadence of their world.

If anything, I felt special.

Pampered. Doted on. Like for the first time in my life, I was the most desirable thing at the party.

Surely, I was drunk. There was no other explanation for thinking something so absurd. And yet…

I thought, fleetingly, of the flight attendant, of the way she'd said, *perhaps you'll end up with one, yourself.* Had she meant more than a tattoo? Had she meant this—this seamless slide into belonging?

By the time I collapsed into bed, my body hummed with exhaustion, my skin still tingling from Denning's touch. He hadn't so much as kissed me since the shower, not after Ever had finished with me, not after he had murmured something unreadable against my temple and carried me to bed. But his presence next to me, solid and immovable, was enough to lull me into sleep.

I DREAMED.

I was at the shrine once more, but this time in the height of bright, golden sunshine. Everything had an iridescent quality, as if just outside of reality.

The altar stood before me, like it had that afternoon, except now the jungle encroached around it, the trees stretching taller, the vines thicker, as if the island itself had grown encircling the shrine. The air hung heavy, suffocating, thick with the perfume of something floral, something rotting beneath it. The woman was there again—the one with the black hair, the one I had seen in the jungle.

But she did not speak.

She lifted a single finger to her lips, a silent command: *Shh.*

I opened my mouth to ask her what was happening, why I was here, why the jungle felt like it was breathing around me— but no sound came. I couldn't even hear the crickets, the waves, the wind through the leaves. Everything had been swallowed by silence.

I wasn't scared. I wasn't anything as I followed her gaze.

She turned and gestured toward the shrine.

The first statue loomed larger than before, taller than me now, its golden face familiar, draped in strands of delicate rubies and lush garlands of flowers. The priestess—if that was what she was—plucked a ruby bracelet from the statue and fastened it around her wrist, her fingers delicate, deliberate. She turned to me, her dark eyes expectant, urging me to *understand.*

I followed her gaze to the second statue.

This one was different. *Colder.*

I felt something different now. A curiosity.

The pile of rubies at its feet shimmered under the afternoon sun, their surfaces slick like wet stones. Something inside me twisted, an animal instinct screaming at me to run—but my body would not move. I watched, helpless, as the rubies began to melt, darkening, congealing into something thick and red. Blood. It pooled around the statue's feet, seeping into the cracks of the altar, filling the air with the sharp scent of copper.

I tore my gaze away, turning back to the priestess, but she was gone.

My nerves tingled.

And, in her place, the first statue had changed.

It was no longer her.

It was *me.*

The sun was suddenly too hot. I struggled to breathe under its suffocating rays.

My own face stared back at me, frozen in gilded horror, lips parted as if I had been captured mid-scream. The bracelet the priestess had stolen was gone from the statue's grasp. I reached for my own wrist, but before I could feel for its weight, a shadow flickered from the corner of my vision.

The second statue *moved.*

Fear replaced the sun's baking light with ice, my blood chilling in my veins.

A knife gleamed in its many hands, the curved blade catching the moonlight. My breath caught in my throat as it turned its head toward me, the motion slow, unnatural, deliberate.

My heart began to pound. The frost spread through me. I

opened my mouth to cry out, to ask for help, but no sound came. I tried to run, but my feet were stuck to the ground.

Then it *lunged*.

I let out a blood-curdling scream, breaking the sound barrier at last as the blade came down—

I GASPED AWAKE, COLD, WET, DARK.

I was not in bed.

Where was I?

The chill of stone bit through my thin t-shirt, chilling my side, damp with the humidity of the jungle. My breath came in sharp, panicked bursts, my heartbeat a frenzied drum in my chest as I pushed into a seated position. The world swayed as I tried to get my bearings, my stomach lurching with the realization that I was no longer in the villa. It was so black. If it weren't for the sliver of crescent moonlight, I wouldn't be able to see my hands in front of my face.

I'd awoken at the mouth of the cave.

"Oh, fuck." I scrambled to my feet, immediately looking to the statues at the cave's entrance. I stumbled backward, staring at the stone women. They were immobile, as they were meant to be. The altar loomed before me, the same one from my dream, only now it was real. Too real. I spun, searching for some explanation, some trick of my own mind—but then I heard something. It was almost a whisper of wind, nearly a breeze, but there was something strange about it. Something lyrical, as if curling smoke carried a sound.

I strained in the dark, heart trilling as I struggled to make sense of how I'd gotten here, terrified of being alone in the jungle.

"Cassidy..."

My real name. The one no one on this island should know.

The whispering grew, a chorus of voices murmuring in a

language I couldn't understand, threading around me like a spell. The jungle moved—not from wind, but from something else. The leaves shifted as if *watching*. The ground pulsed beneath my feet like the island itself was alive, its heartbeat syncing with mine.

I tried to step back, to move, to *run*, but my body would not obey. It was not a dream gluing me to the ground this time, but sheer fight, flight, and freeze. My limbs remained stuck, locked in place by some unseen force. A shadow stretched across the stone before me, tall and unmoving.

Someone was behind me.

A breath ghosted against my ear, warm and *too close*. My skin prickled as something cold pressed against my wrist—a bracelet, heavy and metal, clinking as it was fastened into place.

A gold band, set with a single, gleaming ruby.

The same as the bracelet the priestess had worn. The same rubies that had turned to blood.

A voice, low and rich, poured into my ear.

"Come to me, my golden girl."

A hand brushed the nape of my neck, fingers skating across my skin like a claim.

I screamed—

My eyes flew open, lungs heaving, the sheets damp with sweat. My pulse pounded so hard it hurt. I sucked in frantic breaths, fingers curling into the linen beneath me, my body trembling from the force of it.

White gauze. White duvet. White sheets. Gentle gray morning light.

I was back in the villa.

Back in bed.

The stone altar was gone. The jungle was gone. The whispers, the voice, the presence—gone.

But the weight in my hand remained.

I turned my palm over, barely breathing as my fingers uncurled.

The bracelet lay in my palm.

Heavy. Gold. Set with a single, gleaming ruby.

I choked on my own breath, my stomach twisting into knots, my mind scrambling for logic, for some kind of explanation—but before I could even begin to process what had happened, movement flickered beside me. I tried to escape the bed, to sprint to the cold shower to rinse away the acidic beads of sweat but froze at the sight of my muddy feet the moment I slipped them out from beneath the sheets.

Denning was turned away, still asleep at my side.

I could not speak.

I could not breathe.

I could not escape.

Whatever had happened, I was in the ocean in the middle of nowhere, with no one to save me, and no way out.

I belonged to the island.

13

ISLAND: DAY THREE

I scrubbed my feet until they were pink and raw—eliminating the muddy remnants of my nightmare—as if I could wash away the panic that had me in a vice grip. I slipped the bracelet between the flaps of a fluffy, white towel while I bathed, hiding it as best I could. The moment I stepped out of the shower, I reached for my phone. My hands were still damp, and the screen stuttered under my fingertips as I tried to unlock it. Still no service. Not a single bar. I swallowed down the rising panic, forcing myself to stay calm. It had to come back eventually. The others insisted they'd gotten it to work before. Maybe I needed an eSIM or some sort of roaming plan, there had to be a way to get it to work.

I threw on a loose dress, then returned to the bathroom, pinching the bracelet between two fingers as I fetched it from its hiding place. I grimaced at it as if it was coated in poison. I jammed it into my pocket the moment I heard feet moving in the room behind me. I slid the door open with an easy smile plastered across my face.

"Heading to breakfast?" Denning stopped me in my tracks.

"In a bit." I hedged. "I wanted to take a walk first."

Denning paused, watching me like he knew something I

didn't. His hair was still a mess from sleep, and the imprint of the sheets left a faint crease against his bicep. The sight of him, so effortlessly perfect, sent a ripple of guilt through me.

I had to do this.

Had to make sure I could reach someone off this island if I needed to.

Denning's gaze lingered, but he didn't push. "Don't be gone too long."

I nodded, slipping out before he could change his mind.

THE HUMIDITY HAD BEEN SUCH A WELCOME REPRIEVE FROM Denver's arctic bite when I'd first arrived. Now, I was sick of drinking the air around me. The inability to breathe deeply without half of my lungs suffering from the dew point, feeling like drowning on dry land.

I'd been outside for less than a minute and was already sweating. I was confident that my hair had adopted a halo of frizz to match the batch of sweat between my breasts.

I started on the beach, holding my phone up to the sky like an offering. Nothing. I switched it to airplane mode and back. Nothing. I reset the network settings, restarted the phone. Still nothing.

I'd seen Indie on her phone before. Wei had shown me his Instagram page. They'd been clicking away at dinner and the pool, posting pictures, probably tagging locations. There had to be a way.

Perhaps I wouldn't figure out the cell reception, but there had to be internet somewhere on the island. Maybe the workers had access to a separate network, something they used to order supplies. If I could just piggyback off that...

I hugged the edge of the path, desperate to stay in the tiny pools of shade cast by the palm fronds and vines and whatever other cretaceous-period leaves I hadn't seen before and would never be able to name. A single stray arm in the sun felt like throwing a piece of a raw bacon to sizzle in a frying pan. Maybe I'd just woken up on the wrong side of the bed, but I was goddamn sick of it.

I headed in the direction of Ares's pen toward the practical, understated worker's building. It was only a five-minute walk, but it felt longer every time I took this path. Maybe if Ni Luh was there, she'd help me connect.

The edges of the worker's building poked out of the jungle as I rounded the corner. Despite knowing that I had every right to be on the island, and that the attendants who ran the facilities were paid handsomely to help the guests out, I couldn't help but slow as I walked toward the hidden structure. An odd ache below my throat and above my lungs, like swallowing something dry and being unable to wash it down with water, pulsed uncomfortably within me.

"You're not in trouble," I whispered to myself. "You're allowed to be here."

I didn't know if I believed the words coming out of my mouth. I straightened my shoulders and feigned confidence as I marched up to the structure. I practiced in my head, reminding myself why I was there, what I needed, and repeating the attendant I knew by name.

"It's the twenty-first century," I muttered to myself. "It is perfectly reasonable to hunt down Wi-Fi. This is fine. You're fine."

As I reached the side of the building, the uneasy feeling persisted. I gulped down the papery lump in my throat to no avail. There was no one outside. I heard no evidence of a hustle and bustle. Instead of marching to the front door, I took a few steps to the side and cautiously peered through a window.

My brows furrowed at the odd sight. I squinted, trying to make sense of it. My brain buffered as I stared at what I saw, but it was no mistake.

My blood turned cold.

Under the flat, unyielding wash of fluorescent lights, several heads were turned down to a long table, engrossed in their work. Hands were moving. Arms were bent at strenuous angles. Fabric and sewing machines and garlands and plants and florals scattered the surface. The workers were quietly fixated on their task, weaving something together with wordless precision. A headdress. A skirt. A flower crown.

The rest of the room blurred. It may as well have been empty for it all mattered. The moment my gaze caught the smear of brown hair and white teeth, my head began to spin. At the center of the table lay a photograph, with measurements listed in marker over the image.

It was me. I recognized the snapshot I'd uploaded to Discreet Arrangements.

The spinning increased. The too-humid air was no longer just a struggle to breathe; it was an impossibility. A chill rolled down my spine despite the suffocating heat. My pulse roared in my ears louder than any wave crashing against the beach. I took a shaky step back, ready to turn and run—

And yelped as I collided straight into the pillowy chest and waifish frame of another human.

I grappled with the world to stop on its axis long enough for me to see whose perfectly manicured fingers were digging into my biceps.

I looked up into the blonde hair and blue eyes of Lemon Rothschild.

The expensive yellow dress anchored me, but not in a good way. The papery lump in my throat turned into something as sour as her namesake.

My lips smacked against the bitter tang of her name, barely able to spit it out as I reeled. "Lemon! Hi. I…"

"What are you doing here?" she asked, catching me by the wrist.

I stammered, presenting my phone uselessly. The rectangle

hung limply in my hand. "I haven't had service since I landed. I'm looking for Wi-Fi. I…"

There was an uncanny, doll-like rigidity to the way she tilted her head to the side. The smile remained plastered on her face, eyes wide and glassy as it cocked near her shoulder.

"Not here, darling. *Here.*" She lifted her free hand and motioned to the jungle. "What are you doing on the island? What are you doing with Denning?"

The spinning stopped. I felt the lines that creased my forehead as I focused on her eerie expression. I'd been caught peering into the employee building at something I almost definitely wasn't meant to see, and yet, her question was about…

I blinked away whatever was left of the spiral. I had a role to play, and there was more at stake than my paycheck. The barest of breezes moved a golden lock of her hair around her collarbone, cooling the sweat beading against my brow. Palm fronds waved just enough to cast necessary shade as I grounded myself for the performance of a lifetime.

"We're dating," I said, tripping into my memorized script. "Denning and I met four months ago when he came into my clinic. We—"

"Bullshit," she said. I didn't realize that she hadn't let go from my initial stumble until now. Her nails bit into the flesh of my upper arm as if daring me to get away. The coo of some exotic bird covered my thundering heartbeat, if only for a moment.

She looked down at me with an expression I couldn't quite place, somewhere between amusement and disdain.

"Listen," I swallowed the sour knot in my throat. I could do this. This was what Denning had warned me about. This was precisely why he'd hired me for the job.

I straightened my shoulders, lifted my chin, and pasted the most relaxed expression I could muster across my face. I struck a tone that sounded nearly bored as I said, "You moved on first. You're with Wei. It's great that you're still friends with your ex or whatever this is. I'm not trying to get in the middle of it. But Denning and I are together now."

The almost mechanical thrum of cicadas filled the beat it took for her to recover from my response.

"That's not enough. You can't be this stupid."

I hoped she didn't catch the way my eyes flared. I kept the corners of my lips upturned in a cool, practiced smirk. This couldn't phase me. I wouldn't let it.

"Why you?" she pressed. "Have you asked yourself that? Why Denning chose to bring a girl with no friends, no life, no social media footprint?"

"I don't know what you're implying," I said. I did my best to pluck her hand off of my bicep, but her grip tightened. If she wanted to throw down, I may have to switch gears and change from wealthy actress to MMA fighter. I kept my breathing steady, but I let the unspoken threat glaze my expression.

Her lips peeled back from her teeth, much like the jaguar she possessed. "You shouldn't be here," she said. "You don't belong."

I spoke through the grit of a hollow, clenched smile. "Excuse me?"

Lemon peered over my shoulder at the worker's building, then back at me. She stared into my soul as she said, "The next shift of attendants leaves at sunrise. It would behoove you to leave with them."

I forced a breath into my lungs. "And why is that?"

Her grip slid from my bicep to my wrist. She held it up, twisting it just enough for the morning light to catch the ruby bracelet against my skin. Her lips pressed into a thin line.

"Where did you get this?" she asked.

The breeze picked up. Palm branches scraped together, joining fretful birds and the cacophony of insects in a bizarre, clashing sound as the jungle undulated around us. Yellow hair whipped in front of her face, but she was unmoved.

"I—I don't know," I stammered. "I woke up with it."

Lemon's grip tightened. "You expect me to believe that?"

I forgot the humidity. I forgot the sweat pooling against my sternum, seeping through my dress. I felt only cold.

I stared at her, my own frustration bubbling to the surface. "I was sleepwalking."

Something in her expression flickered. She let go abruptly, stepping back like I was something unclean. "Sleepwalking," she repeated, more to herself than to me. Whatever I'd said, it seemed to make her angrier.

I rubbed my wrist where her fingers had pressed into my skin. "Look, I don't know what you want from me, but I'm not leaving."

Lemon looked like she was going to claw my eyes out. "You *have* to leave."

"Why?"

Her blue eyes were black coals as she looked into mine. "Do you really think he'd be with someone like you? I'm his type, Juniper. Look at me. Then look at yourself. You can't truly think this was real."

The damp air crackled, turned to liquid in my lungs.

Her gaze flickered to the staff quarters, to the table where my photograph lay. "Or be a fool. But if you stay, you won't like what happens next."

The cold I felt had nothing to do with the temperature, and its ice was stifling. A shiver gripped my spine, but I forced myself to meet her stare. "I see what you're doing. You don't scare me, Lemon."

"I'm not the only thing on this island you should be afraid of."

I STORMED BACK TO THE VILLA WITH THE STICKY WIND AT MY BACK, fists clenched, anger burning through the last of my panic. I sputtered out the damp locks of hair threatening to choke me every time I opened my mouth. Lemon had no right to tell me what I could and couldn't do. She didn't know me. She didn't know what I wanted. The tropical birds seemed to be following me, calling after me, mocking me.

Cheep-cha-CHEE.

Get-away-from-ME.

Her stupid threats, her stupid fake smile, her stupid face was the only thing that could have distracted me from the bizarre sight I'd spotted in the jungle.

The green underbrush gave way to the disturbing memory.

I saw the workers bent over the table. I saw the skirt, the flower crown, the picture once more and couldn't believe how silly I'd been. Denning had told me there was an initiation planned for me. This shouldn't have been a shock, so why was I treating it like something terrifying, instead of the welcome ceremony it was? Maybe I was just getting island fever. Maybe I was letting the isolation and the extravagance get to my head. But I liked Denning. I wanted to be with him. And if he was right—if things went well—maybe I could come back. Maybe we could make this real.

I thought of Lemon's words, of the way she'd looked at me like I was something disposable. Something temporary. I stared at the bracelet again, and this time, I laughed.

Indie and Evergreen had sent over clothes, shoes, swim-suits, and filled my villa with unfamiliar belongings, all free for me to borrow. I'd given Lemon the answer I'd needed for myself: I was just sleepwalking.

Paranoia was unbecoming, but maybe it was a natural part of transitioning from someone so small, so insignificant, to this sort of bizarre micro-culture of opulence.

I couldn't let her win.

I wouldn't.

I fit in. I belonged.

14

The breeze pushed me out of the jungle, back to the manicured, Stepford-esque villas with their pristine hedges, clean lines, and ostentatious displays of wealth. The chittering bird flapped overhead, abandoning its relentless call for some new victim elsewhere on the island. I slowed my pace, smoothed my furrowed brow, unclenched my fists, and walked confidently toward the villa. Thatched roof, brushed concrete, curated florals, and billowing linens awaited me, as if the night hadn't happened. As if I hadn't woken up in the jungle, hadn't held a bracelet that shouldn't exist, hadn't listened to whispers calling me a name that shouldn't be here.

As if Lemon hadn't just looked me in the eye and told me I didn't belong.

No matter how poised I tried to look, the storm inside me raged, unyielding. I cast a hasty glance in either direction to ensure my tumult didn't have an audience. Succumbing to my rage, I yanked open the glass door, fingers curling into my palms once more.

That rich blonde bitch was wrong. She didn't get to decide who belonged in her snooty, elitist, too-good-for-broke-med-students world. If she thought I was a mistake, an outsider, a temporary plaything—I'd show her how wrong she was.

I'd show everyone.

But first, needed to convince my worthiness to myself. I shoved the offending bracelet back into my pocket.

I stopped myself just shy of slamming the glass door closed, if only because I had a point to prove, and I wouldn't very well prove it by tantruming onto the scene. I faced the outdoors, back to the room as forced myself to ease the lock to a gentle click. I sucked in a steadying breath of air-conditioned oxygen. I unclenched the muscles running from my back up to the base of my neck. Then, I turned to see the reason I was here.

I was ready to keep acting. I was ready to prove myself.

But something happened when I turned to see Denning inside, stretched across the massive couch. My breath hitched, brain skipping a thought or two as I tried to understand the mess of emotions that overrode any rhyme or reason steering me forward.

His shirt was unbuttoned. It made sense for the tropics, I supposed, but I couldn't help but look at the hard-cut muscles and open shirt as if sex itself had been propped up on the sofa to tempt me. His hair was mussed with the morning. Stubble dotted his chin, celebrating the lazy vacation, a break from razors, reveling in the departure from the demands of everyday decorum. He took a slow sip of something dark from a crystal tumbler, allowing me my reverie as I dragged my gaze southward. Permanently tanned and rippling, I'd nearly forgotten my name by the time he spoke.

His gaze flicked to mine, sharp as ever, assessing. Always assessing.

"How was your walk?" His voice was smooth, unreadable.

I snapped back to reality. The lump in my throat had returned. I swallowed hard. "I ran into Lemon."

His mouth twitched, but he didn't seem surprised. "Did you?"

There was a velvety quality to his puncturing words. The two-word question struck a chord, sending my heart fluttering once more, but the effect it had on me pooled in a new place entirely.

I grazed my lip with my teeth, chewing it gently. "She told me to leave the island."

If I hadn't already nabbed his attention, these words did the trick. His glass clinked softly as he set it down, tilting his head as if waiting for me to explain myself.

"She said I wasn't a good fit. That I should leave tomorrow morning with the workers."

Denning exhaled through his nose, leaning back into the cushions like a king surveying his court. "And? Will you?"

I took a step closer. "No."

His gaze raked over me, thoughtful. Then, without a word, he looked back at his drink. Like he wasn't worried. Like I'd already lost the argument before it started.

Something in me snapped.

In that moment, I wasn't Juniper. I wasn't even Cassidy. I wasn't some desperate loser from the Rockies who came here for some deal. Not anymore. Not after last night. Now, I was a bitch who *belonged*.

I crossed the room and climbed onto his lap, staking my claim. I straddled him, forcing him to see me, to acknowledge me.

"I'm not leaving." This moment, this place on the island, this man in front of me: they were mine. Lemon could go fuck herself.

Denning was elusive, evasive. If I could capture him…

His hands didn't move to touch me. He didn't push me away, didn't pull me closer. Just watched me with that same unreadable expression, like he was waiting to see what I would do next.

I rolled my hips just like I'd done in the pool during our stupid game of Truth or Dare, but this time was different. This time, I was in charge. The evidence of his attraction hardened against me, emboldening me as I gripped his neck for stability. I moved on him again, grinding against the proof that he wanted this as badly as I did, even if his guarded expression said otherwise. I didn't wait for permission this time. I brushed my lips against his, pausing just long enough to suck in the sweet honey of his breath, and kissed him.

A pause.

Maybe I'd expected him to grab me and throw me on the bed, but this was better, somehow. This wasn't a man and his hired actress. This was mine to command.

When he didn't react, I moved forward on my own. Both hands went to the buttons of his shirt, eager to get him naked, to tumble into bed with him, to have him all to myself at last.

I wanted this man more than I wanted my next breath of fresh air. He was like a poison in my veins, corroding me from the inside out, and I couldn't help but be addicted to the pain. I could never tell what he was thinking, could never tell if this was just a game, but at this point, I didn't fucking care.

My need for him superseded any rational thought as my fingers reached the second to last button, popping it free.

His hands caught my wrists before I could push further, tightening—not enough to hurt, but enough to stop me. Enough to remind me that he, not I, decided how this went. I felt the bracelet's weight against my thigh as I moved, my deep pockets reminding me of its safety.

"Slow down," he murmured against my lips.

I bristled. "Why?"

"Because I said so."

I ground my teeth, refusing to let him derail me. "I don't want to slow down."

He laughed; the sound low, indulgent. "That's not your decision."

The words sent a shiver through me, something hot and electric unraveling in my spine. I tensed my legs, trying to stave off the wetness pooling between my thighs. He liked this—the struggle, the way I fought for control just so he could take it away.

His grip on my wrists tightened. "Ask me."

I stared at him, chest heaving. "Ask you what?"

"If you want this, ask my permission."

"I shouldn't have to."

"That's where you're wrong." He let go of my wrists, settling back again like he had all the time in the world. "You don't get to take. You get to ask."

A challenge. A test.

I swallowed my pride and whispered, "Please."

His smile was slow. "Ask better."

He redirected everything. My hands, my movements, the pace, like an artist arranging a canvas to his liking. Any time I tried to take over, he stopped me, corrected me. I was here, in his space, on his terms. And some deep, dark part of myself loved it.

"Let me take your shirt off." I bit my lip. "Please."

"You first," he countered, cocking his brow. "Strip for me."

His words shot straight to my pussy as my hands went to the strings of my dress. I fumbled for the bow, my desire making me delirious.

"Slowly." His gaze raked over me. "Take your time. And don't look away."

The love and hate became an ache. I'd never met anyone like him. I'd certainly never fucked anyone like him. But his words, his need for control, did beautiful, terrible things to me. Need curled within my deepest parts like a pulsing ache. I slipped out of my dress, revealing first my chest, then my stomach, then my legs as it pooled at my feet.

"Leave your panties on." He held my gaze, always testing. "And finish the last button on my shirt."

I complied, keeping my slow, intentional pace. My fingers went for his belt, and he snatched my hand.

"Ask," he said again.

"Can I…" I cleared my throat. "May I?" When no further instructions came, I clarified, "May I take off your pants, please?"

"Please, what?"

I knew what word came next, even though it felt impossible to say. The submissive term, the three-letter word that signed over my respect, felt like lead on my tongue.

"Please, sir."

Standing in the room. Laying on the bed. Me on my knees. Him on his back.

May I touch you. May I touch myself. May I kiss you. May I lay at your feet. May I see you naked. May I tie up my hair. Please, sir, may I suck your cock.

This man had me desperate—feral, needing, begging—to lick his shaft, to choke on his head, to bob up and down, up and down on his dick. Each newly granted permission was a rush of dopamine, a flood of oxytocin, a wild hit of serotonin as I got closer, and closer, and closer.

If I didn't have him inside me soon, I might cry.

My pussy throbbed. My panties were soaked. My heart hadn't stopped pounding. My lips were swollen from endless sucking, slurping, tasting, needing his cum, wanting it in my mouth, on my tongue, seeping down my throat, glowing deep in my stomach.

I felt his fingers on my hair, brushing it gently out of my face, guiding my head away.

"Take off your panties," he said. "Get on top."

"Yes, sir," is what I wanted to say, if the flush of heat hadn't rendered me breathless. I swung my leg over him, righting myself as smoothly as I could manage. I wasted no time tilting my head back, spine arching, savoring the position.

My hand went straight to his shaft, guiding him to my entrance. His head touched my lips, but before I could take the next step, he gave me another command.

"Ask."

I had no dignity left. I wanted this so, so badly.

"Please fuck me." It was barely more than a whimper.

He kept his composure but couldn't hide the hunger flickering behind his eyes. Even his voice, level and controlled, contained the telltale signs of primal need. "Please, what?"

I would have gotten on my hands and knees if he had asked me. I looked at him like he was the last glass of water in the desert. My hand stayed on his member as I hovered above him, feeling the barest evidence of wetness trickle down his shaft from where I waited.

"Please, sir."

It was over. He'd been unleashed.

Denning flipped me onto my back, entering me in one smooth motion. I expected him to slide into me like a hot knife over butter, but he was too big, I was too full, it was too much, and too gorgeous, terrifying, sensual, dominating, perfect.

Fuck, I hadn't been with a man in years, and Denning wasn't just a man… he was a *man,* whatever the fuck I could possibly mean by divine, assertive, self-actualized sense of the word. Holy shit, he was magnificent.

His fingers dug into my flesh, rougher and more animalistic than anything I'd ever experienced. I gasped, wanting him to stop, wanting it to go deeper, confused and drunk on oxytocin over how badly I needed this. My pussy clenched around his cock, desperate to keep him inside me. The pain clashed with pleasure in a euphoria I'd never experienced.

"I…I…" I gasped, trying to say anything, to express a single goddamn thought.

"Tell me," he growled. The force of his cock slid in and out, skin slapping against the flesh of my ass.

"It's too much. I can't—"

His fingers tightened against the base of my neck. "Do you want me to stop?"

I dug my nails into his skin, pulling him closer. I practically screamed my answer through bared teeth. "Don't you dare."

The head of his cock hit my G-spot again and again and again, plunging into me, urging me closer, higher, deeper. I held onto him for dear life, merely a passenger as he took what belonged to him.

The rhythm of his thrusts took on its own hypnotic effect. I was a garbling mess, free of thought, lost to the cascade of over-powering sensations. He could have asked me for anything, and I would have said yes, no matter the cost.

Some tickling thought in the back of my jelly brain let me know, "Oh, this. *This* is drugs. And goddamn—I get it. I'd do anything to feel like this again."

I surrendered completely—sweat and flesh and cum and need—and I'd never felt more whole.

At some point, I lost track of time, lost track of my own breath. Denning didn't, though. He stayed in control, guiding, adjusting, deciding.

Please, please, please, cum inside me.

Please fill me up.

Please make me yours.

And he did.

THE WORLD WAS DIFFERENT, SOMEHOW.

I stared up at the vaulted villa ceiling, undoubtedly crafted by some award-winning architect. Natural elements smeared together with modern simplicity. Beams and linen curtains and brushed cement made the perfect backdrop to my fuzzy stream of cum-drunk bliss.

I dripped with his seed, my inner thighs wet, my muscles aching, my pussy pleasantly plump and sore, my guts inexplicably rearranged, my soul unbelievably happy. I was owned. I was claimed. I was his.

Denning exhaled, dragging the backs of his fingers down my arm, watching the way I trembled from it with a smirk. "Are you satisfied now?"

I blinked, still catching my breath. "Profoundly." After a long draw of air, I asked, "Are you?"

"If I wasn't, do you think I would have let you stop?" His words curled around my skin with dark seduction, and despite having just had the hardest orgasm of my life. The heartbeat between my thighs had the gall to throb again.

I let my head drop against his shoulder, pulse thrumming. "This is where I belong."

Denning tilted my chin up, forcing me to meet his gaze. Something flickered in his eyes, something darker than amusement, more deliberate than simple pleasure. "You think so?"

I nodded.

His lips brushed my forehead. "Then stay. Become part of the island."

Yes.

My eyelids were heavy with bliss. My body needed to rest. I sank deeper into total and utter satisfaction.

I had won.

In the barest moments before sleep, something itched me uncomfortably.

The scratch came from a memory I didn't want to relive. A sight I hadn't wanted to see.

I wanted—no, I *needed*—to relax into this triumph, but the unpleasant, abrasive sensation needed to barb me with one final thought before I fell asleep.

Despite my confidence in my victory, I couldn't help but feel like I'd stumbled into a game where I didn't know the rules. Maybe I was Denning's girl. Maybe I'd outsmarted the island. Maybe I belonged here. But for the rest? I didn't know the pieces to this contest, the scope of the board, or the players. And most of all, I felt in my bones that I had no idea what was at stake if I lost.

15

Warm sunlight filtered through the glass doors, letting us know the blue skies and heavens above had full access to our carnal display. The upscale villa felt too proper for something so depraved, but then again, my brain was starting to shift the way it viewed the wealthy. Perhaps money didn't coincide with conservative values. Stacks of cash just meant that the 1% had to escape to a remote, uncharted island to indulge in the things that truly brought them to life.

The brush of fabric was an unwelcome sensation after the raw, unfiltered skin on skin.

I was still pulling my dress back over my head when the knock came.

A satisfied warmth prickled in my limbs, the kind that made moving slow and thinking slower. Denning was sprawled across the bed, half-draped in the sheets, watching me with that ever-present smirk, like he knew exactly how undone I felt.

Another knock at the door stirred him from his leisurely pose.

"Allow me." He took his time swinging his legs over the bed, as if he couldn't be bothered.

"You aren't going to make me ask to answer it?"

"I could." He offered a crooked half-smile. "But you were already so good for me. You deserve a little pampering."

If I hadn't known before, I was certain now. I wanted to be totally and completely his.

I watched over his shoulder as he opened the door.

"E," came the lazy greeting. "How are you?"

Ever responded with a grin I could only partly see, barefoot on the villa's polished stone floor, dressed in something light and sheer that caught the breeze. "Is your girlfriend free? I have a treat for her."

He kept his arm on the doorframe, blocking Ever from seeing me until I was ready. It was challenging to understand the rules of his game, but being inside his world was intoxicating.

"What do you say, babe?" He asked, turning to me with the familiarity of a couple in love. "Would you like a treat?"

Ever called over the blockade of his arm. "Get dressed, girl! You're coming to the lawn with me."

"What for?" I asked, tying up my dress in time to slip into the space beside Denning. His hand settled on my back as if it belonged there.

"When was the last time you got a massage?" she asked. "All the girls are going. It's a thing."

I glanced at Denning, who just raised a brow, as if to say, *go ahead, see what happens.*

Fine. A massage didn't sound terrible. And if this was another chance to solidify my place here, to prove—to myself and everyone else—that I was meant to stay, I wasn't going to say no.

Ever grabbed my hand and tugged me along, leading me barefoot down the stone path, past open-air lounges and stretches of dense green.

By the time we reached the lawn, a row of massage tables

had already been set up, crisp white linens billowing slightly under the weight of the island breeze. Umbrellas had been erected in every gap, casting each table in cooling shade. The impenetrable wall of jungle thicket rustled at the far end of the lawn, creating the perfect sanctuary for our little indulgence. Attendants moved with quiet efficiency, adjusting scented oils, folding towels, preparing.

Indie smacked her lips at me as I arrived in a hands-free air kiss. Clementine offered a flighty how-do-you-do. I supposed it was hard to be in a bad mood in a place like this. They were both unclipping and untying their bathing suits to reveal perfectly tanned, naked bodies. The women climbed onto their respective tables.

God fucking damn if this place wasn't one serene, luxurious reveal after another.

I counted the tables. Lemon wasn't here.

I opened my mouth to ask, but Ever just nudged me toward an open table. "You're going to love this."

I'd had massages before, but never in the open-air. I climbed onto the table hesitantly, sinking into the soft linens, the heat of the sun kissing my skin even through the canopy's shade. A woman approached, her expression unreadable, her hands warm as they pressed into my shoulders.

And then—

I exhaled sharply as her thumbs dug into the knots beneath my shoulder blades, unearthing tension I hadn't even realized I was carrying.

Oh, hell yeah. This wasn't just any massage. This was what a massage felt like when your bills were paid, the sun was shining, the drinks were flowing, and there wasn't a care in the world.

The woman worked me like she knew me—knew every muscle, every buried ache. She used her forearms, her elbows, her feet. At one point, she climbed onto the table and pressed her weight along my spine, stretching me in ways that made my bones pop, a release so satisfying I nearly moaned.

The oil smelled rich, heady—something floral with undertones of sandalwood. I inhaled deeply, surrendering to the sensation of being unraveled piece by piece.

Beside me, Ever let out a blissful sigh. "See? Told you."

I hummed in agreement, my voice coming out half-drunk with relaxation. "I don't think I've ever had a massage this good in my life."

Ever chuckled. "That's because you haven't."

We lapsed into comfortable silence, the only sounds were the rhythmic kneading of skin, the rustling of palm leaves, the gentle lapping of waves in the distance.

I didn't want to ruin it.

Didn't want to break the spell.

But I had to ask.

"I saw something earlier."

"Ugh, you're a talker," she grumbled. "You don't want to nap?"

I gnawed on my lip. "It's just a quick question."

She moved her head until she was facing me, both of us still on our stomachs while the masseuses worked our muscles.

Ever made a low, barely intelligible sound in acknowledgment.

"The workers," I continued, eyes still closed, body still loose under the woman's touch. I conjured the image that had haunted me from the moment I'd peered through the window. "They were making something. A headdress, I think. A skirt. A flower crown."

Ever made a pleased sound, stretching lazily. "Oh, that's lovely."

"It was for me."

She smiled like that was the most obvious thing in the world. "Of course it was."

I listened for her to say more, but the gentle crashing of salt water against a sandy beach created a lulling, hypnotic distraction. I let the rhythmic sound fill the space between us, reveling in its peace.

Despite the soothing percussion of wave after wave, I pouted, my brow furrowing. "What does it mean?"

"You should be excited." She tapped a playful finger against my wrist. "It's a huge honor."

I tried to process that. "Honor?"

"It means everyone likes you. They've—we've—chosen you."

My stomach clenched at the phrasing. "*Chosen*?"

Knuckles kneaded into me pleasantly. The southeast Asian heat wasn't stifling at all under her pressure. The soft brush of humid wind over my skin felt like a lover's touch. It warmed my muscles, letting my body open up to her manipulation. Her fingers gently coaxed every knot and worry from my body, providing a most welcome distraction to the conversation.

She smiled, eyes half-lidded from the massage, utterly unbothered. "Mmm-hmm."

Taking a risk, I asked, "Does this mean I'm getting a tattoo or something?"

Ever burst out in a giggle. "No, no, silly." She waved a hand. "Nothing like that."

I let out a breath I hadn't realized I'd been holding.

She leaned in slightly, her lips curving. "That's beneath what's coming for you. Trust me."

The massage continued, but suddenly, the weight of the woman's hands felt heavier.

The scent of the oil, thicker.

The heat of the sun beating through the paper-thin umbrella canopy was almost too warm.

I swallowed. Forced a smile.

And tried not to think about what, exactly, I'd just been *chosen* for.

Ever propped herself up on an elbow and faced me. "I'm

gonna be honest, babe, you seem a little uptight for someone in paradise. Is having everything on a silver platter daunting?"

"It's not that..." but I didn't have an intelligent end to my sentence. There was no articulate rebuttal as she looked at me.

When I failed to say anything convincing, she said, "Here's what's going to happen. I'm going to offer you drugs, and you're going to say no, because you're a prude."

"I, what—"

She waved me away. "Let me finish. You're going to say no, not only because you're in med school and have a very convincing list of reasons that drugs are bad, but also because unlike the frivolous wealthy around you, you're sensible. You're a good girl. Drugs are beneath you."

My skin prickled uncomfortably at her words. I was suddenly too conscious of the humidity.

"Ever..." I wasn't sure where she was going with her tirade, but I wished she would stop.

"But the main reason you're going to say no? Is because saying no is what you do."

A beat. The breeze stopped. The leaves didn't rustle. There wasn't even a bird or bug to fill the awkward stretch of silence. Just the gentle sounds of women being touched by the masseurs as Evergreen read me to filth.

"Tell me I'm wrong," she prodded.

But I couldn't. She was right. I'd never been the fun girl. I was not the stay-out late girl. I was not the rave bae. I was not the pill popper—I was barely even the drinker. I was not the threesome-haver, the porn-watcher, the sexually adventurous girl.

I stared at her, lips parted, speechless.

She plucked the little glass vial from her neck and dangled it in front of me. Then she raised her voice, saying, "Indie, I'm doing G. You want some?"

I watched the tiny cylinder of glass pass between them like they were witches peddling a potion. For the briefest moment, the substance disappeared against the blue horizon, matching the way the ocean met the sky as Evergreen held it aloft.

Ever thrust the glass toward Indie, who uncorked her vial and dribbled a couple drops into the glass. Indie stirred it with her finger and downed it in three gulps while Ever mixed her own concoction. Before drinking it, she asked me, "Do you want some?"

It was like the island was waiting for my answer. The tropics were muted. Even the waves seemed quieter as I stared at Pandora's box before me.

Did I?

The obvious answer was no...but Ever was right. I was someone who said no to things. But maybe that version of me no longer existed. I was currently on a private island, surrounded by unholy amounts of wealth and excess, hired as a sugar baby by a man I hadn't known before I took the job. I'd taken a new name, purchased new clothes, and begun my new identity. I was desperate for Denning, and had my pussy eaten by Ever before he'd let me truly kiss him.

Maybe I was someone who said yes.

I held out my glass but hesitated. "I haven't heard of G. What's it do?"

Indie had already swallowed it whole, so whatever it was, it sure seemed like it wasn't going to kill me.

"It's like molly," she said. "A little more like ketamine, I guess. It makes you feel really good, really calm. And, well, it makes you wanna fuck."

Two tables over, Indie shouted, "It's the new rave drug."

"Raves for people who don't want to be too hyper," Ever corrected. "Who want to just feel the music and have the best time."

For the second time since arriving on this island, I thought of rows of plastic desks, of dozens of wide-eyed students, of a local police officer and a television rolled in for educational purposes. Drugs were supposed to come from evil villains lurking in the shadows. We hadn't been trained to resist a substance from a mostly naked woman in paradise who was having the time of her life. She wasn't selling to get me hooked. This social titan was sharing out of the goodness of her heart. Or…something like that.

My fingers tightened on my glass. "A rave drug. For dancing." If ravers were using it, and it was a dance drug, I had to assume there was an amphetamine in it, though perhaps at a half dose, if it was for ravers who didn't want to be overly energetic. I was confused by the comparison to horse tranquilizers but didn't know enough about drug culture to argue. It didn't seem like a fun drug to get a massage on, but then again, I knew that people who'd taken molly loved to be touched.

Ever answered for her. "It's big among ravers who don't want to get overstimulated. Dance but be chill about it. You know? It's great." With that, she stirred the drink with a manicured finger and slurped it back.

I hadn't done molly or ketamine, but I knew enough people from college who'd done both and lived to tell the tale. I ignored the parts of my brain that screamed about its legality, its neurotoxicity, its probable impurity, its—

Fuck it.

"Give me some," I said.

She flashed a row of brilliant white teeth. "You sure?"

"Do it before I change my mind," I said.

My masseuse, as with all of those trained to attend these Dionysian affairs, paused long enough to let me accept the vial.

Three drops of turquoise later, I was following suit and stirring my mojito with my index finger. My drink was a little bitter. The ice clinked against my teeth, then I felt the sharp stab of a brain freeze as I sucked down the dredges.

If the jungle had been on pause while awaiting my answer, my final swallow brought the world to life again. Her fingers resumed against my back as the crackling excitement of delinquency hit my veins long before any drug could enter my system.

"Juniper came to party!" I heard at my side.

A breeze touched my cheek. The grass beneath the massage table undulated in a gentle rustle.

"Juniper's on G!" Indie whooped from two tables over.

I was pretty sure I heard the sounds of Ever passing her vial so Clementine could participate, but I'd nervously plunged my face back into the headrest and was too busy focusing on deep breaths to take in my surroundings.

But, if I was being honest, it wasn't that bad.

It didn't really feel like anything—save for the soothing buzz of downing my cocktail too quickly—as the masseuse continued to knead my muscles. Honestly, maybe I should have done more. The drug did nothing, save for the spreading warmth and intense pleasure of the masseur's ever-prodding touch.

Fuck, it felt good.

The warmth spread through me with vibrational pulses, not unlike the buzz of alcohol but heavier, sweeter. I sank deeper into the massage table, my limbs turning to liquid as the pressure of the masseuse's hands melted the last knots from my back. It felt good. Too good.

"This stuff you gave me isn't working," I said, my words sticking to the roof of my mouth like taffy. I chuckled. "Okay, it's making my lips a little fat."

"Making you feel a little loose, you mean," she slurred happily at my side.

Whatever you say, I sighed happily. God almighty, even if the drugs had no impact, this massage was spectacular. Come to think of it, the previously stifling sunshine was also now the pleasant sort of temperature that matched my body heat completely, as if I was still inside the womb.

I had the vague awareness of her shifting, propping herself up on one elbow to watch me. I kept my eyes closed. I wasn't sure if I wanted her to see me like this—relaxed, vulnerable, pliant.

The hands on my back changed. Not in pressure, not in technique, but there were more of them. I tensed for a split second, and then the sensation settled into something unearthly, the perfect synchronization of two, no—four hands working in tandem. A ripple of awareness rolled down my spine. My head lolled to the side, and I cracked my eyes open to find Ever watching me closely, her eyes gleaming.

Damn, how long did they book this massage? Back in the real world, I knew they could go for an hour, or even ninety minutes, but had this one been going for hours? It was so healing, so spectacular, I sure wasn't about to complain.

The masseuse continued with her deliberate, professional movements, working on my knots and rubbing my muscles. Ever's touches, however, took on a more mischievous nature. Her slow, swooping motions, her circular pumps, the daring regions she grazed…

"You okay?" she asked. "Is it okay if I touch you like this?"

I wasn't sure if it was the drugs or the nerves, but it was twice as hard to swallow. I couldn't bring myself to open my eyes. I'd already crossed blindingly hot boundaries with Ever in the shower. This, though…

"Denning's not here," I said at last, spitting it out like someone caught in the midst of a lie.

"I'm sure he'll arrive any minute. And trust me: he'll be thrilled that you're having fun. Now, is this good? Do you like my hands on you like this?"

Fuck ketamine and molly. She'd given me truth serum.

I didn't want my lips to turn up at the corners like they did. I knew my lids were heavy as I lolled my head to the side to see her.

My throat bobbed as I admitted that yes, it felt fucking amazing. And she was right. Denning had said as much when we'd first landed: everyone on the island was in the lifestyle, and I was welcome to participate.

I heard the smile on her voice, even if I couldn't bring myself to open my eyes. "Good."

The air shifted again, thickening. My thoughts felt slow, syrupy, as the massage changed. The touch on my body was deliberate, exploratory. The heat from Ever's fingertips sent a crackle through me, one like the charged lightning of an oncoming storm that drifted through the open-air pavilion.

"What about here?"

I took a shallow sip of air, dizzy as her fingertips slipped beneath the thin towel the masseuse had used to cover my modesty. The professional continued to work my shoulders while Ever crept closer to my inner thigh, brushing, grazing, caressing.

My innermost muscles clenched, then throbbed. I couldn't help the rush of water that dampened my inner thigh. God, I was soaked.

She reached for me, hesitated just long enough for me to pull away. I didn't.

"You want another pair of hands?"

I looked up to see Indie's flash of caramel hair, her twinkling eyes, her perfectly perky tits as she'd broken free of bikinis, of towels, of whatever coverage one might have during a massage. I laid perfectly still, half terrified of what was happening, and equal-parts scared that if I moved, it would stop. The masseuse gave a slight bow before departing, and Indie took over at my shoulders.

"Shit, Juniper, I've been wanting to kiss you from the moment you landed." My lashes fluttered open just long enough to see the pink and beige blur of flesh and lipstick as she hovered above my mouth.

Holy shit, if a massage felt nice, how would a kiss feel? My eyes practically rolled into the back of my head as I thought of the soft pillow of a woman's lips. I felt so good that my brain couldn't even access the corridors of my brain that used to belong to Amanda, to how she'd hurt me, to what I'd left behind. Come to think of it, she'd never been that good of a kisser. So, if I let Indie press her mouth to mine now…

Yes, I'd fooled around with Ever in the shower, but you know what they said…

The best way to get over someone old was to get under someone new.

Maybe it was the drinks, the drugs, or maybe for once I was just going with the moment. I arched upward, kissing Indie the moment Ever's fingers slipped inside me.

I sucked in a breath.

It was as if I was floating through the most sensual dream—a wet dream, a perfect dream—taken wholly by perfect agents of pleasure. I wanted to live in this dream forever. I wanted more. Another finger. A harder touch. More mouths. More tongues.

Somewhere beyond the haze, voices filtered in. A laugh. The low rumble of a man speaking. The shuffle of bodies shifting on the massage tables nearby. I turned my head in time to see Clementine on her back, Roman between her legs, his mouth moving over her throat as she arched against him. Indie slid between them with a lazy, wicked grin, her fingers trailing over Clementine's stomach before she leaned down to kiss her.

Yes, yes, yes…

Ever used two strong fingers inside me, nudging my inner most wall to call me to attention as she pointed from deep within me. "See? Paradise."

The sound that escaped my throat belonged to the heavens.

"When did…" I wanted to ask when Roman had arrived, but my eyes rolled as I took in my surroundings for the first time in a long time. Indie and Clementine were still somewhere at my side, Ever between my legs, but I hadn't realized that we were not alone. The men had collected near the pool, almost close enough to touch. I could practically count the droplets of sweat dripping down Odie's chest as he clutched Flick's neck beneath him.

My gaze darted across the space, and suddenly, I was struck with a sharp, clear thought: What if I turned my head and saw Lemon? Or Wei?

"Is it everyone?" I asked. I didn't bother with the rest of the sentence: *and could there be more?* To be fucked on a cloud…that was something that belonged to the highest circle of the afterlife.

"Oh, baby," she giggled, dipping to touch her lips to my skin. She kissed the length of my spine, smiling from the drugs, the sex, the delicious speculation, as she said, "You haven't felt anything until you've conquered your first orgy."

A curious moment moved through the cloud. An uncomfortable furrow of the brow that I couldn't understand. I peered through the haze, trying to make sense of the words.

A stroke of unease lanced through my buzz. I shifted, pulling myself up onto my elbows, but my body still felt sluggish, humming under the influence of whatever was coursing through me. I'd been bewildered by my first threesome, but I'd trusted Denning.

Did I trust Ever enough to guide me through whatever was coming next?

"There he is," Ever purred.

I didn't have to ask who 'he' was. Denning had arrived to make the dream perfect again.

I'd hoped to feel him inside me but instead felt the delicious tingle as the rough scrap of his calloused fingers touched my sides.

I peered through my haze as Denning's hand slipped around my waist. "I'll take it from here," he told Indie.

"I'm so glad you came," I slurred, still in a daydream.

I would have been too woozy to maintain much awareness of where she went or what she was doing, had it not been for the giggles and groan as she crawled onto the table with Clementine and Roman.

God, his hands felt so good. I snuggled into him, longing for him to be inside me.

Denning's voice cut through the murmur of pleasure. "What did you give her?"

Ever waved a dismissive hand. "Relax. It's just G."

"For fuck's sake—"

I wished they wouldn't bicker. It disturbed the clouds.

"She consented!" Ever's fingers stilled within me. I pouted, denied the rhythmic pleasure of her full, perfect pumping.

Denning's jaw tensed. "She didn't know what she was consenting to."

"Hold me?" I asked, disregarding their cross talk for the one thing I truly wanted.

He slipped a hand behind my back, easing me out of the horizontal position.

I blinked up at him, the room spinning slightly as I sat up fully. I hated that they were talking around me. "No, I—" I licked my lips, tried to find the right words. "I wanted to."

Denning exhaled sharply, like he was reining something in. I wasn't sure what. He stepped closer, brushing his fingers against my wrist in a barely-there touch. "You wanted this?"

"Very much," I swore. I knew there was more to the message. I wanted him inside of me. I wanted the pleasure. I wanted to be on an island where only good things happened from now until the end of time. But right now, I wished he'd take off his clothes and slip into the frothy cotton of pleasure.

His expression darkened, not with anger, not quite. Something else. Something unreadable.

Ever smirked and leaned in, brushing her lips against my shoulder. "Then keep going."

If I wanted him, I was going to have to take him. I tried to guide him closer, to free him from the prison of his shorts to get him inside me.

Somewhere in the depths of the pleasure, I heard Denning's voice, low and firm. It took me a second to process the word.

"Tundra."

The air shifted in an instant. The hands on me stilled. The heat cooled on my skin. I traded the sun and waves for pictures of slow blowing across the Antarctic. The laughter, the movement, everything drew to a halt like a thread snapped, like a spell broken. My pulse thudded in my ears as I turned my head to look at him, my lips parted in a question I couldn't quite form.

"But—"

"It's no questions, right?" he prodded.

I nodded, suddenly terrified I'd done something wrong. I tried to scramble free but didn't have full control of my arms and legs. My lip did little more than pout. My body was too relaxed for me to fight, to sit, to comply.

He scooped me toward him. "Come here."

"Denning, come on. She's an adult. She wants this."

"I'll deal with you later," he bit off the scold. I felt Ever peel away before I heard her leave. The air changed from indulgent to something heavier, something cautious. Ever sighed, stretching her arms above her head before flopping back onto her massage table.

"Way to kill the mood," she muttered.

Denning didn't take his eyes off me. "I'm taking her back."

My head swam, my body still tingling from everything, from the drug, from the touch, from the heat of so many bodies in one place. But I let him pull me away, let him carry me from the pavilion, away from the flickering candles and low murmurs of satisfaction still reverberating in the air.

The grass swam beneath me as I nuzzled against his tanned, muscled chest, swimming in his arms. Maybe I should have felt anxious, like I was in trouble, like I'd done something wrong, but I couldn't get myself to care. I was too happy.

The world sparkled in a muted, ticklish sort of way as he

settled me onto the bed. He held the back of my head and tilted a bottle of water to my lips.

"I'm sorry." His mouth made a flat line, brows drawn as he looked at me.

"For G?" I choked on the water, sputtering until he dabbed the corner of my lips. "The party drug?"

His expression was difficult to understand past the gauzy film of blurry bliss. "It's a party drug, sure. The crew uses it for chem sex, but they do it with informed consent. When people don't know what they're getting, it's a date rape drug."

The words were an electric volt. My vision cleared. I struggled to see him. "G is...G..." I flipped through every drug I knew. It wasn't a street name for Rohypnol. It was...

"GHB," I whispered miserably. Gamma hydroxybutyrate. "Am I safe?"

He got up from the bed long enough to wet a washcloth and return to pat my head.

I wasn't sure what I was asking. Was I close to a hospital in case of an overdose? The answer was no. Indie and Ever were my size, and they seemed to be taking it without issue, but they wanted whatever was coming. I, on the other hand, hadn't fully understood what it entailed.

He tucked me closer to him, further away from the choices I'd made tonight.

My head whirled. My skin was still sparkling, desperate to be touched. My muscles were relaxed, my head pleasantly fuzzy. The heartbeat between my legs hadn't gone away. The wet, dull throb of unrequited sex continued to pulse as my pussy ached from promised sex that hadn't been delivered.

Was I truly willing to fuck anything on this drug? I'd been in public, surrounded by Denning's friends, and I'd been ready to fuck anyone willing. Maybe it was the drug. Or maybe I had undergone a sexual awakening since arriving on the island.

Everything was different now. *I* was different.

"You're safe with me," he promised, and I believed him.

It wasn't just the words. It wasn't even the act of swooping in and snatching me from what would have arguably been an immensely pleasurable, if confusing, night. It was something in his voice. A hitch. A change. A note both tighter and softer all at once that let me know that something had changed.

I let him pull me into the dark.

As we drifted off, I wondered if I'd been rescued, or if I was so far gone that I couldn't recognize what it meant to be drowning.

16

ISLAND: DAY FOUR

MY EYES WERE HEAVY DESPITE THE CLEAN, BRIGHT LIGHT THAT coaxed me awake. I cracked open a single lid, letting in the blue sky and early morning light beyond our air-conditioned slice of heaven. I smacked my lips, tongue despicably thick with an unbearable coating of dehydration over it. Now *this* was more along the lines of things McGruff the crime dog warned me about.

I reached for the bottle of water at the bedside and gulped it down until droplets escaped the side, dripping off my cheeks and down my neck.

A hot, new day awaited me.

I awoke with a mission. It was my second to last full day on the island, and I still had more questions than answers. I stirred before the sun had fully risen, slipping out of bed as carefully as I could. Denning barely stirred, his breathing deep and steady, one arm draped over where I had been lying moments ago. I held my breath, watching him for a second longer than I should have before I tiptoed across the villa and out into the humid morning air.

You couldn't have paid me to get out of bed at dawn in Denver's frostbitten mornings, but it wasn't a struggle to slide from the room to the grassy paths. There was no shock to the system, as the air matched my blood's temperature, as if I was safe inside the island's womb.

The world was quiet. The tropical birds had not yet awoken, their songs asleep for another twenty minutes or so until the sun breached the horizon. The palm trees loomed dark against the purpling sky, and the only sounds were the distant hush of waves and the occasional cry of some unseen bird. I wasn't even sure why I was doing this, only that I had to. The cave, the shrine—it called to me like a thread I couldn't cut, a mystery half-unraveled, and I needed to tug the rest of it free.

I moved past the monstera leaves, past the fuchsia flowers, past the sweet-smelling blossoms and birds of paradise as quickly as I could without making too much noise, careful to avoid stepping on anything that might snap or crunch underfoot. Despite the fireworks of our lovemaking and my previous resolution to belong, the night before had left me feeling unsettled. Lemon's warning clashing with Denning's reassurances, but this —this was something else entirely. Before I could give myself over to Denning, to the others, to this life, I needed answers.

It was odd how quickly this island had become home.

I'd left the thin windows, the shitty apartment, the cockroaches behind. I walked the familiar path, at ease with the larger-than-life green leaves, with the shock of brilliantly colored flowers, with the coos of electric birds I'd never seen before and may never see again.

I trusted my feet as they carried me forward, no longer as sweaty as I felt at home in the humidity, and nowhere near as insecure now that I knew in my bones that I belonged.

And for that reason alone, anyone who deserved to be here, deserved answers.

It was five minutes to the worker's building, then a two-minute walk and another left past Ares' pit, then continue hugging the leftmost path for however long it took to get to the cave. While ten minutes may not have sounded like a long period, it was an ominous eternity in the dense, jungle silence, completely alone without overhead lights, and knowing a gaping, shadowy maw awaited me.

Nerves wrapped their anxious threads around my throat, tugging it closed until it was hard to breathe, hard to swallow, hard to pump blood. I knew I could chicken out and turn around, but there was too much left unanswered. In order to choose this life, I needed to go in with my eyes open.

I'd never been religious.

I'd also never had sex for money, been flown to a private island, posed as a millionaire, participated in an orgy, done hard drugs, or walked the earth as Juniper before.

There was a first time for everything.

"Hey, rock goddess," I raised my voice, unsure of where to start. I didn't have a respectful reserve of prayers or behaviors to pull on. As it were, something within me told me that pomp and circumstance would come across as utterly insincere. I settled for blatant transparency. "So, uh…who the fuck are you? How do I find out?"

The shrine was just as I'd left it, half-hidden by vines and framed by the yawning mouth of the cave. The two statues stood silent, imposing. The air smelled of earth and old incense, a lingering trace of something sacred.

I reached out to touch the nearest statue—the one draped in flowers, the one that had looked so much like the woman in my dream.

A milky voice curled around me. "What do you think of the island?"

I jerked my hand back, spinning to face the woman standing behind me.

She was breathtaking. Dark hair curled over her shoulders; her golden skin luminous even in the dim light. She wore a flowing dress, something delicate and embroidered, like she had stepped out of a painting. And she smiled at me like she knew every secret I had ever tried to keep.

"Who are you?" I asked, my voice quieter than I meant it to be.

She ignored the question, stepping closer. "What are you looking for at this time of the morning, Cassidy? It's a little early for an adventure."

I gagged on the word.

The jungle pressed in on me, suddenly not offering enough space between me and this bizarre, beautiful woman as I grappled with what she'd said.

"How do you know my name?"

She waved the question away. "The lie was never a convincing one. Denning knew it wasn't your real name, but discretion was part of the arrangement. The others respect your right to call yourself whatever you want." She spoke as if she was plucking information from the air like a shopper might remove things from the grocery shelf. Each new piece of information an unfeeling grab and stuck into her collection with matching idleness. "You think Wei was born with an easy, single-syllable name in Shanghai, instead of a fisherman's son in Qinhuangdao? You think Indie and Evergreen's parents wrote something influencer-ready on their birth certificates? Or do names like Imogen and Francis suit them better?"

Was I still dreaming? I looked over my shoulders for a sign that I was the center of some elaborate prank. Yet, no cameras broke free from the tree line. Nothing shimmered in that mirage-like way to suggest it was unreal. It was just me and a torrent of incomprehensible words from the stranger at the cave.

"I don't know anything about these people," I admitted.

Her lids narrowed, but there was a playfulness to the challenge. "Look me in the eyes and tell me that you think Odie's name was Odie when he was born to a single mother in Johannesburg."

I hesitated, uncomfortable with the line of questioning. "It's not for me to say—"

"Riddle me this, Cassidy Finch," she drummed her fingers against her hip. "Are you Cassidy? Or are you Juniper?"

It wasn't a question.

I looked over my shoulder again, but this time I was scanning for an exit.

I wasn't sure if I felt angry or scared. There was something infuriating over being caught in a lie that people allowed you to tell again and again and again, watching you make a fool of yourself.

It would be insane to take off running over a weird conversation. I convinced myself to be calm, to stand my ground, to ask the question burning in the back of my throat.

"You first. Who are you?" I demanded.

A grin this time. The blackened jewel of her eyes sparkled.

"The real question is: who is she," said the woman, gesturing to the statue. "This is the goddess, Lakshmi; the deity of prosperity and fortune." She smiled. She waited for me to recognize the words, and I did. Flick and Wei had said something ominous about their tattoos on my first morning here. The priestess said, "Surely, you don't believe the lie that the wealthy grew rich based on merit. There is no hard work, no pulling oneself up by one's bootstraps, that results in millions, if not billions, in fortune."

Was she waiting for me to answer?

This was the truest evidence of a dream. Society's upper echelon insisted that they'd clawed their way to the top through hard work, smart investments, and an overall, problematic as fuck, eugenics-laden insistence that they were simply better than everyone else.

It had to be my sleeping mind implying that something more was at play.

Since I couldn't believe what I was hearing, I offered the only evidence to the contrary that I could conjure. Jenna had told me that the Rothschilds' line of hotels had locations closing across the globe. Their stocks were in the tank. This was not evidence of supernatural blessings.

It was a piece of conversation to buy me some time, if nothing else.

"Mmm, yes," the woman agreed. She brushed a lock of inky hair over her shoulder while she considered the information. "Flick and Odie have been uninvited from their roles as hosts at the GLAAD awards. Wei lost half a million followers. Indie was dropped by most of her sponsors. Lemon lost her meal ticket…"

"What?" I didn't know why she was telling me this. "Why? Why would bad luck fall upon—" I was going to ask how they all could have struggled at the same time, but the priestess's look told me that she had a particular brand of answer. As if the goddess had withdrawn their blessing. As if fortune was no longer extended to them.

I prickled. She was saying too much. I couldn't trust any of it. I needed this to end.

"I don't know what you're getting at, but I just came out to see the shrine again."

"Sure." Her eyes flicked over my face like she was looking for something. "And? What do you want?"

I hesitated. Why had I come? What *did* I want?

I was more uneasy now than I would have been if I'd stayed in bed. This was going terribly, and I wanted to leave.

"Do it," the woman said. "It's not too late to take Lemon's advice."

I didn't have to look over my shoulder for an escape this time. I knew what she was saying. I could still get to the hanger, board a jet, and leave with the workers. I could back away right now, turn left instead of right, and be gone before the rest of them woke. And yet…

How did she know what Lemon had said to me in private?

Before I could answer, a second figure stepped into view.

I took a step back, pulse quickening.

How could I not have realized someone else was here?

I swallowed, on edge as I tapped into whatever piss-poor survival instincts might tell me that this was a motherfucking ambush. But first, I needed to assess the new threat.

This woman was different. Where the first woman was soft edges and flowing honey, this one was sharp lines and confidence. Short-cropped hair, striking eyes, a body carved from strength. She stood like a soldier, or a predator.

"She should stay," the second woman said.

I was flanked by strangers. I was outnumbered. Whatever was happening, it was going poorly.

The first woman frowned. "You know that's not wise."

"I don't care. It won't be like last time. I'm as sick of them as you are."

It was like some jungle spider bit into my flesh, its poison turning my blood a chilly shade of blue as my body revolted against me. The dewy glaze of humidity turned to frost on my skin. My mouth was dry, but this time it had nothing to do with the G. "Sick of who?"

The second woman looked at me, then back at the first. "They've played their games and won their prizes. Now, we grow tired of their presence."

The first woman sighed. "They mean well."

"I don't care what they mean," said the second. "You stay in your lane; I'll stay in mine. Okay?"

It's a dream, I tried convincing myself.

A second, louder voice said, *But if it's not?*

I couldn't let my guard down. I kept one foot behind the other, shifting my weight to the balls of my feet. If the time came to run, I needed to be ready.

The first woman pursed her lips but said nothing. Then she turned back to me, her expression unreadable. "Go back to the villa. Relax. Follow the group's lead in the welcome ceremony.

It will sound like it's not going well at some point—I have to reject you, you see."

Speaking to them was like scrambling for footing on the edge of a cliff. I felt like I was grabbing at words while falling backward in slow motion, hands gripping nothing, feet making no purchase. "What do you mean: 'reject me'? What is this ceremony? Is this what they were making the flower crown for? Yesterday, in the worker house?"

The second woman's eyes flicked toward the cave. "It's a good thing," she said. "You don't want to be chosen. Not for this."

"But…" I wasn't sure where I was going with my argument. Still, I stammered through a rebuttal. "I was told I belonged. I made it. I'm one of them. That's good, right?"

The women exchanged a look. One was unbothered. The other wore the barest hint of sympathy in the downturn of her eyes.

The second woman finished her thought. "In that case, don't freak out when things start to get weird. I'll be there."

I stared at her, jaw on its hinge, eyes bulging. "But why should I care if you are or aren't there? Who *are* you?"

The first woman smiled, and for the first time, it didn't feel entirely kind. "Someone who can help."

The second woman's chin tilted down, eyes darkening. "Someone who can change things." Then, to her compatriot, she said, "Let her see."

"Let me see what?" I asked, hoping, praying, *begging*, that this was a dream. It didn't matter if I'd wrestled away the thought. I couldn't make sense of any of this unless I was asleep. It was a dream, it was a dream, it was a dream. It had to be.

The first woman jutted out a full lower lip. She looked at me sympathetically. "You're not going to like what's in there."

The pair pivoted, opening up like a gate. The path between them ended in the gaping, stone maw of shadow and secret.

My pulse thundered in my ears, practically drowning out my question. "What's in the cave?"

The first woman held my gaze for a long moment. Then, slowly, she reached down and picked up a lit candle from the shrine, pressing it into my hands.

"Go in and take a look for yourself."

Perhaps I was in shock. Maybe that's why my fingers curled around the wax. I had no argument. Just numb steps forward.

No, no, no, screamed my gut. *Go home. Go back to bed. Don't look.*

But my feet were moving without my consent. The flame flickered as I turned toward the cave's dark entrance.

The air grew colder as I stepped inside. The scent of old stone and something else—something coppery—filled my lungs. My footsteps echoed as I walked deeper, the candle casting long, curling, dancing shadows on the walls. The same numb feeling kept the chill from making me shiver. It wrapped me in a protective cocoon of denial as I squinted through the shadows. I kicked a rock forward and it made an odd sound— lighter than stone, but not quite wood. I frowned, lowering the candle to see the pale stick, looking at its odd shape…the way it ended in bulbs instead of points. My eyes adjusted and I let out a silent gasp at what I was seeing.

"What…the…"

Dream or not, I wasn't a tourist visiting a cave. I was a med student, and this was no rock.

I tried to suck in a breath, but it caught in my throat, unwilling to reach my lungs.

Inches from my toe I saw the long, white, porous culprit that had made such an odd sound. I may as well have been in the hospital all over again, dressed in a white lab coat, safe in my sterile environment, staring at the X-rays on the wall.

I was looking at a goddamn femur.

I stumbled backward kicking another bone, and another. Piles of ribs, leg bones, all shapes and sizes. My heart began to thunder as I wondered what terrible animal had dragged creatures in here, and what sort of large game had been killed and eaten to leave their broken bodies behind like this, until my tiny candle illuminated something colorful.

I turned and held the candle to the wall, shaking my head at what I was seeing.

Pictures.

The protective layer of shock evaporated. The onslaught of adrenaline was so, so much worse.

"Holy shit. Holy fucking shit." Cortisol-laced water brimmed my eyes as I struggled to stay upright.

Rows and rows of goddamn photographs, mounted to the cave walls. Some were headshots, others were full-body images—women wearing flower crowns, dressed in flowing fabrics, their smiles frozen in time. Some of the pictures had writing on them. Names, maybe. Others had been marked with deep brown smears, as though someone had dragged fingers over them with something thick and dried.

I slipped on another bone and looked down to see a jawbone filled with human teeth.

"No, no, no…"

A human skull, and another, and another.

The goddesses from the altar had been painted onto the stone, their outlines primitive yet eerily familiar. And around them, pinned in careful, deliberate arrangements, were the pictures of the women.

My eyes watered. My head spun. I wanted to sprint. To vomit. To scream.

My breath caught in my throat as I stepped closer, my heart hammering.

At the center of it all, at the very heart of the cave's shrine—

Was my picture.

17

I BARELY NOTICED MY OWN BREATH AS I STUMBLED BLINDLY DOWN the path, my limbs stiff and aching from the tension coiled inside me. The cave, the pictures, the statues—it all rattled in my mind like loose bones in a shallow grave. I just needed to get inside, back to Denning, back to the illusion of safety I was barely clinging to.

I was awake, and that news alone was the worst thing that had ever happened to me.

My sandal caught on a paved stone, tripping me as a lightning bolt of pain shot through my big toe. I lost my breath, unable to cry out as the motherfucking traitor throbbed, ruby red droplets bubbling around my toenail as I struggled to blink the white-hot stars away from my vision. I was sick of the green smear of plants blocking me in. I didn't want blue sky or a sun so close to the equator. I hated the sticky, sweaty hair. I was so sick of cicadas. I wanted to wake up from this motherfucking nightmare, but right now all I had to my name was a dry mouth, a confusing dream, and a stubbed toe.

"Ow, ow, ow," I mouthed, limping forward until I could walk with the barest sense of dignity. Nothing on God's stupid rocky earth was worse than a stubbed toe. Tiny streams of blood dribbled, pooling in my sandal, as I cursed this nightmare of a morning.

I needed to get back to the villa, rinse off, and ground myself. Maybe pour a stiff drink. Whatever was happening, I needed to pull out of a spiral, or I'd lose my mind entirely.

I wiped the sweat-slicked baby hairs out of my eyes as I passed the worker's building, the jaguar pit, putting one foot numbly in front of the other until voices halted my march.

I slowed, disoriented as to why anyone else was awake so early.

Lemon's voice, sharp as a blade's edge, sliced through the humid morning air. I pressed myself against the wooden wall, heart hammering, straining to catch their words.

"How dare you—" Lemon was saying. The second half of her sentence was muffled, but the venom was unmistakable.

"You don't know what you're talking about," Denning clipped.

"You're a monster," Lemon spat. "You're a fucking monster."

A pause. A charged silence. As I flattened myself further, creeping to the corner so I might catch their words. Their conversation was dizzying. I was immediately resigned to bake in the sun as long as it took to make sense of the argument. I moved my hand silently, wiping the beading sweat from my upper lip, my brow, my sternum.

"Then why are you here?" Denning asked. "If you hate me so much, why do you come back year after year? Stand for something, Lemon. But don't criticize me after sticking me in the gilded cage you've all forced me into."

"Cage?" She laughed, a bitter, humorless sound. "You?"

The heat was a third party to their argument. I succumbed to the oven, blistering with both their charged exchange, and the discomfort bubbling on my skin. I tried to regulate, to handle the heat, to know that whether the third degree was physical or metaphorical, I had to hold still.

Their voices continued to carry. Denning's low gravel was next.

"You tried to back me into a corner. All of you. But you underestimated who you're asking."

"Drop dead." Her voice shook with fury.

"You first."

"I can't believe I ever loved you."

My breath hitched, my fingers tightening into fists at my sides. They weren't just fighting. They were at war. And yet, despite the venom, despite the tension, there was something else underneath it, something tangled and deep-rooted that I couldn't quite unravel.

Denning's answering silence pained me. I didn't know what she was doing to him or why she was berating him, but I couldn't take it. I moved back from the corner so I might straighten my shoulders and walk normally, as if I was on a stroll and hadn't caught a word of their exchange.

I tried—and instantly failed.

Too much had happened. The morning was a nightmare from which I couldn't awaken.

I needed a cold shower. I needed a Band-Aid. I needed a stiff drink. I needed to roofie Lemon's drinks and put her in a coma so she wouldn't be a goddamn pest for the rest of the vacation. And more than anything, I needed to look into Denning's eyes and know that everything was okay.

Four steps later, and there he was.

His deep eyes and clenched jaw softened the moment I rounded the corner; his expression was curated just for me. He reached out without hesitation, his fingers closing around mine. "I've got you," he murmured, his grip firm, reassuring. Possessive.

Honestly, it was exactly what I needed.

I don't know if he saw the distress painted across my features or guessed that I'd heard the end of Lemon's rant, but he had me, and that alone allowed me to take a deep breath.

His touch grounded me, but I was still spiraling, the cave's horrors clinging to my skin like salt and sweat. The images wouldn't leave me. The smears of dried brown. The way my own picture had been placed at the center of it all. Denning gave Lemon a final, withering look before leading me into the villa and locking the door.

Behind the safety of our four walls, I choked on my breath, my hands shaking as I clung to his. "I need to go. I can't—I don't—"

"Hey, hey." He cupped my face, his thumb brushing away a tear I hadn't even realized had fallen. "It's okay. Whatever it is, tell me."

Church hadn't played a role in my life, but if it had, I suddenly understood the purpose of confession. I wanted to feel lighter, to purge myself, to give the stress, the fear, the confusion over to someone else who would hold me and make everything right again.

And so, I did. In a rush of words, I told him everything. The cave, the pictures, the blood, the statues, the whispers. My own face plastered on the wall. I told him about the two women, their cryptic warnings, their battle of wills over whether I should stay or go. And then, finally, I admitted what I hadn't wanted to say out loud—I wanted to leave. I wanted out. I wanted him to come with me.

"There were bones, Denning," I cried, hiccupping as tears ran down my face. "Human bones. It was them. It was the women in those pictures. I know it was. You have to get me out of here. Something is wrong with this place, with these people…please, you have to get me out of here."

He chewed on the information, shaking his head in disbelief. His fingers threaded through my hair as he held me close. "Okay. We'll leave tomorrow morning."

It was almost enough. Almost.

I pulled back, searching his face for any sign of hesitation. "Please, can we go now?" The tears wouldn't stop flowing. My voice was hoarse, desperate. "Please, please. Let's go now. Let's call the plane. Please"

My begging sounded pathetic, even to me. I couldn't stop.

"It's too late," he said gently, smoothing his hand down my back. "The plane leaves at sunrise. It's already en route to Jakarta, then needs to refuel. It won't be back until tonight. It'll leave again in the morning, and if you want to leave, we can go."

"Then the boat! We have a boat." There was no dignity in begging. I didn't care.

His expression was stifling—pitying, even—but the message was clear.

I wanted to argue, but I knew I wouldn't win. This wasn't a city with taxis lined up outside, wasn't a place where I could grab my bag and catch the next flight or jump onto some oceanic vessel. I was on an island in the middle of nowhere, at the mercy of their schedule. At the mercy of him.

"What happened to them?" I begged, voice getting smaller as I cried. "What happened to those women?"

Tears welled up again, unbidden, and I hated myself for them. He pulled me into his chest, his chin resting against the top of my head. "Shh," he murmured, his voice like velvet, soothing even as my gut twisted with unease. "I've got you. I've got you."

I needed to believe it was true.

I needed to believe he had me.

Even if just for tonight.

No. I didn't want to go for a swim. No, I didn't care about the reefs, or the rainbow fish, or if the boat would take us to a pod of dolphins. I didn't want to be alone on a boat with these people.

No, I didn't want massages, or drinks, or to go on a walk.

No, I didn't want to talk.

No, I didn't want to leave my villa.

No, I wasn't interested in Ever's pouting, in Indie's goading, in Flick's or Odie's, or Wei's bullying. No, I didn't care if Roman and Clementine made me feel like a bad guest. No, I didn't want to hear another word out of Lemon's mouth.

I would sit here until sunrise, and then I would get on the plane. I would leave. I would text Jenna. I would be safe.

To all other people, places, and things, I had one resounding message.

No.

18

ISLAND: DAY FIVE

I hadn't planned to sleep that night.

I hadn't even gone through the nightly ritual of putting on his t-shirt, as I wanted to be ready to head to the hangar the moment that I spotted the first grays of daybreak. I didn't mean to close my eyes. I certainly didn't think I'd get a wink of sleep. Yet as I stared out the window, begging the coal black night beyond the glass to show any hint of light, I began to nod, then slump, succumbing to the adrenaline crash.

A twitching, restless limbo, something between unconsciousness and the urge to run at a moment's notice put me in a foggy, agitated slumber.

The villa shook like it had been gripped in the hands of an angry god.

I cried out, confused, terrified, scrambling to understand what had happened.

A crack of thunder tore through the night like an explosion. I jolted upright, heart hammering, as lightning illuminated the villa in a blinding flash. A second later, darkness swallowed the room again. I scrambled out of bed, fully alert now, barely registering that I'd fallen asleep sitting up but awoke in bed. I looked down at the large men's t-shirt, knowing I hadn't fallen asleep in it. Denning must have tucked me in after I'd drifted off.

How long had I been asleep? And how *hard* had I been asleep?

It didn't matter. We had to go, *now*.

Denning was already awake at my side, muscles tense. I swung my legs off the bed, but the moment my feet touched the floor, I gasped at a cold shock of surprise. It took me a second in the inky darkness to understand that my toes were submerged in water.

"What's happening?" I demanded, breathless as I clawed for consciousness.

"It's flooding," he said through gritted teeth. I searched for any sign of light, but there was no moon, no stars, just the relentless howling of the wind beyond our glassy doors. The bedside clock flickered once before cutting out completely.

He flipped the light switch—nothing.

Electric tendrils split the sky, giving me the barest glimpse of Denning's hard-set profile.

The rumble of thunder that followed rattled the walls.

"We have to get to the main house," he said.

My brain struggled to quantify the sense of terror and urgency, like waking at 4:00 a.m. to go to the airport, like waking to a house on fire, like waking to the knowledge that something big, something terrible was happening, yet at the same time you were maddeningly and confusingly late.

The storm was the emergency. The flooding was the emergency. The power outage was the emergency.

No, no, no…

I pressed the heels of my palms into my temples. "Denning, the airport. We have to leave. We can't—"

"In this? June, come on."

We didn't even bother dressing. He grabbed my arm, tugging me forward in the oversized t-shirt and panties. Our feet sloshed through the slick inches of floodwater that overtook the villa. He led the charge, running out of the house in little more than boxers, ushering me into the storm.

The world beyond the villa walls was a physical assault of punishing rain, hurricane winds, and natural fury, the likes of which I'd never encountered before.

I understood the true scope of the storm. Rain thrashed down in thick sheets, blinding us, lashing our skin, drowning the pathways. Wind howled through the trees, bending palms until they looked ready to snap. The ocean, once pristine, was an angry mess of slate-gray waves, crashing violently against the shore.

I was soaked to the bone, freezing, disoriented, and doing everything in my power to call to mind what important thing I was supposed to remember. There was something bigger. Something worse than the storm. But fuck, this headache, this rain, this—

Another crack of thunder, louder than a canon going off inches from my ears, defeated any hope I had at stringing together a thought.

"Fuck, my phone—" I braced against the pummeling rain, spitting out the downpour as I choked on the words.

"It's no use," he shouted over the storm. "It's not working anyway. Keep moving!"

I could barely make out the dull flicker of orange through the thick curtain of rain. He dragged me toward the only semblance of light, and I obeyed, grateful to have someone leading the charge as the worst was upon us.

There was no sense to be made, so I slipped forward in bare feet, sopping, hair and shirt clinging to my skin as we slipped over stone and dangerously slick grass, staggering the last stretch of the way until we burst across the threshold of the main house. I wiped rain from my face, water dripping loudly off of my clothes and hair in a puddle as I let my eyes adjust to the flicker of candlelight. The gloomy shadows turned into the dimly lit faces and shapes in varied states of saturated clothes, damp tendrils of hair, and pools of water surrounding shoes and bare feet. Roman and Clementine, perfectly dry, were in host and hostess mode, passing out towels and lighting candles, though the motion was performative at best. Attendants in equal states of flood and disarray fluttered about, the crisis of the storm sending their every action into overdrive.

Denning and I, it seemed, were the last to arrive.

Prior to tonight, every time I'd visited the main house, tables had been piled high with a smorgasbord of food and drinks. On calm island nights, the main house was lit with inoffensive lighting, nature and modernity melding into a cohesive, if expensive, ambience. The flickering candles may as well have been a permanent fixture, their gentle illumination creating the same upscale effect as if the entire island hadn't just been thrown into the dark ages. Attendants bustled about, unable to be victims of the storm, solely focused on caretaking the guests as they passed out steaming cups of coffee, switched used towels for fluffy, dry replacements into the guests' hands, and set up makeshift barriers against the rising water.

I profusely thanked the young man who handed me my fluffy towel and tried not to read too much into his unwillingness to look me in the eye. It was the middle of the night, after all, and he had a job to do.

I wrapped the towel around my shoulders, wasting its warmth on a soaked nightshirt. I was at a loss for what I was supposed to do in such a bizarre scenario. I looked to Ever—disgustingly gorgeous in a rain-soaked silk negligee and natural beach waves from the rain—wondering if she'd cast a welcoming glance or make any effort to usher me under her wing. She, along with the others, remained sucked into their own bubble of crisis management.

I listened to the women fuss over their clothes, their hair, their things.

"My luggage is soaked," Indie moaned.

"Everything is drenched," Ever added, staring at the puddles forming inside.

Denning put a hand on my back, steering me toward the others. He strutted into the center of the room like he owned the place. "This is it, guys. We're done. As soon as the sun comes up, we're leaving."

He spoke like a director telling a scene to wrap it up.

If he was in charge of the movie, others wrinkled their noses like a mutinous cast.

Roman barked a laugh, shaking his head. "No chance in hell, buddy. That jet isn't flying in this weather."

Denning's jaw tightened, but he said nothing. I clenched my fists, throat tight. The idea of staying here—trapped—made my skin crawl.

Another blue-white bolt of lightning unfurled like a skeletal tree, its branches clawing through the roiling clouds. The flash showed every face, every expression, every piece of lingerie and muscular body and inconvenienced wealthy asshole who couldn't be bothered to show an ounce of compassion in a literal typhoon.

"I'm sorry, but is no one going to do anything?" I asked. "Shouldn't we be blotting towels under the cracks in the doors? Head upstairs? Move our valuables—"

"Relax, June," Wei rolled his eyes. He looked at Denning. "As if this night isn't annoying enough. Can you put a lid on her?"

Denning shot him an icy glare, but whether he didn't want to defend me further, or had other tasks on his mind, I remained wet, defenseless, and feeling unbearably adrift.

I took a step closer to the group, grateful for whatever warmth was thrown off by the candles. "Has anyone contacted emergency services? Has the news said—"

I was cut off for the second time, but it was Clementine who lolled her head back in an uncharacteristic display of irritation.

"Who are we calling, Juniper? The island's police? We're alone here."

Roman was quick to pile on to what was feeling like a bully train. "Get ahold of Jakarta's Coast Guard, if you like. Let me know what they say about taking a ship out in this nightmare to save a bunch of rich tourists from minor flooding."

Three of them had actively told me to shut the fuck up, in their own words.

Everyone else had told me to shut up through their silence.

I was wet, cold, and no matter how badly I wanted to belong, they wanted me to know that I did not. I moved closer to Denning, chafing my arms for warmth.

The storm raged on, refusing to let up. Lemon paced near the windows, worry written across her face.

"Ares." Lemon scrambled on her feet. "We have to check on Ares."

Whether I hated her or not was irrelevant. The news of an animal in danger made me tense and ready for action. I looked to the others for the go-ahead, ready for someone to issue a plan.

Wei rolled his shoulders back, utterly dismissive. "Jaguars are rainforest animals. He'll be fine. If it floods, he'll climb. That's what they do."

Lemon ignored him and turned to the attendants. The handful of employees ceased their tasks, towels and beverages and cleaning supplies frozen in their hands, as they awaited her command. "The island is flooding. You need to move him. Get him out of the pit."

A few of them exchanged uneasy glances. There was some quiet arguing, but I couldn't tell what was decided.

A roar cut through our petty grievances.

The new sound, crashing, destructive, powerful, made everyone's head whip toward the too-dark window, eyes wide, crazed for answers.

No thunder and lightning followed. The wind howled. The building shook. The roar happened again, louder this time.

"Oh, shit," Ever muttered, spine straight, staring at the window even though there was nothing to see.

Flick's hand flew to his chest. "Is that the ocean?"

Odie took a step back from the doors. "For fuck's sake, no one said this place could get goddamn tsunamis."

Denning flattened his hands, urging calm upon the room. "Panic isn't going to help anyone. For all we know, it's just a few inches of floodwater and an inconvenient night. We all know that this happens during monsoon season."

"Or!" Lemon's hands balled into fists. "Maybe we're sitting ducks when we could be preparing for a tidal wave."

"It's not a tsunami," I said. Their dismissive attitudes had a calming effect. I was emotionless as I said, "the waves wouldn't be getting higher if we were about to get hit with a tidal wave. It would go out for miles. We wouldn't have a flood right now."

Wei spread his legs, propping his elbows against his knees as he leaned forward. "Okay college girl. So what is this?"

"It's a shitty night, is what it is," I said. "Now are we going to help the workers with the towels or what?"

I thought I was making progress. I'd broken through whatever weird barrier had made everyone pissy and distant, and these irritable, entitled losers were finally listening to me. Maybe if I'd been able to speak for a moment longer, I could have made a difference.

The roar happened again. All eyes were on the little we could see of the ocean's blackened silhouette, darker shapes against already dark shapes. The sky showed the barest sights of light as gray hints of dawn arrived, allowing us to see the tar-like splashes of wave after wave breaking against the beach. The murky shape of a palm tree bent too far, groaning under the strain—then snapped, crashing down.

The room was stifled with an effective hush as the wind roared louder and louder.

It had to stop soon. It had to get better. Surely…

Suddenly, with a sickening crack, the statue fell. A bolt of lightning tore the sky open, slicing the clouds in blinding fragments of silver and white as a horrible noise rocked the island. This wasn't thunder, or a wave, or even some tree. I strained to see the damage until a second streak of lightning—electric fire sending the lawn into momentary daylight—sent a gasp through the house.

The ruins were unmistakable.

At the base of the banyan tree, the enormous, sacred figures lay shattered.

The goddesses had been split in half.

Clementine scurried to the door; fingertips pressed against the glass. "Shit, shit, shit."

Flick grabbed Odie's wrist, yanking on his hand, a stream of incomprehensible demands as he repeated, "This is fine, right? This is fine? Tell me this is fine?"

My face twisted, brows puckering in the middle, as I struggled to understand how this could possibly be the most important thing in the midst of a natural disaster. Maybe I was still asleep, or perhaps there was some wealthy, art-dealer reason for this property loss to be more important than lights or power or safety, but the reaction utterly discombobulating. I reached for Denning, hoping to tug on his shirt, to search his face for an explanation, or at the very least, for a reassuring expression. My fingertip barely missed his arm as he joined the others in their steps toward the glass door.

The energy in the room had a strange new charge, every bit as electric as the storm outside. It wasn't just shock. Whatever they were feeling, the current passing between them was fear.

I squinted into the darkness, discerning one shape against the other, too focused on trying to make sense of the wreckage to turn around and see what was happening behind me.

"We have to go forward with the ceremony," someone—
Odie, I was pretty sure—said. I rolled a single shoulder as if
shaking off his weird, middle of the night rambles. They were
all being unbearable, and I didn't have the space to hear whatever the fuck rich person bullshit he was talking about. How
could he be thinking of parties and cookouts in the midst of a
typhoon?

"We have to wait until sunset," another—Clementine,
perhaps—argued.

"It won't work now."

I was annoyed, I was wet, I was tired, and if they weren't
going to make an effort to include me, I didn't want to elbow
my way into their frivolous plans about parties.

I made no attempt to keep up with who was speaking.
Men and women, they tumbled over each other in an
argument.

"She wants to leave—it's no use."

That line was odd enough to draw me back to the room. I
tore my attention from the window, from the broken statue, to
piece together who was talking about what.

Denning's hand moved down my forearm, fingers looping
around my wrist. He gave it a squeeze and said, "It's not
happening. As soon as the storm lets up, we're leaving."

I opened my mouth to ask for clarification, but the conversation was off to the races.

Roman scoffed. "Sorry, buddy, but it's no longer up to you."

Brows bunched; my gaze whipped from one speaker to
another.

Denning's expression darkened. "Like hell it's not. Come on,
June, we're leaving."

I was so lost; the first sign of movement caught me utterly
off guard. Denning pulled me toward the door, and I tripped,
too surprised to catch myself gracefully on the slick floor. In
three powerful strides we'd moved away from the others and
reached for the furthest opening. Before I could ask if he was

dragging us back out into the storm, my world tipped upside down.

The rain, the storm, the inane arguments ceased to matter.

Feet slapped against the floor. Hands shot out from all directions.

Denning released me as Wei, Flick, Odie, and Roman pinned him to the wall, trapping him before he could take another step.

I choked on a scream, eyes wide, shock bobbing in my throat. My hands went up in a useless show of self-defense as I took one step back from the flurry of violence, head shaking, lips parted, each backward step a baffled, disembodied attempt to create space between myself and the bizarre descent into madness.

"No!" Was the most articulate thing I managed.

The struggle escalated, matching every strange, uncomprehending beat as I watched the terrifying brawl. Fists flew, bodies jostled, and for the life of me, I couldn't make sense of how or why or what the hell was happening. I couldn't look away as Denning threw a punch, sending one of the men stumbling back, but another took his place. Attendants joined the battle, the slew of bodies in a nightmarish tangle with no rhyme, no reason, only madness. The sickening crack of bone made my stomach roil. Another step back and the wet noise of flesh and blood made me dizzy. A high grunt. Fists and elbows and the bodies of men twisted over one another in the firelight locked in an incomprehensible battle.

"Denning!" I shouted; the name useless on my tongue. I couldn't even see him, lost to the pile of anger and betrayal and grunts and strength.

I reached toward him—a shocked, futile gesture—knowing we'd been torn apart.

My next step backward hit a wall of chest and flesh and hair. There was no sense to be made as hands were on me, fingernails digging into my arms, tugging me backward, holding me down.

Fight, flight, freeze, and fawn were meant to be the danger responses, but I'd unlocked whatever the fuck this useless, dissociative shutdown, silent, limp, lost to the lack of reason as senseless tugs and shoves and restraints unfurled.

No screams. No thoughts. Simply three, jumbled words, over and over again played as I was overpowered.

What the fuck, what the fuck, what the fuck.

I tried to cry for help, but who could possibly help me when I didn't even understand what was happening?

The slate gray morning, obscured by punishing rain, cast just enough light for me to gape at my captors.

"Ever?" I choked, barely catching the outline of her jaw, her chin pointed forward, gaze focused. I whipped my head to the others, to Lemon, to Indie, wishing one of them would look at me.

The first words to cut through the murk and mire were so soft, so strange, that they made my ability to think infinitely worse.

Clementine's gentle voice whispered, "Sorry about this."

It was the only human expression, the only semblance of emotion, of connection, of goddamn eye contact, and the sorrow behind her eyes sent a bolt of primal horror through me.

Something pressed against my mouth—the rough scrape of cloth, the sharp, stinging assault of fumes burning my nose, the pressure of the foreign object suffocating me. I jerked my head away, yanking for freedom, but there were too many hands, too many arms, too many scraping, cruel fingers holding me captive. I gasped useless, struggling until I had no fight left in my body, but my limbs were already going weak.

Gray sky, blurry women, swimming rain wiggled, darkening at the edges until the blackness suctioned its way to the center.

I tumbled into a new kind of night, helpless, powerless, as one final sound called out.

Denning's voice was the last thing I heard before the darkness swallowed me whole.

LEADEN EYELIDS COULDN'T LIFT ENOUGH TO SHOW ME ANYTHING more than smudges beyond the curtain of obscuring eyelashes.

Black, amber, fire, shadow.

My head drooped; neck too weak to lift it. I couldn't open my mouth, couldn't move, could do little more than pulled in a ragged breath through my nostrils.

Chemicals, smoke, perfume.

I was paralyzed, but not so numb that I couldn't feel a wild, uncomfortable, all-encompassing sensation on the crown of my head, my face, my shoulders, my torso, everywhere.

Rain, thunder, lightning.

The storm. The rain. I was alive, then. I was on the island. The storm continued. I couldn't open my eyes, but I checked in with other senses, and my ears picked up on dissonant gibbering.

Voices, low and dissenting.

Male, female, other.

It was no one. It was everyone.

"Can she drink? She isn't even conscious."

"Tilt her head back. Open her mouth more."

My body wasn't mine. A mannequin scarcely attached to the bits of my brain capable of thought moved at their behest. I felt fingers on my chin and the mannequin complied, mouth opening, head succumbing to gravity as it rocked backward on its spine.

My mouth burned. I coughed. I gagged. Yet, the mannequin didn't move. Its eyes did not open. The only sight that belonged to me was the same sliver through the screen of lashes—little more than colors.

Sound required no motion, no muscles, barely even the capacity for thought.

The voices went on, and the mannequin received them, unresponsive, uncaring, barely present as their words wove from bad to so strange, so unreal, that I only heard one word as I listened.

"That's it. By the time she's awake, the drug will be in her system. She'll be ready."

"Will the goddess take her? Doesn't she have to drink willingly?"

"We don't have a choice."

The word swirled behind my eyes, the cursive of the drug slurring into one resounding message. This wasn't bad. The word stamping itself behind my eyes wasn't even scary.

This was clearly, and unmistakably evil.

19

"CASSIDY…" MY NAME TUGGED ME FROM THE DEPTHS OF A FEVER dream too terrible to comprehend.

My eyes fluttered open, stinging as rain droplets blinded me. I blinked through the assault, writhing against jarring discomfort. The storm hit me with a brand-new sensation. The paralytic had worn off. I didn't have the luxury of being eased into this nightmare. I jolted into feeling absolutely everything.

"Cassidy…wake up."

Rain gripped my skin with insistent fingers, plastering my clothes to my body, my hair to my face, shaking me into alertness. I tried to suck in a lungful of air, but I'd never experienced such an insistent, relentless deluge before. Choking on the rain was like breathing in smoke—smothering, drowning, helpless.

"Help," I gagged on the word, unsure who I was begging. The pathetic word was too quiet, stolen on the wind.

The color was wrong.

I had to focus. I had to shake the dredges of the drug from my system.

The sun had come up, but everything was washed in charcoal and sepia. The lightning cut through the blue-gray clouds, setting the world ablaze with its cold light. Muddy, brown water flowed over my feet as the banks forsook their soil, and the world became a boundless river.

This was the island. I knew it was. The storm had torn a scar through the land, smearing the earth, blurring the plants, tilting this resort-like prison on its axis. Still, I shook myself awake. I couldn't pass out. I couldn't freeze. I couldn't leave my body again. I couldn't move my hands, and that meant my mind was my only chance at survival.

I searched the relentless sameness of trees, vines, fire, stone, a cliff, and... I knew where we were. The rocks curved into a gaping, shadowed mouth. We were at the cave. They'd dragged me to the foot of the altar.

Focus, focus, focus!

The world swam as I tried to lift my head. My limbs were sluggish, my muscles thick with something unnatural. I gagged, my mouth coated in something bitter. I tried to spit it out whatever remained of the drug, but my tongue was heavy, disregarding my commands, dead in my mouth.

"Cassidy..."

The statues of the goddesses loomed ahead, somehow seeming fifteen feet taller amid the chaos.

I dragged in air through my nose, one breath after another.

Hands, bound. Feet, immobile. Heart, thundering.

I racked my mind for what I had at my disposal before the only answer smacked me in the face. My mind was the only thing to rack because it was *all* I had...but it was not nothing.

You're a fucking med student, Cass. You've been drugged. You can figure this out.

Another pull of air through my nose.

Step one, you can't panic. If you hyperventilate, the CO2 drop will only make you weaker.

I peered through the rain as the water stung my eyes. It was like keeping your eyes open underwater, but unlike the watery blur, every raindrop pummeled me with bullet-like intensity.

Neuro check. Do it now, I growled, grounding myself,

screaming at myself as if the budding doctor within me and terrified victim were two divorced entities. *Person, place, time… I know my name. I don't know the hour, but that's fine. Double vision…? No. Whatever they gave me, I'm not stroking out.*

The voices, low and rhythmic, weaving in and out of the storm's howling breath. Chanting. Music. A drumbeat, steady and slow, like the heartbeat of something waiting. Something ancient. Something hungry.

I opened my mouth again, if only to test the muscles. I was so relieved that it responded to my signals that I succumbed to impulse, yelling the moment I was capable.

"What do you want?" I screamed, spitting through the storm.

My hands balled into fists uselessly behind me. I knew I should be angry at the restraints, but the white lab coat talking me through the trauma was relieved.

Your mouth, your tongue, your hands are all responsive. Good grip. CNS intact. You can fight if you need to.

I caught the bright orange of a drenched dress and knew I was looking at Indie, even if the thick, pounding headache struggled to let me focus. Ever's green dress broke free from the tree line—a living, moving piece of flora, coming closer, chanting louder.

But they weren't saying my name.

I homed in with laser focus.

The cadence was right. Three syllables. Nearly a rhyme…I heard it again, and again, until the jumbled sounds became clear.

"Bound to thee…"

I battled the warbling vision, forcing myself upright, blinking against the rain. Every second that passed was a new moment for me to take in information, to assess my surroundings, to make sure I'd be ready to run, to fight, to do whatever it took the instant I had an opening.

The confusion and fear had already soured into a new emotion entirely.

The more I grounded, the more I prepared, the more I hardened.

Something strong, something bitter, seeped in through my pores. Every muscle I could straighten, every fiber of my being that regained control felt this new, glorious, freeing feeling.

I hated them. And hell, was it great.

Torches burned in the gray downpour, defying what I knew of fire and water as the resistant flames lined a path ahead of me. The storm churned overhead, flashing lightning across the jungle canopy, making the faces around me flicker in and out of shadow.

I was surrounded.

Make your list like your life depends on it, Cass.

Navy blue—that was Flick. Odie was in a soaked white shirt, stark against rich skin. Roman and Clementine held hands as they stared straight forward.

A slice of yellow pulled my desperate, panicked vision to the side. I could barely discern that Lemon was yelling—her voice cutting through the others, sharp and petulant.

"You can't just—this isn't how it was supposed to—"

I tried not to look like I was following the conversation too closely. I was above this.

That rhythmic...what was it? A poem? A prayer? A goddamn haiku? Whatever it was, the chanting continued while Indie snapped, "Oh, give it a rest, Lemon. You're just pissed it didn't happen with you and Denning."

Denning. With painful clarity, I remembered that he'd been attacked, ambushed, dragged before they'd jumped me. I tried to keep my movements subtle as I scanned the area, searching for any sign of him.

The sounds, rhymes, bickering, whatever it was, were both incomprehensible and painfully clear. I could hear the words, but the meaning didn't matter.

They paid me no mind, which was great. Let them ignore me.

A few murmurs of agreement after Denning's name was dropped. A sneer from Indie. I would have remained observing, strategizing, but jolted the moment someone grabbed my arm. I looked at Roman's thick fingers wrapped around my forearm as if a viper had sunken its teeth into my flesh. I yanked back, but he didn't let go. His stood in front of me, blocking my view.

"Please, don't." It wasn't a lot, but I knew the moment it left my lips that it didn't matter.

"Trust me," he said, "You're the lucky one."

He didn't share the soft sorrow Clementine had offered. His gray eyes were darker, dead, utterly checked out from seeing my humanity.

Going limp was my only defense mechanism. I balked, resisting them with every step. I wished I was clever, that I had a silver tongue or money to bribe my captors, but in the heat of the unthinkable, my mouth supplied utterly useless words before their futility reached my brain.

"Let me go," I begged.

"The path is ready," Clementine said, talking as if I hadn't said anything. I may as well not have been there for the attention they were paying me. She gestured toward the cave ahead. The torches swayed, their fire flickering wildly in the wind. "Follow the trail."

I was wrong. The hate wasn't as impenetrable as I'd hoped. Fear crept back in as I followed her point and looked into the blackened hole before me. They wanted me to join the bones.

I sputtered through the rain, trying and failing to dig my feet into the mushy lawn. "No."

Ever sighed like I was a stubborn child. "Don't be difficult, Juniper."

Juniper. I was about to die, and they didn't even know who they were killing.

My pulse roared in my ears. Breathing techniques failed me as I stared into the mouth of the cave, so dark it swallowed even the barest hints of grim, stormy light. The wind carried the scent of wet earth and burning oil. The statues along the path loomed taller than before, their carved eyes catching fire-light, watching. Waiting.

"Walk," Roman ordered, giving me a shove forward.

I staggered, hitting the ground and staying down when I landed. When I turned to glare at him, his expression was empty. Like this wasn't even personal. Like I was already gone.

The music swelled, sharp notes from an unfamiliar instrument cutting through the storm. Javanese gamelan. I'd heard it before, in restaurants, in documentaries, on the plane as we touched down in Jakarta, in the spa music played by our masseurs. But here, now, it sounded… Less like music. More like a summons. I sank into my knee, wishing the earth would open up and swallow me whole.

I found my voice, spitting out a demand. "Where's Denning?"

Clementine made a noise as she shifted out of the way.

I gasped, choking, all the more wild as I realized there would be no rescue.

Denning was on his knees, held back by Wei and Flick. His lip was split, blood seeping down his chin. His breathing was ragged, his muscles flexing as he struggled against them.

"Don't do this," he snarled. "You don't have to do this."

"Oh, we really do." Ever gave a mocking pout. She took a knee at my side and tucked a knuckle beneath my chin. "You were a lot of fun, babe. Thanks for the fuck."

"Fuck you," I snarled, yanking my head to the side and shaking off her touch.

"You did," she winked. Ever smoothed a hand down the side of my face, her touch infuriatingly gentle. "We're just asking the goddess to join us, Juniper. That's all. A simple request."

I glared up at her from my place on my knees. "You've lost your minds. All of you."

"You're the one fighting logic," Ever laughed. She lifted her hands up, catching raindrops on her palms. "You have the chance to be a goddess, and you're fighting it. Let this happen, June."

Nothing they'd said had made any sense before. Why should it start now?

I looked at the others, desperate for a glimpse of sanity, of hope, of a shot at my freedom, but saw none.

Ever smiled. "We're offering her a way to walk among us. To bless us."

The torches flickered, and for a moment, I thought I saw something move in the cave's yawning mouth.

"What are you even talking about?" I swallowed a gulp of rain as I snarled at them. "You're fucking insane."

Ever stood and gestured toward the statues. "What do you know of Batara Guru?"

I stared blankly. Was she serious?

"Figures," she shrugged, unbothered by the elements raging around us. She pitched her voice above the rain so we might hear as she said, "Shiva is the god of destruction. He's one of the most important gods in Hinduism. But when you come to Indonesia, the Javanese teach us something important: Shiva can take an avatar and walk among the humans."

"Please, stop," I said, but the words washed away.

The hate returned. I didn't want to hear a word out of their mouths.

"Batara Guru was Shiva's form on the islands as the great god walked among us," she said, gesturing to the sky, the sea, the whole of Indonesia. "Our forefathers knew how to summon the most powerful being in the Hindu pantheon. And when our time came—six friends, long before our wealth and riches and partners—we hatched a plan."

My lips pulled back in a snarl, but I couldn't look away.

Every word felt like poison, and I was its unwilling subject once more.

"Lakshmi, the goddess of fortune, is one of two goddesses who bless this island," Indie said, joining Ever at her side. "She's brought us prosperity beyond our wildest imagination. All she asks for is an avatar."

"I don't understand." I practically gargled the words, lips slick, eyes stinging. I didn't understand. I didn't want to understand. I didn't want to hear the words that came next, but the moment they were spoken, they stole whatever hope I had with them.

"You're a human sacrifice, dumbass," Wei said.

The fight within me deflated. My vision swam once more.

"Hey!" Clementine turned around to scold him. "That term is barbaric."

Wei continued to speak. "I'm new to the group, right? I got to come this year, because Lemon made good on her turn two years prior and the goddess accepted her offering. When you do right by the goddess, you're blessed, and your next partner gets to stay. Right, Flick?"

Flick rolled his eyes. "I had to pretend I was straight when it was my turn. Can you imagine? That poor girl did *not* have a fun vacation."

The priestess. The dreams. The pictures. Their words made my head throb.

Flick mock-pouted. "But now Lemon gets Wei, and I get to keep Odie, and if you care about Denning, you'll step up and do this for him so he can find love the next round."

I began to shake my head, to reject the insane premise, when the sickening memory of bones clanged around in my head. The visions of women in floral crowns bled behind my eyes. The rain did nothing to cleanse me of the fear I'd felt then—a terror that paled in comparison to what I felt now.

I wanted to fight, to cry, to run, but Roman and Clementine held me fast.

Denning fought harder. His captors grunted, struggling to hold him back.

Indie's voice cut through the wind. "It's too late. It's the goddess's decision, now."

I searched for the speck of yellow, hoping she might intervene, but Lemon was nowhere to be seen.

"You're not even fucking Indonesian," I said miserably. "Denning is the only one here with Indian heritage and a tie to the gods."

"Don't be a snob," Ever shrugged. "Hinduism is an open pantheon."

They were shitty last words, but I had no way to fight. With teeth clenched and feet kicking, Roman and Clementine dragged me the rest of the way to the altar. The chanting began again in earnest. The music swelled. Stopped fighting altogether, head hung to let the water drop onto the ground before me as they forced me to kneel before the shrine.

The moment stretched, long and unbearable. My skin crawled, my breath shallow. The weight of the storm, the fire, the eyes—real and carved—pressing down on me.

Nothing happened.

No goddess. No answer. No possession.

I was still me.

The silence dragged.

Ever's hand fell away. She cocked her head, something unreadable in her gaze. Then, after an agonizing beat, she sighed. Shrugged.

"No worries, peaches," she said, voice breezy. "Like I said: the island has two goddesses. If Lakshmi won't inhabit you, then Svaha will take you as a living sacrifice."

20

I was a rabbit, feet scrambling beneath me, diving through the thicket, weaving like crazy, while the jaws of every ravenous fox on the island snapped behind me.

I pulled in a burning drag of air, arms pumping, as I tried to escape into the forest.

I took off in a dead sprint, slipping and colliding into rocks and trunks as my feet failed me. They'd released me the moment they'd offered me to the island, leaving me to plunge deeper and deeper into the belly of the sentient slice of sand and terror. The world was a blur of rain and shadow, lit only by the white, jarring, blindingly violent slashes of lightning overhead. I knew the thunder was coming, but the explosive, ear-splitting crack reverberating through my core, reminded me I was in the trenches of a war zone. I gagged on the rain through each deep breath as I sprinted through the mud.

My ankle twisted on a root and I went sprawling, sliding through clay, face, hands, arms, shirt, painted by the earth, erasing the color from my skin, my clothes, my hair. I scrambled, crawling when my feet failed me, until I found my footing once more.

I jerked my head from side to side, desperate for the tiniest sliver of relief that came when I saw no one was upon me. The moment I could stand, I was back to running.

A voice carried over the rain from somewhere behind me. "Free Ares! He'll get her!"

Claws, fangs, speeds of, what, 30, 50 miles per hour? They had an apex predator at their disposal, and I had the only thing any creature felt the moment before death: the frantic, unrelenting desperation to do whatever the fuck it took to survive.

The chorus of expletives streaming through my mind was interrupted only by base, primal commands. I truly was the rabbit. Monosyllabic thoughts and cold commands drove me.

Tree. No! Move. Left, left! Good. Faster. Faster! Branch. Branch, now! Duck! Good. Move, Cass, move.

Juniper, Cassidy, I was both, I was neither, I was *no one* if I didn't get the fuck out of here.

I already had a murderous hoard of blood-thirsty lunatics after me, and now I had to worry about their goddamn jaguar.

I was too close to the pit for comfort. The closest building—the worker's house—was still five minutes away if I was walking. I was ready to cut that down to sixty seconds.

A new kind of terror jolted through me, just when I thought I was incapable of any further reaches of terror. That goddamn cat distracted me from the important, basic things before me. My mind conjured the image of the jaguar in its pit, its golden eyes glinting in the torchlight, its body coiled with muscle and quiet, restrained violence. If they let him loose, he'd be on me before I could blink. Claws, teeth, muscle ripped between powerful jaws, a solid black demon that stalked in the darkness. I didn't stand a chance.

I ran harder, the rain blinding, the jungle swallowing me in its drenched embrace. My lungs burned. My legs ached. Every inch of me was slick with mud and something warmer, something coppery—was I bleeding? Could it belong to someone else?

The path was clear, save for the slick stones. I'd left the

chanting freaks and their gaping cave maw behind me. Every time I slipped, I leaned to the edge of the path for a tree trunk to catch me. I was completely blindsided when I ran headlong into something soft and warm.

My ankle twisted again. It didn't waste its time with a roll. My leg crumpled as the joint released a sharp, angry pop.

I went flying—hands skinning against the slick stones as I sprawled at someone's feet.

No, no, no.

I wanted to cry. How had someone found me already? How could they have beat me? How…

I planted my hands as I craned my neck up, remaining on my knees as I looked into the eyes of a goddess. Dark hair, huge eyes, glowing skin, somehow unaffected by the deluge—this woman had been present when I'd met the priestess who wasn't a priestess.

Hands firmly in the mud, I craned my neck up to look into the face of the person who'd stopped me.

I was still thirty feet from the corner of the worker's building. I was desperate to get away from this crazy woman, away from the threat, but the stranger stood between me and the door.

I had no idea how I recognized her, but I knew I was looking into the face of Svaha.

My pulse skipped. Time warped as I stared, no longer compelled to sprint, frozen in her presence. The animal brain slowed. I could do little more than stare in wonder.

Hibiscus and smoke rolled off the powerful woman before me—scents I'd once mistakenly attributed to the upscale spritz of villa linens—and I knew they belonged to her.

Her short-cropped hair was spared from the rain, still dry despite whatever plagued the island. The striking, warrior figure was even taller than I remembered, or maybe it was the way the lightning twisted her features, making her dark eyes look endless, her lips sharp with something like amusement.

The goddess of sacrifice. The one they should have feared more.

Either I was hallucinating, or the rain parted, encircling us. The downpour continued, its rhythmic curtain obscuring the world around us. For the moment, we were in a perfect circle that seemed to exist outside of the island and its torment.

Her gaze flicked over my shoulder, to the chaos behind me. Her expression didn't change.

"You're faster than I expected," she mused. "That's good. You'll need to be."

My chest heaved. I swallowed, small and crushed with insignificance beneath her stare.

"Please—" I didn't even know what I was begging for. The gagging tang of copper choked me as blood filled my mouth. What did I want? Mercy? Help? A way out? I thought I'd have more time. I thought I'd get a real chance to run. Instead, here I was, thirty seconds into my escape, and already in the hands of the enemy. I stopped short of begging her to spare me. I wasn't sure what synagogue, mosque, or mass would have prepared me for this shit.

Why had I bothered running? I was a human sacrifice, and the goddess had found me.

I winced as she reached into the folds of her garment. I was no coward, but anyone flung into a ritual against their will and sent to die at the hands of a god deserved their moment of fear, as far as I was concerned. I didn't know what the sacrifice would entail, but I wasn't sure I wanted my eyes open for it. Barely daring to peek through squinted eyes, I watched as she pulled out something wrapped in cloth. She extended it toward me.

"I like you, Cassidy," she said.

This wasn't what I braced myself for.

I...I hadn't been stabbed? My throat wasn't slit. I touched my chest, though I felt a bit silly doing so, if only to ensure my limbs still belonged to me.

I blinked up at her pathetically, staring at the impossible soldier, too beautiful for humanity, too strong for a physical body, too impossible to be speaking to me.

Her eyes sparkled, mouth to the side, hip popped out. "Or maybe I'm just bored and you're here. But you're a fighter, and that's fun. Here."

She nudged the object toward me.

Sure. I was long past arguing against the nonsensical. I'd swallowed everything whole, and if the worst was happening, this strange turn of events might as well be happening, too.

I extended my fingers for the carefully wrapped bundle—first one hand, then another below it, cradling the hidden gift as if I'd been given a baby.

The fabric fell away, revealing the gleam of a blade…but not just any knife. I knew the word for this one, if only in the distant reaches of my mind from a nearly-forgotten archeology class. It was a *keris*—a wavy dagger, its blade almost hypnotic in the flickering light.

My hand tightened around the hilt of the weapon.

As my fingers closed, so did my resolve. My breathing slowed. By the time I was ready to look up into her face, my spine straightened. Maybe I didn't know what she was about to say, but I'd been given a fighting chance, and that could only mean one thing.

The shrewd goddess tapped her wrist. "I see you're still wearing my sister's present." My gaze went automatically to the gold and ruby bauble flecked in mud. She continued talking, the same hint of a smile lacing every word. "Keep it on. You'll be glad for the luck it brings you. She's the goddess of fortune, after all."

I gaped at the bracelet. I hadn't remembered putting it back on. I certainly didn't feel fortunate.

"This," Svaha said, "is a gift from me."

She smiled, slow and knowing. "Give me a sacrifice, Cassidy Juniper. If you want, you can press the blade into your flesh now. Open the red river and end it. Take yourself far away from here before anyone else can touch you." A pause—the same curious, amused compassion tugging the corner of her mouth upward. "Or...if you have the fight that I think you do, try your luck and see what other blood there is to be spilled."

"Please..." The blade was cold in my grip. Heavier than it looked. More real than anything I'd ever held.

"You kill them all before sunrise," she continued, her voice like the rain, steady, inescapable. "And I let you go."

I must have hallucinated the words, because what she'd said...

I couldn't check out, though I was desperate to dissociate into the insanity of her words. My eyes widened as a high-pitched ringing assaulting me, but I forced myself to stay grounded.

Her expression, unchanging, was unmoved by my unrelenting stare.

My pulse roared in my ears. I was too hot and too cold all at once. Mud and water stuck in my nose. I was going to vomit. I tightened my grip on the weapon. "You want me to—?"

"Someone's going to die, Cassidy. This is how the night ends."

"You're a goddess!" I didn't know what I was arguing, but I petitioned any prayer, any belief, as I sputtered, "Put a stop to this! You can end this now!"

There were no words to explain the comforting, patient, longsuffering way she looked at me. She reached for my face in a way that would have been condescending if it had been anyone—*anything*—else.

"Sweet Cassidy. Don't make the mistake of putting human morals on a tradition that has existed since the first man struck fire in a cave. For what it counts, I'm rooting for you."

It wasn't enough. I couldn't stop myself. Clearly if she was powerful enough to keep the rain at bay, to put us in a protected space in this natural disaster, she could stop this. She could end the nightmare before it started. I had nothing smart to say, nothing worthy of a goddess, beyond the pathetic sentence. "This doesn't have to happen."

When her lower lip lifted in a pout, the sincerity wounded me. "They've already sacrificed you to the island. But the island is bored, and you seem like a fighter. What do you say? Are you going to let them kill you?"

Was this a joke?

I looked at the perfect circle of water, the green beyond, the beautiful, miserable thicket of rainforest plants that trapped us on this island.

"But…" I didn't know why I was arguing, but I couldn't help the words from tumbling out. "Aren't they your practitioners? Aren't you here to…help them?"

Her laugh was a short, staccato sound. "I'm a god, babe. And they annoy me. What about you? Will you annoy me? Or, answer one better: do you think there's any world where they let you go? The rich fucks who brought you to the island: do you really think if you make it to the jet, that they'll just let you fly away?"

It wasn't the first time I'd swallowed something whole.

Even the scientist within me knew it would be a disservice to continue to question the stone-cold evidence.

Alright, she was a powerful deity. Yes, blood was demanded. And for whatever twisted reason, I was not only trapped in this swirl of otherworldly nightmares, but I'd been given a fighting chance.

The next breath sent me into supernatural calm.

No. I knew they wouldn't. Roman, Ever, Wei. For fuck's sake, their names didn't deserve space in my brain. They didn't see me as a person. I was an ingredient in their ritual. These pieces of elitist trash needed their sacrifice. If the goddess of fortune wouldn't take me, then they'd try another way. And if the goddess of sacrifice was rooting for me…

The sharp slice of dark hair swished around her chin as

Svaha took a step closer, lowering her voice. I could smell her perfume, my skin tingling with electric shock at her nearness. "You don't have to do this, of course. You could run. You could let them find you. And they will. I'll get my blood either way."

I said the first honest thing I'd expressed in ages. I abandoned whatever quivering, pathetic urges had motivated me and said, "You've told me who and what you are, and I believe you. You need blood. And you don't want it to be mine…. So let's give them a show."

My exhale was magical.

It was like screaming the chorus at a lifechanging concert even if my voice cracked.

It was like confessing my love to a childhood crush, whether they liked me back or not.

It was release, it was dedication, it was the only vulnerability that mattered.

Dragged out of my bed in a storm wearing nothing more than an oversized white t-shirt and panties hadn't given me a lot of tactical options. I glanced at the blade for the barest of moments, then worked the tip of the blade into the white fabric at the bottom of my shirt. I cut the long strip free, then quickly re-tied it against my thigh, wrapping it twice in a makeshift sheath. I slipped the blade into the snug space between the two strips, securing it to my body.

Practically purring, she smiled, "There's a good girl."

It was so disorienting, borderline sexual, it rocked me to my core.

I released my grip on the dagger, trusting it to hold. I held her gaze and nodded.

She was right. This was my only path forward, whether I liked it or not.

The reprieve nearly let me relax, practically letting myself think I was safe, until the moment shattered. A new voice, sharp and familiar, cut through the downpour.

"Juniper!"

Any calm or confidence I'd achieved crackled. The knot in my throat returned as I jerked my head toward the source of the noise.

The safe circle, free from rain, collapsed in an instant. A magnetic pull snapped them to the center, drowning me in monsoon rains once more. One hand clutched the hilt of my knife, the other flew to my brow, protecting my eyes from the downpour as I readied myself to face the enemy.

Slick, red hair, freckles, manicures and screams. I didn't know who I expected to find me first, but the soaked dress and royal energy of the most obscenely privileged woman I'd ever encountered was not at the top of my list. I set my feet, lifted my chin, and stared down the woman before me.

Clementine was holding a bottle of chloroform like it was a Molotov cocktail.

I might as well have hallucinated the goddess' existence for how utterly alone I was, and yet...I looked at the curved keris in my hand.

I turned back to ask for Svaha's help, but this ginger motherfucker and I were completely alone.

There was no monologuing, no build up, not even the social decorum of a second for tension. The bitch moved before I had a second to think.

I whirled just as she lunged for me, something white clutched in her hand. She was too small, too weak to have this agility. She was a blur of pale skin and anger. I dodged the threat as she swung for me once more. The chloroform rag. Again. *Again.*

She was fast, but I was faster.

We circled like boxers in a ring, huffing, twitching for whoever made the next move.

"What do you think you're going to do with that?" Clementine's *eyes were wild. "Put down the knife, June. And just go to sleep."*

Svaha had changed my brain chemistry.

This wasn't about morality.

I couldn't hold an ancient god to my human conception of good or bad

Clementine twitched, and I matched her motion. Every step, I mirrored. She bared her lips, and a resurgence of hate baptized me. I pulled my lips in return, reveling in my snarl.

"Do it," I growled.

"Go," a step that I matched, "the fuck," another movement, closing the distance between us as I tensed my muscles, prepared to spring, "to sleep!"

She lunged on the last word. She was fast, but I was ready.

I swung for her like the wave slamming down on the reef. I swung my knife like my life depended on it, and a punishing tidal wave laying waste to flimsy wreckage beneath. A sickening pop and crunch broke through the rain, skin bursting, metal plunging into the esophagus as the goddess-sharpened blade sliced through her throat as if it was little more than butter. Clementine gasped, stumbling, hands grasping at the wound blooming in her neck, red spilling down her dress like ink in water.

The world slowed as I watched the impossible.

I stopped breathing.

The second-hand ticked as I stepped outside of my body, aghast as I stared at the nightmare. The hate, the pain, the gore, played on a staticky record, looping in the background as if it didn't belong to me as I stared at the crimson, wet evidence of our brawl.

"I...I'm sorry..."

I released my grip on the blade as Clementine stumbled backward.

My tension, my readiness, my willingness to fight was nothing against the flesh and blood reality. I thought I was prepared. But looking at her now...

Her mouth opened, but no sound came out. Her knees buckled. She collapsed into the mud, her body convulsing once before going still.

My fingers twitched, wanting to catch her, to save her.

Direct pressure. That's what she needs. Years of training, of my oath, of a lifelong need to save people fought for control. *If I move right now, if I use the heel of my hand, lean into it, keep the blood from pouring out… If it's arterial, she's only got minutes…*

In our final moments, we were two strangers staring, wordless, motionless.

The flood washed the blood away, erasing the evidence of something so huge, so unfathomable…

Clementine's eyes met mine, and I broke.

My feet carried me forward. I crashed to the ground, knees hitting the stones with bruising force. I reached for her, suddenly unsure where to touch her. One hand flexed above the wound, then retracted, knowing how utterly futile it was.

Blood bubbled on the edge of her lips as she stared at me.

"It's okay," I said, one hand going to her face, the other finding purchase on her shoulder. "It's okay. It's okay."

It was a lie.

If she tried to whisper something, to give any last words, they were stolen by the wind. Saltwater prickled against my lids, robbing me of the chance to cry as I clutched her uselessly.

"It's okay," I said again. What I meant, I couldn't be sure.

It was a compulsion as if the words didn't belong to me.

She wanted me dead. She, and everyone with her, was going to do whatever it took to ensure I didn't make it off this island. She would have gut me like a pig if she'd had the chance. And yet…

I sniffled, breathing in through my nose, and out through my mouth.

My eyes shut tightly, and when they opened once more, something within me shifted.

I looked at her corpse, silk nightgown, stab wound, bloodied lips, open eyes and all.

"I'm not like you," I said, pressing my palm against her lids. I expected to close them, to put her to rest, but couldn't bring myself to do the motion. I shifted my weight out from underneath her as I got to my feet. I stared down at her body as the words flowed freely. "You tried to murder me because you, your friends, everyone on this goddamn island is fucking evil. And I was supposed to die…because I'm not."

Whatever shock, sorrow, or human emotion one was meant to experience from a life-altering trauma seeped into the feeling I craved—no, the one I *needed*. The hate returned, not for some moral failure, but because these motherfuckers deserved it. I was meant to be sacrificed for my innocence.

My lip twitched as I let the reality fill me.

No one would die, not now, not ever, if these soulless bastards hadn't brought it upon themselves.

I puckered my cheeks, mouth filling with salvia, and summoned the final insult. I spat on her corpse, glaring at someone so vial, so unworthy of the breath she drew, that she dared to take me in a battle to the death.

Thunder rumbled through the sky, shaking my blood, chilling me to the bone. I trembled as the equatorial rain turned icy.

Clementine deserved exactly what she got, and I wouldn't spare another second mourning her.

I turned to walk away, skidding short at a figure mere feet from the display.

A warrior with short, dark hair looked between the body, then back up at me.

Svaha exhaled, almost pleased. "One down."

I felt nothing. I couldn't. Not panic, not fear, not even the folly of premature victory.

The cut of light didn't just flash against the smoke-gray sky, it crawled through the clouds, its tendrils cutting into the world above as it illuminated my sins.

The thunder rumbled, and deep in my belly, I knew it might as well be the slap of a half dozen pairs of feet. Clementine was dead, but the others were coming.

"You're going to want that," came the goddess's near-playful voice, the sound growing thinner, echoey, as she faded from existence.

She was right. I had one weapon, and I couldn't waste it on this bitch.

I sprinted toward Clementine's corpse and plucked the weapon from her throat. The downpour cleansed the knife from the bright, red blood the moment I tore it free. I cast a final glance down at her wide, unseeing eyes, knowing they'd never blink again.

I'd killed someone.

I looked at the blade, now cleansed of my mortal sin by the relentless storm. I could never take back what I'd done.

I'd love to lift my chin, march off this godforsaken rock, and never spare a thought to what these pigs had made me do.

But this wasn't finished.

Not even close.

HOLY SHIT, HOW DID PEOPLE LIVE LIKE THIS?

Blinding rain, impenetrable foliage, ocean on every side.

Get it together, I demanded of myself through gritted teeth.

This was impossible.

This was insane.

This couldn't be happening.

Green, blue, and brown swirled in a soggy blender as I slipped forward. I didn't know where I was going, only that nowhere was safe. The villas? Too exposed. I'd be slain the moment someone opened the door. The main house? Roman knew every hiding spot better than I did, and my soggy footprints would take them straight to me. Hiding in wait was out of the question.

The jungle was alive with shadows and storm.

My breath was ragged, my pulse a living thing clawing up

my throat. I had to run. I had to hide. But there was nowhere safe. Nowhere that wasn't drowning in darkness, in the roar of the wind, in the whispers of something far worse than thunder.

Then—

A voice, playful, sing-song.

"Here, kitty kitty…"

Motherfucker. I'd barely had a moment to recuperate. Survival of the fittest didn't care if I was still catching my breath.

The man's voice called again. "Kitty, kitty, kitty…"

The hardness calmed me. I clutched it, allowing the stone in my heart to anchor me.

I should have known that if I killed Clementine, her husband would be right behind. I swallowed the terror rising in my chest and pressed my body against the trunk of a thick banyan tree, trying to steady my breathing. His steps squelched through the mud, slow, measured. Hunting me. He was enjoying this.

Hate would distract me.

I had to be calm. To feel nothing.

I strained my ears through the water that doused our footsteps, hiding our next moves.

I listened for the space between the drops that broke against the earth. I heard the others in the distance, shouting, searching. The storm masked my exact location, but it wouldn't for long. I needed to move, but if I did, he'd hear me. He was too close.

His heckle wasn't just a taunt for me. It was a clue.

My chest tightened as the image of a powerful jaw, outstretched claws, and the king of the jungle dominated any thoughts of threat.

Instantly, I knew where we were.

The same monosyllabic doctor that had barked orders once before had a new set of instructions. The words were short, loud, and I knew they were life or death.

The pit.

Ares.

I'd passed the turn to the jaguar's enclosure in my sprint to the worker's house. If I could backtrack…

An idea came, half-formed and reckless. I shifted slightly, just enough to let a jagged intake of breath escape.

Roman's footsteps halted.

"Oh, sweetheart, you know you don't stand a chance, right?" He chuckled. "Come on. Let's not make this harder than it needs to be."

"I know you're going to kill me." I pulled my shoulders back, straightened my spine, and stepped out from behind the emerald curtain of leaves. I lifted my chin as I stared him down. "But you're going to have to catch me first."

His expression shifted as I turned and ran. I heard him cry out for me to wait, to stop, before he succumbed to the chase and unleashed his speed. My feet slammed into the earth, arms pumping, hands slicing through the air. I counted on the rain to conceal me as I skidded to the side, carving a serpentine trail just enough to confuse him.

"Stop it, Juniper!" he shouted. "You know this is a dead end."

They'd dangled an apex predator as a threat. The jungle contained more danger than I could possibly tackle, and if I let myself flinch, if I spiraled for even a moment, I'd be done.

I didn't know if they'd freed Ares, and I didn't care.

I looked at Roman for the barest of moments, and an unintentional smile—one I couldn't have controlled if I tried—cracked my face. Even in the rain, his designer shirt, his soft hands, even the lilt of his voice all screamed of a coddled, pampered opponent.

Roman was stronger. He was taller. In a sheer battle of weight thrown one to one, he would win. But my smile spread wider, though scarcely more than a second had passed. All he had was his size. This asshole had no idea how to battle intelligence.

I sprang into action, letting the callow, delicate man charge me with the only attack he possessed.

Three things happened at once.

Roman rushed forward, muscles flexed, face betraying his bloodlust.

In the time it took for him to take a single step, I marked a big tree, a twisted rock, a viny coil and knew I'd arrived. I extended a hand and grabbed a pale vine, wrapping my fingers around it and clinging to it for dear life.

I slid to a halt at the lip of the enclosure, scrambling to come to a stop as I slipped in the mud. He did the same, finally posed for the kill.

He grinned, veneers cutting a ghostly white sneer as he declared his victory.

"Nowhere to run," he shouted, jogging up to me. Roman came to a stop a few feet away, lips pulled back from his teeth in a diabolical grin. "You want to nap with the kitty?"

I gripped the stone within myself, clinging to the calm, anchoring sensation.

I took another breath, shaky, panicked, letting him think I was breaking. I needed him closer. One more step. Two.

"You are the kitty, after all, aren't you?"

My skin crawled. I sneered but didn't want to distract him. I hated this man with every fiber of my being. I let him monologue, let him tease, let him goad me as he took one step, then another, then another.

"Kitty, kitty, kitty…"

He pounced.

I dove.

A flash of motion, a stumble, my body flailing forward. He lunged, gripping my arm hard, yanking me back—

Right over the edge of the pit.

Everything happened in an instant. Time slowed as I twisted at the last second, my foot striking his knee, sending him careening into the darkness below. Science and brawn were locked in a deadlock for a single, terrifying moment as I trusted physics with my survival. I held onto the vine for dear life as he tried to pull me with him, but the thick coil held true. My hand burned. My arm strained. I heard a crack. A cough. He let out a choked scream. I peered over the edge to look at his twisted form, arms, and legs in an unnatural position as he coughed up blood.

I stared at him until he stopped coughing—his frozen corpse, blood on his lips, an echo of his wife.

Roman swung, little more than a muscular doll, lifeless, nothing.

I stood at the edge of the pit as he twitched, the pendulum of his body swinging on the rope-like plant knotted around his throat. The bough overhead groaned as it leant its vine to my nightmare.

I tried to look into his eyes, ready to feel something, searching for guilt, for an emotion, for whatever a human was meant to feel as she stared into the dangling cadaver of the man who'd just delighted in the plan to murder her.

Back, forth, back forth.

I slipped the knife back into the makeshift band. The smile returned, because I knew what I felt.

I knew at my core that I'd fight tooth and nail for a life who deserved to live.

And if they deserved to die…

I watched him swing one more time. With a parting breath, I turned and ran.

21

Two people were dead because of me.

I'd murdered them.

I'd been horrified by the image of Clemetine's sputtering death. With Roman, however?

I shuddered as bile rose in the back of my throat, then spit the acid into the mud.

I touched the knife in my sheath, chest aching, heart pounding as I felt the firm bulge of its hilt. I had to do it. I had to do it again, and again, and again.

I continued to sprint with no destination in mind. I was running from the wild storm, the unhinged chase, the shame of my crime. I was running from what I'd done, and toward what I still had to do.

Tears bubbled in my chest, fighting the panting, wheezing claustrophobia of being on a goddamn island. I was trapped. There was nowhere to go.

Svaha had told me the sole path forward.

The only way to escape was to kill everyone else before they killed me.

Which meant there were six more beating hearts that need to be silenced before the sun came up.

I was so fucking sick of being wet. I glared at the sky as if it made a difference. If anything, my irritation brought me peace.

The storm, like the people, like the wealthy and their heartless, unforgivable ritual, was below me.

The rain hammered down in heavy sheets, turning the jungle into a churning mess of mud and water. My breath came in ragged gasps. Roman and Clementine should have brought me relief, I couldn't take comfort in their death. I'd murdered two humans, and it barely put a dent in the murderous assassins hellbent on my sacrifice.

Roman's swinging body.

Clementine's slit throat.

And me? What would I look like if a single one of these silver-spoon jackals got to me before I got to them?

I stumbled forward, heart slamming against my ribs. My pulse was a roar in my ears, nearly drowning out the sound of rushing water and the distant shouts of the others hunting me.

I needed a plan. Running aimlessly was going to get me killed. I needed a second to regroup, to gather my thoughts, to bring my heartrate back to resting, if only for a moment. If I was going to hide, I'd need water, I'd need shelter, I'd need somewhere out of the rain. If I was going to run, and the plane wasn't an option…

My mind flashed to the boat. I knew the waters were treacherous, but I was ready to take my chance with a possible capsizing against the definite, intentional murder that awaited me if I stayed on this island one second longer.

I took off down the path toward the villas, hugging the trees in case I needed to dive into the jungle for cover. Fortunately, my path remained unobstructed as I rounded the bend and found the pristine, civilized structures. The villas. The main house. The lawn. The pool.

I scrambled to make sense of the building, but my brain hitched on the structure, incapable of puzzling this together for better or for worse.

Did I want to hide in the house?

Were the others waiting inside?

Should I sprint back into the forest?

I tilted my head back, grounding myself beneath the punishing, watery staccato. I wasn't fighting it anymore. It was a part of me—of *this.*

I still had a ways to go to get to the cliff, to carefully make my way down the stairs, to get to the dock, but I could do it. I gathered a few rallying breaths to make sure no one was going to jump out from around the corners before I started running to the edge of the lawn.

A man slipped into view from his hiding place near the main house.

I slid to a halt, trapped between the pool and the house as Flick blocked my exit, blue button-down linen shirt glued to his carefully cultivated muscles, white shorts pasted against his thighs. I had no idea when he'd made the time to get dressed when the rest of us had stumbled into the forest in our nighties, but maybe he'd intended for my death in panties and an oversized t-shirt to be some final insult. He stood near the edge of the pool, chest heaving, hands braced on his knees. His grin was wild, teeth a streak of light in the gray-blue storm.

I widened my stance and offered him the most basic of challenges.

"What?" I snapped. "What's your plan, Flick?"

His recoil was slight, but I caught it. The challenge caught him off guard.

If he wanted me to be scared, he was too corpses too late.

We sized each other up while he cast hurried glances around for weapons, for strategy, for whatever he could use to finish the job.

I clucked my tongue before I knew what I was doing.

A goddamn loser. I didn't know where the thought came from, but it was as true as the ground on which I stood. *This parasite is here to murder me for what? His bank account? And he didn't even bother to make a plan?*

It was insulting.

He found no blunt object, nothing sharp, no surprise machine gun or whatever the hell someone with a silver-spoon mentality thought would be laying at his feet so he could cleanly do away with a human life.

I had no patience for his bullshit.

"Hurry up and do it," I goaded. "Don't be a pussy."

The quizzical twist of his face only enraged me.

I'm sorry I didn't make this murder more convenient, you worthless jellyfish.

Flick may not have a thought in his head, but while he struggled to understand why the dripping blood of a human sacrifice wasn't handed to him on the platter, I'd pieced together what I needed.

I still had no semblance of a plan, but strategy was a luxury not afforded to those of us trapped on a private island with a rich cult of goddess-worshipping maniacs.

I took a step backward and reached for the ornate garden lantern. It was tall enough for the mounted transformer that channeled power into the main house. Black, corded power lines reminded me of the vine that saved my life in the battle against Roman. The blue water churned in the storm, the reflection of the firelight from the nearby torches flickering on the surface. I barely noticed—I was staring at the power line. It was still attached. Still whole. Still intact.

The cord swung like a slackline; a black rope set free from its hooks.

I knew what I had to do. It might get me killed but so would standing still.

The cord rocked back and forth like an inky viper; a snake filled with its own electric poison.

The anxiety that kept shifting my weight from foot to foot, shaking the nerves out of my hands like a track star, was different entirely from the incompressible mark on my head. This was science, and for once, I had no idea if it was on my side.

Flick relaxed as he watched me dance. He had to think I was stalling. "Where's your bravado now?" He taunted.

Damned if I do, damned if I don't, I thought.

I puffed out a breath, bouncing on the balls of my feet, readying myself for a suicide mission.

"There's nothing you can do, baby girl," Flick called. "Just let it go. Stop running. It's over."

I pulled out my dagger. I could keep him talking long enough to figure out if there was any other option than the half-baked, self-destructive plot twitching in my peripherals. I brandished the keris, the curvy blade holding his attention. "I thought you were my friend."

He chuckled. "Why, because I'm gay? You thought we bonded and I was your gay bestie? That's a harmful stereotype, sis."

Exhaustion seeped through me. I was bored of the game. Bored of the bravado. Bored of whatever the hell he thought he was doing by flexing at me from across the pool. "Get fucked, Flick."

"I plan to. I'll make love to my boyfriend on a pile of cash as soon as the island's fed."

"You're sick," I spat.

The man-made turquoise sparkled between us, the pool rippling with its miniature white caps as nature made itself known. If the thunder and lightning continued, I'd stopped paying attention. I couldn't be rattled by mother nature's fireworks while I readied myself to wrangle a livewire.

I shook my free hand out again, unable to keep the nerves from what had to be done.

He laughed like he had no care in the world. "You have no idea what rich people will do to defend their money. Try me, gorgeous. Let's fight."

The smile that ticked me was a balm. There was almost pity in my voice as I said, "You think the wealthy can fight? You have no idea how scrappy those of us can be when we have nothing to lose."

My fingers tightened around the knife in my grip. I lifted it slowly, let the blade catch the light as I angled for the power line.

Look at the knife, look at the knife.

My debut performance as an illusionist was all or nothing. I didn't need to be a med student to know that the electricity running through the cord could kill a man. I also needed to face the fact I'd been avoiding: if I cut into it, I'd die before I had any chance to use it against Flick.

His smile widened.

"Be my guest," he taunted. "Cut it. Kill yourself. End the futile chase. It'll be quicker than what's waiting for you."

The threat caught me by genuine surprise.

He knew my plan?

I hedged, suddenly at a loss.

Time didn't wait for my delay. Palm fronds slapped one another relentlessly. The pool sloshed. Beach waves crashed in the distance. The island was set to drown in this goddamn monsoon whether or not Flick and I made good on our threats.

But the same sickening truth ran its rusty nail down my back, reminding me of just how dire things were.

I didn't have to kill one.

I didn't have to kill two.

I didn't have to kill most.

Every single one of them was out to get me. Each and every one of the prim and proper, well dressed, snooty, poised leeches would be coming for me, no matter how far I ran, or how hard I fought.

He was trying to goad me into it. I could use that. He wanted me to hesitate. To make a mistake. To be weak. I wasn't weak.

He had muscle.

I had grit, and three-fourths of a goddamn medical doctorate.

This buttoned-up would-be murderer could choke on his cockiness. It was now or never.

I controlled the smile, knowing my confidence would do me no favors. I turned the knife in my grip until I held it in a reverse hold, my fingers steady despite the trembling in my limbs. I took a step closer to the power line, feigning indecision, waiting, waiting—

Odie's voice came from around the corner. "Flick?"

He was distracted for just a second, but it was long enough for me to take three furious steps toward him. Flick lunged, but his timing was off, his angle compromised.

I twisted sharply, bringing the hilt of the knife up and slamming it into his temple. He stumbled, his footing slipping on the wet tile. I hit him again, harder, knocking him off balance. His arms pinwheeled as he fought for control, but it was too late—his heel caught the edge of the pool, and with a sharp cry, he went down, splashing into the water.

His boyfriend screamed across the lawn.

Odie sprinted toward the pool; his eyes wide with panic. "Flick!"

I turned sharply, my gaze darting to the power line. Something inside me screamed that I needed to move, needed to finish this, needed to take my chance. My heart pounded in my throat as I lunged for the wire.

And then the sky cracked open as if on command.

A bolt of lightning split the air, my companion, my cohort, searing through the darkness, striking the power line in a blinding flash. The force sent it whipping free, a live wire sparking and snapping as it writhed wildly through the air like a living thing.

The bracelet pricked against my skin with painful, needle-like intensity—a new jolt of pain with each cracking, whipping squirm from the power line. I had no intelligent thoughts as I felt the effects of fortune—luck coursed through me with wounding strength as the line snapped.

I couldn't move. Odie and I locked eyes.

We both knew what came next. He could abandon his partner to fight another day, or—

Whether he understood basic conduction was instantly irrelevant.

Odie dove into the pool, his arms cutting through the water as he swam for Flick. If I could just catch the insulated part of the cord, if I could guide it toward the water... My breath hitched, and I ducked and dove, reaching for the wire—

For fuck's sake, when would I get the chance to breathe?

I gave myself over to instinct, shutting off my brain entirely as I trusted my body to seize the reigns in my single second of advantage.

A gust of wind blasted through the courtyard. It was as if the island itself took control, its stormy hands snatching the sparkling, furious line from my grasp. The wire snapped away before I could touch it, flung by the storm's fury—

The thick, black cord struck the water.

My gasping, shocked, relieved inhale matched a thunderous crack.

A single cry battled for attention against the tumult. Despite my grit, my heart lurched painfully at the noise. My ears rang. I gagged on the electric tang of metal on my tongue. A violent burst of blue light erupted from the pool as the electricity surged through it. Odie barely had time to scream. The sound was cut off as his body seized, convulsing in the water. Flick twitched beside him, their limbs jerking as the current tore through them. Their mouths hung open, eyes bulging, fingers clawing uselessly at the surface.

Then, just as quickly as it began, they went still.

They didn't move, and neither did I.

The crackle of a livewire sang its threatening song, jerking in and out of their final resting place.

A different version of me—Cassidy the med student, Cassidy the kind, benevolent, naïve girl from Colorado—would have fought to secure the wire, to end the danger, to jump in after them. She would have lamented over their bodies, pounding their chests, giving every bit of herself as she sent every gust of oxygen she possessed into their lungs.

But me, the girl who stood at the lip of the light blue disaster charged with the flickering, was Juniper. And she was an unfeeling executioner.

Electricity didn't give a shit who had money or what weird ritual they'd intended. Current served its only god: basic physics. Flick and Odie came to play, but they had no idea how I'd play to win.

Two dolls, eyes forever open, lips parted in a silent cry, bobbed amidst the aquamarine. Never again would they laugh or joke or love. They'd also never get another chance to murder an innocent Westerner in cold blood. I watched them dip, twist, and turn until their eternally still bodies lay face down in the chlorine.

The rain hammered down, hissing as it struck the electrified water. My breath came in harsh, uneven gasps as I staggered back, my stomach twisting violently. The scent of ozone and scorched flesh filled the air, mixing with the acrid tang of chlorine.

"…Flick?"

It was an involuntary reaction.

I didn't mean to call out. I don't know what made me do it. I watched their twitching, jerking bodies bob in the choppy pool water. Hot, painful tears lined my eyes, but I didn't know why I was crying. I was scared. I was angry. I was betrayed.

But I wasn't sad.

Not for this.

Two more bodies. Four deaths on my hands. One bloody

dagger. Two immortal goddesses. One night so wicked, so impossible, that if I let myself think about it for even a moment, I'd shut down completely. And I was nowhere near done.

I backed away, my pulse thundering in my ears, my limbs shaking so hard I nearly dropped the knife. My reflection shimmered in the water, distorted, fractured, unrecognizable.

I looked at the keris, almost expecting my hands to be blood-stained despite the fact that the electrocuted pool had done the work for me. The ruby bracelet was the only splash of red in the stretch of pale skin and steel. My fingertips had completely pruned, shriveling under the relentless torrent. I couldn't believe I'd ever liked this place. This wasn't paradise. It was a murder soup with a deceitful PR team.

"Cassidy..."

I jerked my head away from the reflection but knew I wouldn't see anyone. No one human, anyway.

"Shut up." I gritted my teeth, shoving the dagger into the tourniquet-like garter on my thigh. I didn't care what the island —what some goddess of blood and sacrifice, or some deity of prosperity and fortune—wanted. They weren't *my* gods. This wasn't my fucked-up faith. I hated them. I hated everything. And god, did it feel good.

The next silver scar of lightning cut through the heavens, sizzling, casting a moment of near daylight on my crime.

"No..." I shook my head, denying the thought. "This is your crime, you motherfucker. Drown in it." Their bodies continued to bob limply, steam rising from the surface of the pool.

The thunder cut my tirade short. The sound shook me back to reality. I couldn't stand here in the open. I'd already wasted too much time without any cover, anywhere to hide.

What was I thinking?

I staggered back, pulse hammering against my wake-up call.

It hadn't come soon enough.

I didn't have time to escape.

My brain hadn't even had a chance to wake back up, to form a thought, to force my feet to move.

I was rooted to the spot, the vice-like grip of powerful, unkind hands crushing my shoulders as I realized it was over. I'd been found.

I wrenched my body to the side, wriggling as much as I could, hoping to see Denning, yet knowing in the rotten depts of my gut that I wouldn't be so lucky. The firm grasp, the solid chest, the shirtless wall of muscle and threat belonged to another.

I wanted to be angry, to be scared, to feel anything, but I'd been robbed of the chance to pull myself together. It wasn't fair. I deserved a chance.

"Did you do this?" Wei demanded.

My eyes burned with the depths of my loathing as I stared at the symmetrical, plastic, sculpted, six-foot-whatever intersection of vanity and bumbling stupidity. He didn't deserve to be the one who beat me.

It. Wasn't. Fair.

I squirmed in his grasp, writhing for a chance to grab my dagger. "Let me go!"

"No chance, princess," he sneered. "Lemon! Lem, where are you!"

I tried to throw elbows, tried to kick, to do *anything*, but he twisted my arm into a painful vice grip at my back. I winced as he guided my feet helplessly to the ground, forcing my arm into a tighter bend as I choked on my plea.

"Lem!" he shouted again over the rain.

I couldn't let him call for reinforcements. I may not be his physical match, but there had to be something. And if Lemon was coming, the clock was ticking on my options...

He filled his chest with air again, ready to call out, and I cut him off.

"Listen," I struggled for a defense, eyes wide, doing my best to sound confident even if my lips quivered. "You're new to the group, right? That's what you said? You don't have to be one of them. You don't—"

"What do you mean? I *want* this." Wei gestured with his free hand. "Flick and Odie over there? Rest in peace, brothers, but a murder free for all? That's fucking awesome! Once I realized what they were doing, I begged Lem to let me in."

My hopes were dashed in an instant. Any chance of begging for my life turned to ashes. I snarled. "Kill me yourself, then," I said. "Why wait for your girlfriend?"

A snag in his expression. A beat of hesitation.

I wasn't totally sure what I'd stumbled upon, but I dug into it with both claws.

"This is my first sacrifice, okay? I don't want to fuck it up."

I didn't know how I had the space to feel baffled, but something about this man was so profoundly stupid that even in my last moments, I took the space to feel amazed at his breathtaking idiocy.

And then I had it.

He was an idiot. I could work with that.

Wei began shaking. Was it from his admission? These shivers weren't from rage, not from adrenaline, but from pure uncertainty. He gripped my arm too tightly, and his breath came fast and shallow, the way someone pretending to be in control might breathe. He was scared of fucking up the ritual.

It wasn't a lot, but I pulled on the cord of his insecurity and yanked.

"You can't just kill me like this," I blurted, planting my feet. "It won't work."

Wei hesitated. He glanced around, like Lemon might appear out of the rain to guide him through the process. She wouldn't. It was just us.

"What?"

"The rite," I gasped, widening my eyes, letting fear and urgency coat my voice. My soul floated somewhere outside myself as I watched my mouth sputter the words: "You *do* know the steps, right?"

The wind howled through the jungle, whipping my soaked hair against my face. Lightning flashed, and for a second, I saw the doubt flicker across his features. I could practically hear the wind rattle the empty nothing between his ears. I clung to that stupid, pretty hope for dear life.

"I—she told me the steps," he said, but it fell flat. A boy caught in a lie.

I sunk my teeth into the chance, sucking deeply on the vein of opportunity.

I nodded, hoping he'd mirror the motion.

Yes, yes, yes. This is true. You believe me.

"Then you know you have to say the invocation first." I took a ragged breath, trying to look as frantic as possible. "Word for word."

His brows pinched. "Lemon said—"

"Lemon isn't here." A roll of thunder backed me up, as if the island was on my side. "And if you do this wrong, the goddess will be furious." I paused for dramatic effect, begging the words to sink in. "Do you really want to risk your *first* sacrifice being a failure? Do you want to be the reason the ritual falls apart?"

His grip on me loosened, just slightly.

It was no time for a premature celebration. I held still, unwilling to spook him, and reeled him in.

I swallowed hard and leaned in, lowering my voice. "The others have done this before, right? Do you think they're watching? Judging?" I shook my head, eyes darting as if expecting something terrible. "You messed up already. You touched me with your left hand first." I gasped, giving a breathy little shudder. "That's bad. That's really bad."

Wei's mouth parted. He looked down at his own hands, uncertain now, trapped in his own paranoia.

I pressed harder, nodding once more. "You have to start

over. But if you say the invocation, maybe—maybe the goddess will forgive the mistake."

He mirrored the nod this time, if only slightly, and I knew I had him. I just needed one more push.

"The first words of the invocation are—" I drew in a slow, measured breath, pretending to recall something sacred. Stalling.

Another flash of lightning. A crack of thunder.

Wei glanced behind him, just for a second. The beautiful, simple idiot.

And that second was all I needed.

I stomped onto his instep with every ounce of force I had. Something cracked. He let out a yelp of pain, his hold loosening just enough for me to wrench my arm free.

I was back in the game. The resurgence of fight within me was a beautiful thing as I scrambled for the dagger at my thigh —too slow.

Wei recovered, faster than I expected, rage overtaking hesitation. He lunged at me, one massive hand clamping around my wrist. His grip was iron. Pain shot up my forearm, my fingers spasming, and I watched in horrified slow motion as the dagger clattered uselessly to the ground.

I dove for the weapon, but I was too small, too weak, as a muscled body crashed over me. Wei wrapped me in the hook of his left arm while his right arm searched for the dagger. I coughed as he flexed his bicep against my throat. The world began to dim. I threw useless punches in a feeble attempt to free myself, but he had the upper hand.

The light began to dim as he tightened his grip.

He wouldn't have needed anything else. I was lost to the breathless lock when he struck again.

Stars exploded in front of my eyes; vision blinded by white-hot agony as something pierced my side. A terrible glint of steel reflected in the storm, and I knew it was over. The chase was done.

A blade to the belly was a cruel way to go. I wish I'd never studied medicine, hating that in lieu of pleasant childhood memories or important milestones, the last thoughts to flash before my eyes resigned me to the curse of knowledge.

Perforated bowels bleeding into the abdomen. Pain. Sepsis. Agonizing, lingering torture.

Wei, you are such a failure you couldn't even kill me right.

I closed my eyes, feeling the beat of the throbbing wound just below my ribs. I heard him lift his hand once more, ready to repeat his handiwork and finish the job.

Good. Get it over with.

Wei tightened his chokehold one last time, holding the sharpened knife aloft as he prepared to end me once and for all.

Despair was a dull, aching nothing as I said a quiet goodbye.

I almost wished I believed in a god to pray to as I said goodbye. Two of them were real, at least, and given this bullshit, I couldn't say I wanted my last breath to be for them.

I sucked in a final sip of air, relaxing as I gave myself the peace I deserved and let it happen.

The peace did not come.

The instant I said my goodbye, the world erupted into chaos.

A fist flew from nowhere, slamming into Wei's cheek. The unknown third, my rescuer, threw a brutal, bone-shaking blow that sent his head snapping to the side. He staggered, the force knocking him clean off me, his arms flying out for balance.

Holy shit. It really *was* a savior.

I wasn't alone. Someone had come to save me.

I took a life-saving breath and scrambled away from Wei as I stared at my hero.

Denning—wild-eyed, rain-soaked, his chest heaving like an animal forced into a fight. The relentless blue-white veins arced across the sky, casting the foreboding shadows across his face, rage carved into every line of his body. His shirt was ripped, soaked through with rain and blood, clinging to the defined cut of his torso. I was torn between the urge to run into his arms and the ache to relax in the safety of a teammate amidst this madness, but the danger had not ended. The men were gladiators, and this was a fight to the death. The flat, open space between the pool and the house made for an excellent arena.

Denning's body collided with Wei's, a perfect predator's strike. They hit the ground hard, rolling, fists flying. Teeth. Elbows. Knees. The sound of knuckles against bone was like gunfire in the storm.

The caveman brain in the back of my skull spared me from thoughts. Now was the time to move, to react, to survive. Another powerful blow and I gasped, pushing myself up. My limbs were sluggish, from running, from fighting, from brush after brush with meeting the end, and at long last, someone had gotten close enough to take me to the edge. I was losing blood. I knew I needed to pull it together, but with two against one, we might just stand a chance.

"Denning, what—" My hands flew to my side, fingers clutching the wound as I stumbled.

"I've got him," he snarled through gritted teeth, his voice raw with exertion.

Wei tried to throw him off, but Denning was faster, stronger. His arm looped around Wei's neck in a brutal chokehold, his bicep bulging as he tightened, tightened, tightened. The fight turned desperate. Animalistic. Wei flailed beneath him, his heels digging into the mud as he tried to kick free.

Denning didn't look at me when he spoke, but his voice left no room for argument.

"You have to go."

I was shaking, heart hammering, my fingers still twitching from where the dagger had been buried inside me mere moments before. *Thud, thud, thud,* went the rhythmic throb of my puncture wound. I was going to bleed out. I pressed my hand against the hole, knowing it did little to stop the bleeding.

He wanted me to go? Go where?

I tried, "I can get to the boat—"

"There is no boat," Denning grunted, tightening his grip. "Go and stay gone until sunrise. I'll come find you. Just stay out of sight!"

Wei choked out something unintelligible, his eyes rolling back.

I looked down at the crimson liquid leaking through my fingers. "But I—"

Denning's gaze finally met mine, fierce and unyielding. "I'm commanding you. This is an order."

The air between us burned.

I shook my head once, but I wasn't disagreeing. I wasn't even confused. He wasn't in charge of me. I didn't need a master to issue commands. But that wasn't what this was. He was cutting through the haze of trauma, of primal panic, and giving me something unwavering to hold onto.

My stomach twisted.

"Go, Juniper." His voice softened, just barely. "Whether you're Juniper, or Cassidy Mae Finch, you need to live."

I hesitated. One second too long.

"Go!"

The word ripped through me like a gunshot.

I stumbled backward as Wei's struggling slowed. His limbs went limp. His chest stopped heaving. I slapped my hand into the puddle, grabbing the fallen keris before I took off into the sodden hell.

Another body down.

Three more to go.

22

My side ached. My head swam as blood leeched from my body. I couldn't run forever.

I had to find shelter, but hiding in the villas wasn't an option.

I stumbled past a tiki torch that had sloughed to the side, tilting out of the rain and leaning toward the villa wall just enough to spare its flame. Acting on instinct, I grabbed the head of the torch and pressed my back against the wall. I took a deep breath behind whatever imagined safety I allowed myself to feel underneath the nearly opaque sheet of monsoon water and did the only thing I could think to save my life.

I pulled out the keris, stuck the blade into the flame, and began to count.

One...two...three... there's no way it was hot enough. It would take several minutes to get the dagger hot enough to do what needed to be done. I clamped it down over the flame and yanked the torch free from the soft earth. I limped around the building, hiding against the back of the structure as I forced myself to stay perfectly still. Yes, I had to run, but if I didn't stop the bleeding, I'd be dead before anyone had the chance to find me.

I pulled the blade free and grimaced at the lava-like glow.

This wasn't going to be pretty.

I stuck it back into the fire, if only to buy myself three more calming breaths.

The storm covered my tracks, concealing me long enough for me to pull the glowing metal from the torch. I yanked up my shirt and shoved the dagger's fiery edge against the wound.

The shock of pain was more than I'd bargained for.

The goddess of fortune granted me the kindness of a bolt of thunder as I screamed.

A guttural, animal noise escaped my throat as my skin sizzled against the metal.

This is good, I forced myself to believe it. *This was exactly what you need. Everything is fine. Everything…is…fine…*

I shook my head abruptly, a sharp sniff and odd jolt my body's way of keeping me conscious.

One thing after a goddamn other.

Maybe Ni Luh would shelter me if I made it to the worker's house.

Maybe I could get to the caves, and Svaha would tell me I'd done enough.

But I knew that whatever happened here, the workers enabled it. They turned a blind eye. They got matching tattoos. They belonged to the island.

The goddess was worse.

Yes, she was giving me a shot at survival. I knew I had to be grateful for the lucky bracelet, but it felt like a handcuff, chaining me to the island. Sure, I wouldn't have gotten this far without the keris, but there was more to it than that. She—*they* —was real, and these immortal beings wanted this. The goddesses were no safe harbor.

I was on my own.

Sweat and grim clung to me despite the rain. Soaked, white cotton stuck to my chest, my sides, my upper thigh, with an enormous, bloodied gash exposing me for all the world to see. My fingertips went to the puncture wound, grimacing through the pain as I prodded the sticky, reddish-purple scab. It wasn't perfect, but it would have to do. I just needed to buy myself enough time to get off the island, and the only other place for shelter had to be the jet's hanger.

Two birds, one stone.

With a rallying groan, I continued moving.

I ran down the path, my breath ragged, my feet barely feeling the slick mud beneath them. The world was a blur of green and gray, branches whipping past me, the storm ensuring the island remained a nightmare. The rain slashed at my skin, drowning out all other sounds but the drumbeat of my own pulse. I was no longer sick of the rain. It was a part of me—its pummeling warmth like living in the womb.

I tripped on an exposed root, stumbling off the path and into the bramble. A slick, enormous leaf slapped me in the face while stray branches tore at my face, my arms, snagging my shirt. I hit my knees wallowing in the mud as I choked on the frustrated scream desperate to come out. Whatever spirits I'd angered didn't want me to have any time to breathe.

I swung a foot underneath me, ready to push myself up, to keep running, when I saw a flash of orange.

An icy calm replaced my frustration.

I knew that color. That was Indie's dress.

Good. Better they come to me than I have to hunt them down.

I crouched down further, ducking beneath the umbrella-like cover of the wild yam. The deluge drummed against my tiny shelter as I watched the orange dress slip between the trees.

"Let's kill this bitch and get it over with," I mumbled.

Blinding buckets of rain made it nearly impossible to see the crazed shape that emerged, but I knew who it was. Indie had found me.

She moved like a starved animal, hunched forward, eyes

scanning the undergrowth, nostrils flaring as she struggled to see through the downpour. Her hair, usually styled in loose, effortless waves, hung in soaking, tangled ropes around her face. Mud splattered her legs, her bare feet sinking into the soft, drenched ground.

And in her hands—a thick, gnarled branch.

Her weapon of choice sickened me. My lip twitched against my disgust as I watched her clutch the blunt object, her knuckles bloodless, her posture twitching, erratic. Every so often, she would jerk her head in a different direction, her eyes too wide, too wild, her breath coming in sharp, angry gasps.

She wasn't moving in self-defense. She wasn't even looking for me. She was hunting.

I swallowed hard and moved.

I was an animal on the jungle floor, slithering from my hiding place beneath the plant to the nearest trunk. My gaze never left her as I rose to my full height, concealed by the underbrush, trusting the tree to conceal me. Hand over hand, I climbed the massive, twisting banyan, feeling the slick bark beneath my palms. The trees groaned under the weight of the wind. I pulled myself up into the thick crook of the branches, balancing on the wide, moss-covered limb. It was sturdy enough.

Sheer, animal survival tugged me forward, giving me the pitiless, steel resolve I needed as I let Indie walk straight into my trap.

I crept forward, my body low, my weight distributed carefully. Indie hadn't looked up.

She kept moving forward, oblivious, the stick clutched in both hands, her shoulders rising and falling with each panting breath.

I tightened my grip on the dagger.

Wait for it.

She stepped directly beneath me.

Now.

I was more beast than man. I dropped from the tree like a winged raptor diving on its prey, my dagger aloft as I fell from the sky.

Indie's eyes flicked up too late. She barely had time to let out a strangled, gasping "No—" before I crashed into her, full weight, full speed.

We hit the ground hard. The impact sent a shock through my knees, though her body absorbed most of the blow. Her jagged tree branch snagged against the bare skin of my upper arm, ripping the skin open as fresh blood sprung forth.

I saw stars as I rolled onto my side. My fingertips went numb, but I commanded my grip to tighten against the knife whether or not I could feel the hilt in my palm, preparing to fight.

I would have kept fighting, scrambling, tearing, cutting, biting, killing, but the grotesque, wet crack of bone against stone snapped me out of my craze.

Indie's head whipped back on impact, slamming against the jagged rock half-buried in the mud. Her body convulsed beneath mine, a sharp, garbled noise escaping her lips—a sound that didn't belong in the throat of something still alive.

She wasn't dead.

But she was about to be.

Gone was the feral hunt in her eyes. She was weak, helpless, desperate. She blinked against the water that clung to her lashes, her big, doe-brown eyes panicked as she tried to make sense of what had happened.

She stared up at me, her chest rising in ragged, hitching spasms, blood pooling beneath her head, spreading in inky ribbons through the rain-soaked ground. Her lips worked around words she couldn't form, a drowning fish gasping for air.

"June—" crimson stained the edges of her lips. She looked at me with wild, desperate eyes. "Help me."

I twisted the keris in my hand, adjusting my grip as I gritted my teeth.

"Go to hell."

I pressed the dagger to her throat and sliced.

A spurt of warmth across my hands, my arms, hot, sticky, cleansing.

Then—stillness.

I knelt there, breathing hard, the rain diluting the blood, soaking the torn fabric of my shirt, staining it pink with our shared baptism. I plunged the knife into the good sleeve of my shirt and cut it free, cutting in a coil until I had another thin strip of fabric. I bit down on the cotton, securing one end with my teeth as I looped it around my torn arm, tying off the fresh injury. I couldn't keep tying off wounds and cauterizing stabs all night. And, as long as I kept moving, I'd continue opening the injuries. Every heartbeat was a fresh pump of blood escaping my body and soaking the island soil.

Either the others would find me, or I'd bleed out before sunrise. My medical training could buy time, but it couldn't stop the clock.

Indie's body was still warm beneath me.

I swallowed back the bile rising in my throat, wiping my hand over my face.

Two more before I had to deal with Denning.

I shoved off her corpse, discarding her, and kept moving.

I PEERED BETWEEN THE OVERSIZED LEAVES, MOVING VINES TO THE side as I took in the final obstacle. The open, treeless field was a blessing, if only for the barest of seconds. It meant I'd reached the airfield. It also meant I was about to enter an area with no cover.

"Those mother fucking liars," I said, eyes landing on the jet.

The plane must have arrived in the night, before the storm

had begun. Maybe it couldn't take off until this typhoon cleared, but god almighty did it feel good to know there was an option, a hope, however small. I'd slash my way onboard and hold the pilot at knifepoint all the way to Timbuktu if I had to.

Jets were sealed, though. Only a fool would risk getting caught in the open, stuck clawing some door I couldn't possibly unlock. I had some work to do before I could hijack an aircraft.

I waited by the trees, legs shaking, eyes wild as I searched for a sign that someone was watching. I didn't see an elitist prick waiting to assassinate me, but that didn't mean I was safe. I chewed on the inside of my cheek, dancing on the balls of my feet as I waited for my chance to run.

I could only be cautious for so long before bleeding out. It was now or never.

"Fuck it."

I sprang from the trees, pumping my arms, forcing my legs to move faster than they'd ever moved before, ran toward the enormous garage as another crack of lightning gave me away.

I STAGGERED INTO THE HANGAR AFTER THE SPRINT OF A LIFETIME, gasping for breath, my legs trembling beneath me. The incessant, nagging, hateful, miserable, borderline obscene rain wouldn't stop, wouldn't relinquish, wouldn't give me reprieve for a single goddamn second. I could scarcely distinguish from the other sounds that I was royally fucked—the distant crashing of the waves, the echo of my own heartbeat slamming against my ribs, the voices in my head telling me to *go, go, go.*

But there was nowhere left to run.

I pressed my back against the cold metal of the jet, my chest rising and falling with each ragged breath. I was soaked to the bone, every inch of me freezing, blood and rain mixing in a slick layer over my skin. The fluorescent lighting inside the hangar flickered, the generator somewhere in the back struggling against the storm.

The place reeked of gasoline, oil, metal, and something else.

Something faint. Metallic. Rotten.

I ignored it. I just needed a second. A second to breathe. A second to think.

Lightning flashed outside, illuminating the cavernous space in a sudden, blinding burst. Shadows stretched long and distorted, flickering against the walls, and for half a second—just a second—I saw something move above me. A blur of green. The sharp snap of metal.

I whipped my head up.

"Hey, babe," Evergreen flashed her teeth. "Where do you think you're going?"

She was above me, perched in the scaffolding, crouched like a predator preparing to pounce.

"You've gotta be fucking kidding me."

I skidded backward; eyes locked on the demonic nightmare clinging to the bars.

My goddamn karma seconds after I'd jumped out of a tree and murdered her friend.

I continued moving away, desperate to put as much space between me and the predator dangling overhead. I cast a panicked glance to the hangar door, at the open field, at the exposed storm and its unknown terrors just beyond the barn and decided to take my chances with the bitch inside.

"That's a pretty knife," she said, eyeing the sheath around my thigh. I expected to feel a sense of comfort that I was armed, but Ever pulled out an enormous, razor-sharp sushi knife, twice the size of my weapon. "I've got a blade of my own."

She had no business looking that serene.

I plucked mine from the ragged cloth against my leg and held it tight.

Her dress had once been a soft, elegant thing—emerald silk, gold embroidery, delicate straps. Now, it was ripped and soaked, clinging to her like a second skin, splattered with mud and whatever else stained her fabric.

There was something so despicable about her changing from her nightgown into formal attire for the ceremony. She'd wanted to look her best for the human sacrifice, I supposed. Of course, I hadn't been allowed a similar shred of decency.

Her eyes gleamed in the dim light, her mouth curling into something between a smile and a snarl. Had she always looked this vile?

"You made it all this way, peaches," she said.

I mimicked her teasing cadence, even if my words came between ragged breaths. "Come down. Congratulate me in person."

Ever tilted her head. "Oh, Junie. You don't give the orders here."

"Fine, then, you just going to stay up there? Leave me unfinished, like you did in the shower?" I challenged.

She gave an exaggerated pout. "Are you trying to hurt my feelings? You can't fake an orgasm like that."

The bitch was right. I came all over her tongue that night. I rode a face I should have pissed on. "Why did you bother? Why seduce me? Just to toy with me?"

"Fuck no!" she said. "That was all real, babes. Not only were you a blast, but the goddess prefers a happy vessel. She only inhabits joyful bodies. The more relaxed you are, the more fun you're having, the more likely she is to take you. Or…*was*." She clucked her tongue pityingly. "Sorry you ended up with the alternative, but one way or another, the island needs to be satisfied."

I gave a dark chuckle. "I've met your goddess. Or perhaps you haven't heard?"

Her brows met in the middle. She sipped in an acidic breath, looking genuinely skeptical as she waited for me to continue.

"Oh, *peaches*," I repeated the word, enjoying the acid as I spit on the nickname. "How did you think I've made it this far? Your goddess picked a favorite, and you, *babe*, aren't it."

A twitch. "You're lying."

The wicked pleasure warmed my core like molasses. "I met Lakshmi and Svaha several nights ago. They were calling me to the cave long before I knew who they were."

She shook her head once but remained silent.

"I didn't know what I was agreeing to. But we planned this. She had no plans of taking my body. Instead, they were going to see if I had what it takes to upset the balance of things."

Ever's eyes darkened. Her face scrunched sourly. "Bullshit."

"Whose knife do you think this is?" I asked, brandishing Svaha's dagger. "Ask me where your friends are. Ask me who's still alive. Ask me who's *winning*."

Hysteria tinged the edge of her echo. "Bullshit!"

"Your goddesses have forsaken you," I spit.

I barely had time to react before she dropped.

I threw myself to the side, rolling across the concrete as the blade slammed down where I'd just been standing.

With a scream and a flourish, Ever landed with a grace I could never have matched. She moved too fast, her dagger flashing in the dim light. She lunged again—I dodged just in time, my shoulder slamming into a tool chest that rattled on impact.

"Where's Indie?"

I grabbed a wrench, hurling it at her—she dodged effortlessly.

She was playing with me. "Where are my friends?"

I wiggled my dagger. "Get over here and join them."

Something wild in her eyes replaced all remnants of sanity. Terror, amusement, and downright glee gave a reptilian sparkle as she watched me tense for battle.

Another flash of lightning.

But I was no longer on the defensive. And hell, she wasn't the only one amused.

Her blade swung wide, nearly catching my ribs—I barely twisted in time. I lunged, aiming for her neck, but she caught my wrist, twisting my arm until I gasped in pain, the dagger slipping from my fingers.

Shit.

"Come on, baby," she cooed, unhinged, feverish. "Is this really the best you've got? I thought we were closer than this."

She threw me.

I hit the metal stairs leading to the upper scaffolding, pain exploding in my ribs, dull and hot and deep. My vision swam. I could barely get my feet under me before Ever was there again, pressing the blade against my throat.

"Just let it happen, Junie," she whispered, her breath warm against my skin. "We could have had so much fun."

No.

No, no, no.

I gritted my teeth so hard I felt a molar crack. I jerked my head forward, slamming my forehead into hers.

She reeled back—not far, but enough.

I was a caged animal released for a death match with an explosive burst of survival adrenaline to prove it, I lunged upward, tackling her, driving both of us into the scaffolding above. We crashed onto the grated platform, rolling, thrashing, grabbing, clawing.

Ever got on top of me, straddling my waist, pinning me down, sushi knife raised high.

This was it.

I was going to die.

I thrashed, fighting to push her off, but she had the advantage. The height. The strength.

Her curly hair clung to her skin, dripping with rain, with sweat, with blood. Her smile was wide, manic, euphoric.

She was soaking this in.

And then, suddenly—I stopped fighting.

I went completely and utterly limp.

A confused twitch—a questioning hesitation—as Ever's brows pinched. Her thigh muscles relaxed around me. The second of hesitation as all I needed.

I seized it.

I grabbed her wrist, twisting the dagger from her grip. She snarled, jerked, fought, but I was savage now.

The knife came down hard, its polished metal pushing seamlessly into the wet flesh of her stomach. I urged it in deeper, the razor-sharp steel meeting no resistance as I filled her up.

"Take it," I said through my teeth.

Her hands flew to the entry wound, grabbing uselessly for the knife.

"Every last inch," I practically growled.

Her body jerked, a drowned, strangled sound escaping her lips. I didn't stop.

I stabbed her again.

And again.

And again.

I screamed as I stabbed, carving, gouging, slashing, digging.

Hot blood gushed over my hands, over my arms, drenching me.

Ever made a soft, breathy noise, her mouth forming words she never got to say.

I drove the knife in deeper.

"June—" her eyes rolled backward.

I could barely hear her through the crimson haze.

She spasmed, her hands clawing weakly at my wrists. Still fighting.

I pulled the knife out only to plunge it into her again.

Again.

Again.

The ruby pool of her life did not stay on the ground. Each frenzied stab, each maniacal puncture over and over and over filled the air with ruby-red gore. We bathed in the violence, born again, drenching completely in red.

Her weight slumped forward, her body collapsing against mine, pinning me to the scaffolding as her blood ran down my face, my throat, my chest.

I trembled beneath the hot tidal wave of carnage.

Ever shuddered against me, a last, slow exhale ghosting against my ear.

At last, she went still.

I lay there beneath her, panting, shaking, drenched in blood and rain and sweat, my vision blurry, my pulse thundering in my ears. I wanted to sob. I wanted to puke. My arms ached. My soul twitched. My head pounded.

She was dead.

Finally, dead.

I shoved her off of me, my hands slipping in the mess of blood and viscera. She landed with a thud, sprawled across the metal grating, her lifeless eyes staring at the ceiling.

I gasped for air, my whole body shaking.

I wanted to be sick.

I wanted to scream.

But all I could do was continue to stab.

Again, again, and again.

23

THE KNIFE WAS SO SLICK THAT I STRUGGLED TO MAINTAIN MY HOLD.

I'd painted my face, my arms, my skin with Evergreen's blood.

Somewhere, distant and drowned by the storm, a voice called my name. A woman's. Was it the goddess? Was she telling me this was finally enough bloodshed?

"Juniper! June, stop! It's done! You got her!"

My vision continued to swim, unable to see anyone or anything.

I barely heard Lemon over the ragged sound of my own breath, pale hair plastered to equally pale skin, a dripping wet yellow dress, painted lips gaping down at me with so much pity. My hand trembled as I wrenched the knife free one last time, my whole-body shuddering with the force of it. Evergreen's head lolled to the side, eyes wide and empty.

I stared at her. At what I'd done. My heartbeat slammed against my ribs, my breath coming in short bursts.

"Get back," I rasped, stumbling to my feet, my voice raw. I pointed the knife at Lemon, every muscle in my body spasming from what I'd done. "Get away from me."

She didn't flinch. She didn't step back. If anything, she softened. Her expression twisted into something I didn't understand.

"You should have left," she said. "You were supposed to take my advice and leave. You could have avoided all of this."

I swallowed hard. My hands, my arms, my entire body was covered in red. The rain washed through my hair, streaking it down my face like war paint.

Lemon reached toward me as though to steady me. "Come on," she said. "Let's go."

I was delirious. Up was down. Night was day. And Lemon wanted us to leave.

"Go where?"

"To the jet," she said. "It's over, Juniper. It's done."

I looked at my trembling fingertips, too weak to maintain my hold on the hilt.

"Come on," she urged. "Put it away. Let's get off the island."

Away? I almost nodded. I may have, in fact. I couldn't quite tell if my thoughts matched my expression, but I put one bloodied foot in front of the other as I stepped away from Evergreen.

"Let's get that blood off of you before we get on the jet. Hurry," Lemon coaxed.

I continued to move, each step robotic. Leaving. Yes. That's what I wanted. What I needed. The jet was the only way off the island. All I had to do was put one foot in front of the other.

We stepped out of the hanger into the storm. I tilted my face up, hoping the rain would free me from the crimson nightmare soaking my skin, my clothes, my hair. In the distance, the jet's yellow lights were aglow. The sealed door was propped up, letting in the rain. For the first time, I thought—maybe, maybe she was on my side. Maybe she was going to help me. Maybe—

Between the returned onslaught of rain and the rush of my own adrenaline in my ears, I almost didn't hear her. My thoughts lagged a second behind, each word out of her mouth making less sense than the one before.

"Unfortunately," she continued, her voice almost sad, "you didn't leave. And now, if you don't die, everything is lost. You're the sacrifice, Juniper. You missed your chance."

My stomach dropped.

I was awake now.

Whatever brief retreat into shock came to an end.

I turned toward her fully, my grip on the knife tightening. An earth-shaking boom shook me to my core. I thought it was thunder, then realized the sound of my own pulse roaring too loudly to give me the chance to think. An icepick of lightning crawled across the sky, illuminating her face, her rain-slicked skin, the cold certainty in her dead, blue eyes.

"You can't be serious," I whispered. Goosebumps ran from the back of my neck down my spine as I realized my mistake. "Then why would you try to get me to leave? Why would you—"

She couldn't help herself. She cackled, shrugging away her plan.

"If Denning failed at his task—if you'd left and he botched his turn, then he'd be out, and I would get his shares of the island."

The pounding in my head grew worse.

I was sick. I was dizzy. I couldn't, I didn't, I wouldn't, I—

I couldn't help it. The argument that burst forth was automatic.

"But the two of you were fighting! You were calling him a monster!"

She just stared at me. Then, slowly, she raised a hand and pointed over my shoulder.

"It's your fault."

Too stunned to react, too petrified to do anything more than watch, I followed her gaze, my breath catching when I saw who she was pointing at.

The betrayal in her voice was venomous. "You fucking monster," she spat. "You can't even hold up your end of the deal. The rest of us brought an offering to the island, and you try to scam the goddess out of her avatar. You've always been a selfish prick."

Their fight from however long ago slapped me across the face.

That was it. That was why she'd accused him of being a monster.

She wasn't disgusted by the horrible things a man could do to an innocent woman. She'd never been on my side. She was angry because he wasn't going to go through with it, and she wouldn't have her cut of paradise.

In Lemon Rothschild's world, that's what constituted monstrosity.

Denning said nothing. His jaw was clenched, eyes black, shoulders set as he approached.

I pressed my toes to the ground, widening the triangle between the three of us.

Everything in my body screamed at me to run, but there was nowhere left to go. I'd exhausted the entire island. I'd reached my only way off. I was frozen, caught between them, between everything I still didn't understand.

This couldn't still be happening.

Surely, I had died and this was Purgatory. Clementine had killed me the moment she'd chased me down with her Molotov of Chloroform. Maybe it had happened before that, at the cere-mony. Worse still, perhaps I'd overdosed on GHB the moment I'd been tempted by the sinful indulgence of hands and mouths and pleasure.

This was my punishment. I would fight these rich assholes forever. None of them were safe. No one offered reprieve. That was my sentence.

Lemon turned to me again, her voice coaxing, gentle. It matched the pitter patter of the rain, washing away whatever thoughts I held dear. "It doesn't have to be this way. I told you —I told you to leave. But you don't have to go out in a body bag, June. You know there's another path."

Her tone had flipped so hard it gave me whiplash. I shook my head. "You're crazy."

She laughed, tilting her face up toward the sky. She lifted her hands as if in prayer, savoring the torrent as if she was receiving sacrament. "And yet I'm about to give you the only sane advice you'll hear: You could live on, June. You don't have to die, if you give yourself over to the goddess. But when I look between those eyes..." She lowered her hands, chin leveling, meeting my eyes once more. Her blue eyes scanned mine as if reading a disappointing book. "No. You're still the same pretty idiot he hired to come here and die. You're too foolish to realize he isn't going to save you."

I cast a glance at Denning but wasn't foolish enough to let down my guard. Lemon was no friend of mine. I'd come to close to the end to trip at the finish line over such an unimaginative trick. I held my ground.

Her lower lip lifted in a pout. "And apparently you *don't* know that, if you still think he's going to let you off the island."

My stomach rolled.

I couldn't help but look this time. I held one hand up, keeping her at bay, unwilling to lose an inch to her trickery, but I had to look at him. I stared at the way the rain dripped down the hardened set of his jaw. I tried to make sense of the shadows across his face. When the storm split the sky again, it showed me a curious, unnamable darkness behind his eyes.

I lifted my other hand self-defense, closing out the triangle as I forced more space between us. Until lifted my right hand, I hadn't realized I was still holding the dagger. The earth beneath our feet shook as the thunder answered the light. I couldn't tell if it was a warning, or a wakeup call.

He raised a hand of his own. Broad, flat, calming, as if he was attempting to soothe a frightened creature. The straight carve of his nose, the muscled width of his shoulders, the strength of this tall, controlled, powerful man, all positioned to tame the beast.

"Don't believe her," Denning said.

Lemon's laugh was a haughty, bitter sound. "Who are you fooling?"

The open field was an empty coliseum for this battle. Palm trunks bent like eager viewers leaning in to watch the show-down. I cast a desperate glance to the only stretch of beach visible from the air strip, sick to my stomach at the size of the waves. The grey stretch where sea met sky reminded me that we were in the middle of nowhere, and no one was coming.

Another electric crack and the fight went on.

Lemon's fingers were bent like claws, poised to rip out Denning's eyes as she shouted. "She shouldn't believe me because...*Why*? Because you're so trustworthy? You still brought her here. If it weren't for you, she'd still be in safe and snug in Podunk Nowheresville. You did this to her."

He hadn't looked at her a single time. His gaze remained locked on mine. "She's going to say anything she can to rip away your only ally. She wants you to think you have no one, but it's not true. You have me."

Lemon mirrored his behavior, though for different reasons. Her voice got louder, eyes harder, shouting with her full chest as she stared him down.

"You still sourced a sacrifice, Denning! You found one with no friends or family, one with no digital footprint, one who wouldn't be missed." After an agonizing pause, she tore herself away from her tirade long enough to address me. "Is this the one you trust? The one who got you into this in the first place?"

"Stop talking," he snapped.

"Just like our fucking marriage," she snarled. "Denning knows best, right? Well sometimes I know best. And right now, I'm the only one who can get us out of this mess."

My head spun. I tried to cling to something—some

semblance of reality, some indication that anything I knew was true.

Denning took a slow step forward, his hands raised in a careful, deliberate motion. He was looking at me, not her.

"You can't trust my ex-wife," he said. "She's an absolute *hippo.*"

He hinged on the last word. It was a jarring insult, a bizarre comparison to the very thin woman who, though insane, was by no stretch of the imagination…the word clicked.

Hippocrates.

It cut through the noise, the wind, the storm. It sliced straight through my panic, and I blinked at him, confused, shaking.

Trust me.

My lips parted, a breath catching in my throat. My fingers curled around the knife, but I didn't move. He was waiting. Watching.

Rainwater rushed in rivers over my hair, over my eyes, into my mouth. I took a shaky breath and reminded myself of one thing I knew to be true: Lemon had never claimed she could get me off the island. She'd only said I didn't have to die. I could give my body over to the goddess. That would spare me a bloody end.

But it didn't make her a friend.

Another flash of lightning split the sky. And in its electric glow, I saw the muscular, stalking shape of nightmare personified. The only thing on this island more terrifying than armed, wealthy lunatics, was the apex predator.

My heart sped up and stood still. My ears rang, and yet I could hear everything with perfect clarity. My vision swam, certain I was hallucinating, insistent that this was another layer of the Hell I'd been delt. But with cold, terrified certainty, I allowed the reality to sink in.

I tried not to react. I took three shallow sips of air, muscles tense, blood prickly with cortisol as I took two careful steps backward, staring at the only thing at the island that didn't give a fuck what god we served or how much money we had. There was only one power that mattered, and its name was Ares.

Behind Lemon, low to the ground, muscles coiled, was the jaguar.

I barely had time to react before Lemon sneered and took a step toward me.

"Juniper—"

The next lightning strike blinded me.

The cat's eyes flashed. Its inked fur shone as powerful muscles sprang into action.

The answering thunder married the guttural noise of true, primal attack.

The jaguar roared, its throat unleashing a deafening snarl. He lunged, face contorted as predator pounced upon its prey. Ivory pillars gleamed, his fangs impossibly sharp, claws extended.

I barely had time to choke on my scream.

Denning held his ground, though his face betrayed his abject terror.

The beast sank its teeth into her supple skin in one, puncturing snap.

Lemon was hit from behind so hard she didn't even have time to feel afraid.

The colossal hunter pinned her to the ground with its massive paws, ripping her jugular clean from her throat before she had the chance to scream.

Denning was already moving, already reaching for my wrist.

"Get to the jet!"

24

An unyielding wall of water created a physical barrier between Ares's feast and our only means of escape. I had no idea how I'd tolerated the monsoon before this moment, but now that there were no trees to soften the storm's intensity, hurricane winds attacked me with full force.

I clutched the wound in my side, teeth grinding together with popping force as I ran.

Denning and I ran through the downpour, gusts nearly knocking me sideways, my limbs aching, my body running purely on adrenaline and survival. The runway stretched out before us, slick with rain, the jet already powered up, its lights cutting through the darkness like beacons.

The plane opened its door—the gilded, shimmering finish line at the end of a marathon. My feet hit the smooth pavement the moment I left the grass behind, splashing through the lakes settling over the asphalt. Even in my hysteria, I knew this was strange. The door shouldn't be opening. Not for me. Not now. But we were so close.

I was so close.

I barreled toward the glow as if it was the light at the end of the tunnel. If I'd died long ago, I needed this to take me to the other side. Every slamming step through inches of water, every stride covering the final bits of man-made runway.

Twenty feet.

Ten feet.

Five.

I extended my fingertips for the railing, but slammed into the stairs, unable to slow myself as I reached the jet. Clanging metal against metal let me know I hadn't released my dagger. It was fused to my right hand whether I wanted it or not. I gripped the railing with my left hand, but I couldn't control my steps. I didn't know if the jaguar had grown bored of its first attack and taken off behind us. I didn't know if every island employee had lined up to take their turn with me. I didn't know if the goddess herself was at my heels, reaching for an avatar. I wouldn't even let myself look back to ensure Denning had made it.

I slammed into the boarding stairs. My shins exploded in pain but I didn't give myself the time to feel anything. I was a gecko on the wall, scurrying up the airstairs.

I gripped the cold metal railing as I hauled myself up, heart hammering, lungs burning. The wind screamed around me, the jet engines humming as if impatient.

I took the last step up.

I wanted to cry, though I couldn't explain the swell of emotion. My chest burst as if it contained the typhoon itself.

I was close enough for the cool rush of air-conditioned air to kiss my face. Tastefully carpeted floor, indulgent seats, dim lighting, wood-grain panel, and all of its obscene displays of luxury were inches from my grasp. I'd made it.

And yet…

Before taking the last step onto the jet, I stopped. Hair stuck to my face, white sleep shirt shredded, stained in blood, hanging by a thread, makeshift garter strapped to my thigh, tourniquet protecting the gash in my arm, and cauterized wound on my side, I was not the person I'd been when I'd walked down these jet stairs.

I let my body move, let my eyes look for something that would help them understand, let my mind search for reason as I turned my back on the jet long enough to assess the view behind me.

Denning was fast approaching, soaked and breathless. His dark eyes were wild as he reached for me, mouth cracking in an exhausted, hopeful smile, ready to shove me inside.

I widened my stance, blocking the entrance.

His smile faltered. His brows gathered.

"Why did you stop?" he looked up at me, urging me forward.

I rooted myself to the top of the stairs. I couldn't stop staring at this beautiful, complicated, selfish man. In all my life, I'd never witnessed someone so wealthy, so powerful, so self-assured. I'd never been touched by someone so strong, so chis-eled, so unique.

He stood a head and shoulders above any man I'd ever met.

He was complicated, and strange, and sexy, and perfect, and yet....

The words were a part of me, somehow. They belonged to me before I knew what I was saying.

"Lemon was right."

Denning's puckered brows became all the more furrowed. His forehead was a stack of unfamiliar creases. His posture shifted, reminding me of the man who'd lifted his hands to calm an irrational beast when he spoke to me.

He shook his head, droplets cascading from his dark hair. He used his hands again to try to usher me forward. "What are you talking about? Go, June! Get in there! Ares is still—"

My feet cemented to the top step as if I didn't have a choice. I couldn't have moved if I wanted to. I was as sick of the rain as I was of their bullshit. All of it. I shook my head, savoring the calm.

It was my turn to look at someone with pity.

"You brought me here intending to kill me," I said, my voice as steady and empty as I felt.

"Put down the knife," he said. This time, he wasn't talking to me at all. He was assuaging a petulant child so it would stop crying. He was manipulating a frightened creature so it would let down its guard. He was lying with his eyes, with his calming hand, with the air in his fucking lungs.

"You found me with the intent that I would never leave this island."

Denning flinched.

"June—"

"My name isn't Juniper," I said. "My name is Cassidy. Cassidy Mae Finch. That's the broke student you hunted. That's the life you didn't care enough to get to know. And that's the bitch you tried to kill."

The lightning coincided with my arc. My wrist came down so fast he didn't have time to see the decision I'd made.

I plunged the blade deep into his thigh, hot blood spilling over my hand.

It was like putting a butterknife on toast. Natural. Necessary. Final.

His gasp turned into a snarl, his grip crushing my wrist as I yanked the knife free.

Another crack of lightning as I kicked him off the stairs.

He stumbled backward. His disbelief coincided with his groan, face contorting in pain and rage.

I relaxed at the way his face twisted in disgust. I was comforted by the hate, the disdain, the violence in his scream as he raised his voice to let the venom out.

"What the hell? June—Cassidy! Whoever the fuck you are! What the fuck did you just do!"

The rain was a curtain around our tiny circus. A screaming, angry man. The violent woman he'd dared to underestimate. The thunder caressed me, its sound brushing comforting vibrations against my cheek as the stayed witness for my swan song.

I peered down at him, savoring the little river that ran from the crown of my head down my cheek as I tilted my head.

I'd never experienced such serenity as I asked, "Your family's hotels are underwater, right? You need this money. You need me to die."

Water poured down his face, dripping off the cut of his jaw as he gaped at me. "The island has had its blood, Cassidy! They're dead! Whatever debt I owed has been paid."

"And I paid it!" I practically screamed. My cry was joyful, feverish, maddening.

I adored the daylight-white flash of lightning that revealed the twist of his features.

God, the delirium was almost delicious. I allowed my eyes their manic flare, my teeth the threatening smile.

"I'll give you the same choice I had," I said over the rhythmic pounding. "The same voice you gave me when you brought me here. Survive the island. If it lets you live, then you live."

"June," he sucked in the word.

My pleasure hissed out like a puncture in a balloon.

"Cassidy." My eyelids snapped to slits. "Say my name. Say the name you tried to snuff out. Name the girl you tried to kill."

Blood soaked his hands. He was done pretending. "Listen here you psycho cunt—"

He lifted a hand as if to strike me, but I had the high ground. His leg was useless, his hands were occupied, and anyone who dared to raise their voice to me like that deserved whatever was coming to them. I gripped the railing, lifted my knee, and kicked him with every remaining droplet of strength.

Denning tumbled onto the asphalt as I stepped backward into the temperature-controlled cabin. I smiled and waved my fingers, a lazy little goodbye as the door sealed shut between us.

I stared at the tiny window for one final proof of life as the lightning revealed a man raging against the elements on the ground beneath us, and I savored the first slice of silence I'd had since I'd awoken that fateful morning. The storm still raged outside, but here, inside the lavish, dimly lit cabin, it was like stepping into another world.

I flexed my fingers, lamenting the loss of my keris, especially if I was about to hijack a plane and force a pilot to fly at knifepoint. However, I'd come this far and was ready to let my survival instinct carry me all the way back to the Western Hemisphere.

I twisted to see who awaited me.

The aura within the plane was utterly unbothered. Luxuriating, even.

I recognized the flight attendant who moved gracefully down the aisle, a tray of champagne flutes balanced effortlessly in her hands. It was the other two bodies—the women relaxing in the jet seats—that my brain had trouble processing.

The two women seated near the front of the plane turned to look at me.

"Brutal," Svaha laughed, gesturing to Denning. "I knew I liked you."

The air in my lungs evaporated.

Lakshmi, radiant and serene, her presence demanding devotion. Svaha, sharp and playful, a predator lounging in silk, greeted me with their smiles.

"Is this it, then?" I said. "Now you take my body?"

Svaha rolled her eyes. "If that's the case, don't do it sober."

The attendant offered the tray to me.

I was too broken to care.

I took a flute, my bloodstained fingers wrapping around the delicate stem with all the grace of a gorilla. I pounded it back, slapped the flute down, and grabbed another.

Lakshmi tilted her head. "Where are we off to?"

I dropped into one of the buttery leather seats, my limbs

aching, my pulse thrumming. I brought the champagne to my lips, the cold fizz biting.

"We're going somewhere? You're not going to step into my vessel and keep me on the island?"

The women exchanged a laugh. "Oh, hell no. Have you seen yourself? Humans become legends when they battle the gods and win. Now, while our darling here fetches you another bottle of bubbly, tell us: where would you like to go?"

Fuck it.

I succumbed to the heaviness of battle. I was spent. I could scarcely keep my eyes open. If there was any chance I could make it home...

"What the hell. You guys ever been to Denver?"

Lakshmi smiled, something knowing in her deep, ancient eyes. "I'm sure there are many blessings to be bestowed off the island."

Through the curtain of heavy eyelashes, I witnessed Svaha's wink. "Though you may have to do something for us first."

Lakshmi's hand found mine, a soft, cool touch against my feverish skin. Novocain leeched through me. Healing waves sparkled and buzzed beneath my skin. The goddesses allowed me to be tore apart, then put me back together again.

I opened my mouth to ask how long we'd have to wait to leave, but the question was unnecessary. Beyond our tinny walls, the storm shuddered, then, it parted.

Gray clouds boiled to either side, allowing the first gentle pink of dawn to peek through the windows.

The jet began to move.

I exhaled, watching the clouds split open, watching the runway stretch out ahead.

I kept my hand in Lakshmi's as if she was an IV. I needed her. And even if I didn't...Hell, I *wanted* their blessing. I'd motherfucking earned it.

"Your champagne, ma'am?" the flight attendant asked.

I ignored the flute, grabbing the bottle instead. I sucked the bubbles down from the neck.

A sacrifice had been made. I was now the lone recipient of the blessings. But now she had no more cult of followers, no band of merry murderers, save for me. The sword arm of power, fame, and fortune.

The plane surged forward, and I realized I had no idea who was flying it. My fight was over. My shoulders pressed into the seat as we accelerated, then released all together as the wheels lifted from the earth. My stomach tipped, not with fear, but with the dizziness of surrender as gravity let me go.

The jet rose into the sunrise—unmoored, unburdened, free.

I savored the bubbles as I swallowed down a glittering irony.

The island let me leave. That didn't mean it was finished with me. I closed my eyes as the world turned orange, feeling the warmth of the sun on my skin as I sat between two incomprehensible powers.

I wasn't running anymore.

I was just beginning.

ACKNOWLEDGMENTS

At the advisement of my betters, the deeply vulnerable love letter heavily featuring mental illness, now reads as follows:

Please do us both a favor and picture this section as voiced from a version of me on a white sand beach, working on my tan, sipping a mojito, instead of the bleak reality of ██████████████. It takes a village, and sometimes that village becomes life or death.

Katrina, you showed up in the middle of the night to ██████████████████████ when I ███████████████ and was on the verge of ████████, because damn them all to be flushed to Double Hell. Madison, thank you for the extremely personal and unbelievably powerful ██████████. ███████████████ I can't believe I'm saying this out loud, but without you, I would literally ███████ and to think, we nearly gave it to that snowman! All of this took place in the middle of the night, where at the tender hour of four in the morning, Bela ████████████████ which I swore I'd never tell anyone, after Haley stole a succulent Laotian meal. Lindsey, you ████████, and thanks to Cera, Allison, and Kelley for ████████████████ evert step of the way.

Kat, my incredible editor—for the love of the goddesses, you ██████████████ until nothing could keep me sane, but you're off the hook for that one. Thank you for believing in this story and for polishing it up for me. (Y'all, hop over to her page [@kathrynkeeneart], check out her fore edges, and hire her to edit your next project).

Chris! I am not sorry for the thousands of insecure messages I sent you (and will continue to send) for having such a talented fancy accomplished artist on lil ol me's project. (Friends and fae, you have to check out his Emmy-winning art on IG over at @welchdraws and believe me when I tell you that someone that cool and talented is also unbelievably kind). Oh, and while I'm spilling secrets, let me just say, ██████████████████████████████, which is why we'll have to rematch in Mario Kart.

Helena, thank you so much for always being on my team and bringing the graphics to life. You continue to creatively live inside my brain. Zachary, I never want to call upon anyone else for my formatting.

And finally: I want to acknowledge the opportunity to hack and slash one's way out of situations. I think women should get at least 1 free murder per year, and if elected president, I'll run on that platform. Very specifically, this final paragraph goes out to ████████, because how could you. May ████████ find themselves inconspicuously on a luxury island. Whatever happens once they arrive is none of our stabby business. Though I can think of a goddess, or two, who would like to have a word.

Stay bloody,

Piper

ABOUT THE AUTHOR

Piper CJ, author of the USA Today bisexual fantasy series *No Other Gods* and *The Night and Its Moon*, and New York Times bestselling series *Fern's School for Wayward Fae*, is a photographer, hobby linguist, and French fry enthusiast. She has an M.A. in Folklore and a B.A. in Broadcasting, which she used in her former life as a morning-show weather girl, hockey podcaster, and in audio documentary work. Now when she isn't playing with her dog, she's gaming, binging cartoons, dissecting fairy tales, or disappointing her parents.

Website: pipercj.com

instagram.com/piper_cj
tiktok.com/@pipercj

TRIGGER AND CONTENT WARNINGS

Slasher-genre blood, gore, excessive violence, death, murder, blood, human trafficking, drug usage, drugged sex, dubious consent while under the influence of drugs, on-page sex, explicit group sex, threesomes, orgies, body image issues, disordered eating, mythology and deities modernized and personified, themes of others (the antagonists) misusing and appropriating cultural practices, human sacrifice, cursing, language, issues of classism, class warfare, and eating the stupid 1% (…not literally, unfortunately. Maybe we'll do cannibalism in the sequel).

Note on Sex Work and Queer Stories

There is no trigger warning for sex work, just as there are no trigger warnings for loan officers, real estate agents, veterinarians, or authors. Sex worker empowerment and destigmatization is an issue that is important to me and is prevalent in many of my works. If something about sex work causes you discomfort, my goal is not to make the environment more comfortable for you, but to encourage you to confront thoughts and feelings of whorephobia. For more information, please read the lived experiences, articles, and input from sex workers themselves as they contribute to https://tryst.link/blog/tag/articles/ and other resources.

There are no trigger warnings for queer stories, and unless we begin putting in a trigger warning for straightness, there never will be.